BACK *to* BACK

By Jo Fletcher

2024

Butterworth Books is a different breed of publishing house. It's a home for Indies, for independent authors who take great pride in their work and produce top quality books for readers who deserve the best. Professional editing, professional cover design, professional proof reading, professional book production—you get the idea. As Individual as the Indie authors we're proud to work with, we're Butterworths and we're *different*.

Authors currently publishing with us:

E.V. Bancroft
Valden Bush
Addison M Conley
Jo Fletcher
Helena Harte
Lee Haven
Karen Klyne
AJ Mason
Ally McGuire
James Merrick
Robyn Nyx
Simon Smalley
JJ Taylor
Brey Willows

For more information visit www.butterworthbooks.co.uk

CATALOGING INFORMATION
ISBN: 978-1-915009-65-4
CREDITS
Editor: Nicci Robinson
Jacket Design: Nicci Robinson & Jo Fletcher
Production Design: Global Wordsmiths
Cover Design: Lou Designs

Acknowledgements

Big thanks to Nicci Robinson, my editor, for her killer edits and constant support. I've learned loads over the past couple of years from the team at Global Wordsmiths and the network of fellow authors they've created.

Huge thanks to my author friend and confidante Iona Kane for being my sounding board and letting me crash at their place in Ireland while I got this thing down on paper. We did some good work on that trip. And the Guinness was a bonus.

To my awesome fellow sapphic authors: thanks for always lifting each other up and making this journey a blast. Whether we're on a writing retreat or catching up at events, it's great to be part of the sapphic writing community.

Massive love to my wife and son for giving me the time and space to write my heart out. I know sometimes it's annoying when I withdraw into my little bubble for an hour or so at a time. Thanks for the tea and hugs.

And of course, a big thank you to all the readers of my debut novel. Your feedback and reviews have given me the courage to keep writing. Special thanks to those who have called or messaged me directly—you know who you are, and I'm very grateful.

Talking of readers, massive thanks to the advance readers of *Back to Back* who took the time to give feedback and help shape this book.

Last but not least, a huge shoutout to my close friends and family for always supporting my dreams and keeping me going when I need it most. You're the best!

Dedication

To my own Fred and Ruby. Love you loads.

To anyone who happens to meet the love of their life at work: lucky you.

CHAPTER ONE

"Get it over with, I can't bear the suspense." Ruby twisted her hair. Whatever her best friend said next, she'd have to respect. She was her boss after all.

"It's not as bad as you think." Trix frowned. "You've done an amazing job on the perfume launch and the client is, quite rightly, over the moon."

"I sense a 'but' coming my way." Ruby screwed her eyes shut, awaiting the news of her next assignment. It was always tense, finishing one contract and starting afresh. But she'd proven herself on the last job, delighting everyone. "Why so edgy? It can't be as bad as that bloody fish and chip account you parked me on a couple of years ago."

Trix grimaced. "I know you were expecting to launch the art gallery, but the guy in charge has hit a funding snag, and it's been delayed. It might not even happen, which will be terrible for our bottom line." She doodled in her open notebook.

"Tell me, will you? I'll be fine."

"You're moving over to construction and demolition."

"Who says?" Ruby asked, folding her arms. Construction was the worst move. She'd be stuck on a building site with a load of smelly men for months.

"DJ himself."

"Right. No point in arguing then." She slumped. "I gave everything to that last contract. I really wanted to be moved onto arts, or even beauty."

"Don't whine, Ruby. It's deeply unattractive."

"Bugger off." The thought of getting dusty in construction for a year filled her with dread. Maybe it was time to cut loose and call it a day? There were plenty of other PR agencies begging for skills like hers. But none had the prestige and talent they shared at Liquid.

"Don't leave," Trix said.

"Since when did mind-reading become your new skill?"

"You're brilliant, and everyone knows it. Listen, this isn't any old demolition project. Boot Street is one of the most visionary, iconic schemes in the northwest—maybe the country."

Ruby shrugged. "You have my attention." She didn't want Trix to know it bothered her when every ounce of her feeble self-esteem rested on the next gig. If she wasn't good enough for the prize jobs at the agency, who was she?

"I'll explain on the way to lunch. We're meeting one of the top team."

"Now? I'm not ready to meet a new client. I haven't had time to prepare anything. I'm not even dressed to impress."

Trix inspected her collar. "Be your dazzling self. This isn't an interview. They've already hired us and asked for you by name."

"Yeah, right. They'd come across little old me in the trade press or something?"

"Sort of. They saw you'd won the last dynamite award. So, fix your lipstick because I'm taking you to Dresden's for an expensive meal and small talk with a fancy exec."

Ruby's fingers hovered at the gloss on her lips. Winter had been cruel this year, which was fine when she'd been tucked away in a cosy seventeenth-floor office, putting the finishing touches to a photoshoot. The temperature up north was sure to plummet.

Still, she had nothing to lose by popping out for a free lunch. She always could woo the clients, and they knew her by reputation, which was precisely what she'd worked for the last five years to achieve.

At the street corner, Ruby regretted her choice of heels for the day. She hadn't anticipated this jaunt across town. Narrowly missing a puddle, she reached out to Trix and steadied herself on the kerb.

"Easy, tiger, we've not even had a drink yet. Save your wobbles for the way back." Trix laughed.

"Sorry. I shouldn't have worn these stupid shoes." She squeezed Trix's arm. If there was anyone she'd want to lean on, it was her old friend and manager. They'd been together since they were interns at the agency. Trix had made a quicker journey up the career ladder. She knew what she was worth and what she wanted, whereas Ruby had nailed neither of these things. She measured success by how many people she'd pleased that day but deep inside, she wanted to make more of a difference than shifting perfume off shelves.

"You okay, Ruby? You've got a weird face on." Trix hesitated at the entrance to the restaurant.

"I'm fine." She sighed, knowing deep down that she'd have to admit her feelings. She couldn't hide anything from Trix for too long. "I'm thrown by not going onto the art gallery contract. I was really looking forward to something more creative."

"New York and Berlin will come, my friend, but not this year. You're heading to Manchester." She blew her a quick kiss. "It's not so bad. You can visit your sister at the weekend."

"Yeah, I guess." Ruby was engulfed by a rush of warm air as she held the door open. She followed the waiter to a table where a woman with flowing blond hair rose to greet them. *Okay, maybe this gig won't be so awful.* A year in the company of this bombshell could take the edge off a disappointing project. There was only so much all work and no play that Ruby could handle.

"Hello, you. Virtual meetings are great, but it's lovely to see below someone's shoulders." The stranger air-kissed Trix and turned towards Ruby, flashing the white of her perfect teeth. "And here we have…"

"Ruby Lewis." She extended her hand, pleased she'd squeezed in a manicure this week on her short, square nails. "I'm very pleased to meet you."

"Adrienne Banks. I'm global director of external and community relations for Design Futures."

Ruby pondered the ridiculous job title. She could have fun fantasising about that blond hair draped over her pillow.

"Please, let's sit and get to know each other." Adrienne passed Ruby a leather-bound menu. "I'm in town for a couple of days. Usually, I'm up in Aberdeen at the head office."

"Thanks for making time for us," said Trix. "I'm pleased you could meet Ruby in person so early, before she starts leading your account."

"Can we expect you on-site this Friday? Some of the team are gathering to look over drawings and next steps. It would be a good chance to meet the guys."

Ruby's heart sank further as she thought of the crowd of tea-swigging, denim-clad blokes she'd face on arrival. "Friday, I'm due to be –"

Trix kicked her under the table. "Of course, she'll be there. When and where?"

"Come for ten o'clock, and I'll meet you personally. I need to warn you that the place is a demolition-site at the moment." Adrienne leaned in. "Now, tell me more about Liquid Communications and what you've been up to. I saw your recent accolade for that futon company. Very impressive."

"Thank you so much." Ruby nodded. "I really enjoyed that project. It was a family firm, and the grandpa and grandma were still choosing the reams of cotton fabric themselves. It was so sweet."

Trix took over the sales spiel, and Ruby sipped at the table water, remembering the job that had brought home the silverware. She'd had to dig deep for that angle; most of her time had been spent selling the product's safety features. She wanted more from her career but had no real plan for how to make more of her skills, to feel more fulfilled. So, she followed Trix from one contract to another in the hope that one day she'd land on her dream job.

Resigned to the fact she'd have to be in Manchester by Friday,

Ruby ordered a large glass of white wine, decided to loosen up a bit, and put on her best show for Adrienne Banks. She hoped that she might see more of her on-site, or that she might have to make the odd trip to Aberdeen. It wasn't exactly New York, but it was over the border.

A few hours later, she pushed at the swing door of the bar, and squinted in the low light. The stench of stale beer rose from the worn floorboards and sticky tables. She'd managed to leave the office early with Trix's blessing, a sweetener for this morning's complete letdown. "I'll have a measure of your finest whiskey, please, sir."

James shook his head. "You know, you shouldn't really drink before your session, Ruby."

She held her index finger to her pressed lips. "I won't tell if you won't."

"She'll know. She always does," he said, reaching for the top shelf. The amber liquid he poured barely covered the bottom of the tumbler.

"Make it a double."

"No." James stood firm behind the bar. "You can have another after you're done."

"Spoilsport." Ruby threw the drink into her mouth, and it burned her throat. She counted the seconds until it faded, relishing the feeling. She nodded at James and walked towards a black wall at the rear of the bar. As she neared, the sealed entrance became visible, and she pushed at the door into the back room.

She shrugged off her coat and scarf then piled them onto a wobbly stool. A single bulb lit the space, casting shadows into the filthy corners of the room. Ruby picked up the axe on the table and brought it to her cheek. The cold steel stung for a few seconds. She stood back and considered the length of the flight that she knew so well. She raised the blade and appreciated the weight of the handle, before bringing it down. It flew towards the target on the wall with a reassuring thud.

"Hey." Laura Speedy crept out from the shade behind her.

"Hi, Speedy."

"Didn't expect to see you this early. Something wrong?"

"I've been dumped."

Confusion flickered across Speedy's face.

"I don't mean *dumped*. That'd be a shock." She giggled at herself, embarrassed. "More like bumped."

"What do you mean?" Speedy perched on a stool.

"I thought I'd be moving onto an amazing job, but instead, I'm off to the arse-end of Manchester on Friday to work on a bloody building site."

"How long will you be gone?" she asked.

"I've no idea yet. Could be six months. Maybe a year."

"Sounds shit. What are you going to do with the flat?" Speedy raised her eyebrows.

"Get a tenant, I guess." Ruby hadn't got as far as sorting the logistics of her studio above the bar.

"Damn, I'll miss your face around here." Speedy winked and polished an axe on another table. "Why are they sending you on that sort of thing? They'll eat you alive."

Speedy looked her up and down as if she was undressing her with her eyes. They'd never acted on it, but the buzz between them was ever-present.

"I know, I'm dreading it." Ruby launched another axe at her target and pierced the crimson centre. "I'm sick of it, to be honest. So, I left early and came here to let off some steam."

"Best place for it. You know you're welcome here." Speedy nodded at the target. "You're throwing too fast though. Slow down and take your time. Enjoy the moment."

"Is that life advice or axe-throwing technique you're dishing out?"

Speedy turned towards the door to the bar. "We've got a birthday party in at six o'clock. So you might want to be gone by then, unless you want to put your hard hat on before you even get to Manchester?"

Ruby chuckled. She lifted her chin towards the target and narrowed her eyes. She wriggled her toes and stretched her shoulders. Her muscles relaxed, and she smiled for the first time in hours. Maybe it wouldn't be so bad after all, and she could keep an eye on the job listings for something that would really fire her up.

"Can you ask James to get me another whiskey, Speedy?" Ruby shouted after her.

"Nope. You know the rules, Miss Lewis. If you're throwing axes, you can't throw shots." Speedy closed the secret door behind her, leaving Ruby in the shadows.

She stood with her thoughts for company, circling back to the optimism she'd had going into Trix's office this morning. She'd pick herself up eventually, but for now she wanted nothing more than to wallow in her frustration. She threw her last axe, and it sailed north of the target, bounced off the board and fell to the floor with a disappointing clunk. *Ok, Manchester, what have you got for me to play with?*

CHAPTER TWO

FEAR GRIPPED FRED IN the barrel of her stomach. Boot Street was the biggest job she'd ever taken on in her sixteen years with Design Futures. Until now, she'd been a gofer, a chauffeur, and maybe a solid wing man. But never the site manager.

"All right, boss?" Champ shuffled into view as he kicked a loose stone into a pile of rubble.

His red cheeks brought a smile to her lips. He reminded Fred of the enthusiasm she'd had while coming through the ranks. When you're the deputy, the pressure's on, but it's not all on your shoulders. "I'm taking stock. There's an awful lot to do on this one."

"If anyone can, it's you though, Fred. You've got all the boys behind you."

"Thanks for the vote of confidence. It means the world to me." She patted his skinny arm through his oversized coat. Champ bucked the trend of burly builders, and she loved him for it. "We need the lads here first thing to take delivery of some more cabins. They're due to arrive at the crack of dawn, and we'll crane them in place. With a fair wind, we might even have a site office by lunchtime." Fred scratched at her hairline, lifting her hard hat. As a fresh-faced apprentice, it had rubbed the skin around her ears, but eventually her skin had hardened against it.

Shadows fell onto the battered terraces ahead. Dusk set in and the temperature fell another degree, the dull cobbles shimmering under the moonlight with the threat of frost. "I reckon it'll be a rough winter for the demolition, but come spring, we'll have made a dent in this." Fred turned out of the wind and a shiver travelled down her spine. She hoped that Champ hadn't noticed. She hated the idea of looking weak on-site. They needed a leader because this job promised to be brutal. "You should head home soon, Champ. Get yourself warm."

"You too. What time is security due?"

"They're here already." She nodded towards a black van beyond the gates. "Hiding out until the office is built."

"Right. That'll be me, then. See you tomorrow, bright and early."

"Good night." Fred settled into her boots, considering her lot. She'd come a long way since that day her mum had marched her up Stockington Road to the job centre. Once she'd grown strong enough for the manual work, she'd never even thought of leaving the property firm that had taken a chance on her scrappy teenage self. She pushed away the creeping unease that this was all going to come crashing down with the next wrecking ball. She had to believe in the team she'd handpicked. She had to believe in herself.

An hour later, the familiar rise and fall of her brothers' opinions grew louder as she approached the house, and she pictured them talking over each other at the kitchen table. She ignored the seldom-used front door and headed around to the back and scraped her boots off in the porch before she entered.

"Fred's in," her youngest brother, Thomas, said like he'd won a prize.

"I saw her coming up the alley," her father said as she kissed his cheek. "How was your day, love?"

"Not too bad. All coming together on-site. I'll be glad to make a proper start."

"Good lass." Her dad ruffled her hair.

"Don't. I need a shower. I'm thick with dirt."

"Urgh, Fred's filthy, Mam." Tommy screeched and ducked behind their brother Brian.

He was almost into his twenties now but took every chance to play the baby of the family.

"Give it a rest, Tommy. Don't torment your sister." Her mum rubbed a stained tea towel in her wrinkled hands. "Sausage and mash for tea. Go and get washed before I dish up for the lot of you."

"Thanks, I will." Fred kissed her mum's cheek and headed to the narrow hallway. She stretched her hamstrings, taking two stairs at a time, enjoying the release of the day's graft. She flicked on the shower, peeled off her thermals, and tossed them into a pile. Her skin prickled with goosebumps, and she stepped under the warm water as soon as the temperature rose.

As one of five kids, there'd never been much time to enjoy the bathroom when she was growing up, so she was used to hopping in and out with barely the chance to wash the suds from her skin. She closed her eyes and breathed the steam into her lungs, allowing herself a rare moment of calm, solitude, and naked warmth.

"Tea's on the table, Winifred."

Fred bristled at the use of her full name. She'd been christened after her grandmother, who lived two doors down until Fred was ten. It hadn't taken long for the family to realise that Winnie junior was much more of a Fred.

She shook the water from her hair and ran a towel over her head and neck, not worried about how her hair would fall. Her shoulders ached from the day's work.

She threw on a T-shirt and joggers and padded downstairs to join her brothers at the table.

"Brian's been taken on at Wyncroft's today," said her mum.

"That right? Good for you. They're a nice bunch, and the boss is sound. Keep your head down and it could be long-term." Fred smiled at her brother.

Brian shrugged like it was no big deal, and Fred avoided her mum's eye contact. She didn't want to get into another argument about her younger brother's career prospects. He'd been in and out of work for a couple of years and hadn't settled anywhere. Fred sighed between loading forkfuls of mash into her mouth. She'd take him onto her site, but she couldn't trust him not to completely tarnish her reputation. That had been hard-earned, and she'd never forgive him if he damaged it.

"Brian will be grand at the new place. It's a fresh start. Now, Tommy, tell your sister about your college trip next term."

"They're taking us to Snowdon in April. We're going for survival skills, and we're staying in a massive dorm with all the lads together. It's gonna be a right laugh." He squirted ketchup onto his plate, sending splatter marks across the white ceramic.

"Sounds brilliant, Tommy. You behave yourself while you're there, won't you?"

"Here she goes with the lectures. Miss-bloody-perfect," Brian said through a mouthful of sausage.

Fred turned away, avoiding the bait.

"None of that, Brian. You're all adults; act like it." Her dad rested his fork on his plate and locked eyes with her brother, daring him to make another move.

"Sorry, Dad, I didn't mean it."

Fred took a breath. It was a near miss. Brian's temper could be explosive, and he would goad any of them into an argument. After she'd finished her meal, Fred made her excuses. She pulled on her wellies and a fisherman's knit, stepped out of the house, and blew her breath visibly into the night. Before she reached the bottom of the garden, a figure appeared across the fence.

"Evening." The security light bathed her neighbour, Mr Jensen, in a white glow.

"Hi there, Mr J. How's it going?"

"Not bad for a cold one." He blew into his hands and rubbed them together. "How's you?"

"Much the same. I'm heading into the shed to get away from the boys."

"I don't blame you. They get louder each year, that lot. How're the other two getting on?"

"Doing well by all accounts." Fred kicked at a soft patch of dirt beneath her feet. "Arthur's in Kent with his two little ones. Oliver's still growing cabbages on the east coast. Sounds marvellous.

Speaking of which, you got much in the allotment this winter?"

"I struggle to get down there, so it'll lay dormant till the spring. I might need your help come February or March to get the ground ready. We'll see when the weather starts to turn."

Fred took a long, freezing cold breath which almost made her cough. She was grateful for the peace and quiet of Mr J's allotment. It was a sacred space with no site lads or brothers begging for her attention. "You say the word, and I'll be down there. I've got a big job on this year, so you might not see as much of me generally. It'll be loads of late nights and early mornings."

"No change there then, Fred. Your mum said you'd got a promotion at the builders."

"Yeah, something like that. I'm running the site this time, so it's a good step up." A single butterfly persisted in her tummy at the thought of the lads looking to her for every direction. "Keep me busy, eh?"

"I should think so. Anyway, you get yourself inside; it's Baltic out here."

Mr. J disappeared into the black of his garden, and Fred opened the shed door. She flicked the oil heater and battery lamps on and settled onto a sofa, frayed with age and sagging in the middle. It'd seen it all, that couch. She drew her knees into her chest and rubbed at the scar on her shin bone. It ached every now and again to remind her of running from the tyranny of her brothers and falling onto concrete. She'd lived a childhood full of bumps and scratches and not much had changed.

She selected a playlist on her phone and rested her head against the couch. It was chilly but exactly what she needed. Fred looked out of the dappled shed window towards the house and smiled. The lights flicked on and off upstairs as her family moved around in their evening routines. She looked away, aware that she was here, part of her family, but separate from them, trying to carve her own way in life. A knock at the wooden door interrupted her thoughts.

"Fred, can I come in?" Brian asked before his head popped through the gap.

"Yeah, come on then." She made room on the sofa by folding her legs underneath her.

"I'll not stay. I'm just sorry about being a dick at teatime. Mum and Dad are banging on about this new job, and it's making me dead nervous." He picked at some peeling paint on the window frame. "What if it all goes tits up?"

"Then you'll find something else, Bri. But don't go in there thinking you've already failed. And don't listen to Mum and Dad too much. They're proud of you. They don't mean to put the pressure on."

"Yeah, I guess."

Fred loved her brothers, despite their faults. Mulling over Brian's doubts, she hoped that she wouldn't be the one to let her family down on this next job. So far, she'd done well, but that meant she had everything to lose.

"You need to believe in yourself, kid," she said to herself as much as to Brian. As long as nothing got in her way, and she stuck to her tried and tested methods, everything would stay on track.

CHAPTER THREE

RUBY DUSTED HER SKIRT in the back of the cab, regretting leaving her trouser suit hanging on the back of her hotel room door.

"You sure this is the right place, miss? It looks like a bomb's hit it." The driver twisted around with an incredulous look.

"I think so. It's a building site, so it's bound to look a bit desolate." Nerves swirled around her empty stomach. She'd skipped breakfast, and black coffee with three sugars wasn't nearly enough fuel for this kind of first day.

"That'll be fifteen quid then." He shook his head. "I haven't been this way since I was a kid. Thought it was all boarded up."

"I guess it was." Ruby passed over some crumpled notes. She tightened her grip on her work bag and got out of the car. "Can I get a receipt?"

"'Course you can." He scribbled it on a business card. "Looks like it's going to pour down. Cheers, love."

She got out of the car, and he drove off. The sky lay heavy on the rooftops, and the clouds threatened to burst. She sidestepped a patch of mud and sighed. This was it. This grubby piece of abandoned land was going to be her working life for the foreseeable future.

She spotted a gap in the fence, rounded the corner of a cabin, and jumped straight into the path of an oncoming labourer.

"Careful there. You need to check what's ahead," a female voice boomed with authority.

"I'm sorry, I didn't see you coming." She lost her footing in a pothole, and her flimsy heel gave way in the sand. She reached to get her balance and stumbled into the stranger's arms. "Shit, I'm so

sorry." Ruby gripped the woman and forced herself upright. Heat
rose to her cheeks.

"You okay there?" The woman smirked.

"Yeah, I'm fine." Ruby brushed her skirt for the fourth time that
morning and tried *not* to focus on the woman's sharp cheekbones.

"What are those shoes? You need safety boots if you're crossing
through the gate. This is a building site."

The young woman was as tall as the six-foot perimeter fence
they stood against. Her legs stretched for days towards a solid,
muscular frame, and her shirt was loosely untucked at her waist.
Ruby followed the trail of buttons towards the stranger's neck,
where tufts of blond hair poked from beneath her hard hat. Cobalt
flared across her irises as she waited for Ruby's response, and her
lips pursed like she was stiffened with annoyance. This wasn't the
start Ruby had hoped for. "Can you point me in the direction of the
meeting room, please?"

"The meeting room?" The labourer shifted onto one foot,
putting a hand on her hip. "Yeah, sure. It's past the ballroom, to the
left of the hospitality suite."

Ruby frowned. "Are you making fun of me?"

"Sorry. The joke's on me, not you. We don't have a meeting
room yet. The site offices arrive today." She smiled, her face
transforming.

"Where might I find Adrienne? She's one of the directors." Now
aware of her inappropriate dress for a building site, Ruby shrunk
into her two-piece suit and wanted to explain herself.

"Adrienne is due this morning. Why don't you come and get
a cuppa in the shed? It's the one place we have got." She wiped
her fingers against her thigh and offered Ruby her hand, "I'm Fred
Caffrey, the site manager."

So, you're in charge. Ruby's heart stuttered at the thought
of running a construction project with a female site manager.
That could be interesting. Maybe she could work with this little
banishment that Trix had forced upon her.

"Wow, I wasn't expecting that." She caught the flicker of frustration across Fred's brow. "I mean, I'm really pleased to be working with you. I'm Ruby. I've been assigned to your project to run the promotion."

"PR? Great. Exactly what we need." Fred turned and marched towards a metal shed.

Disappointment bubbled in Ruby's stomach. "I know what you might be thinking, but you don't need to worry. I won't get in the way."

"You lot always get in the way," Fred said without looking back.

"Not me." Ruby followed, looking out for any more sandy potholes. "I'm here to help. I'll manage the relations with the local residents, talk to the press, make sure we hit the headlines for the right reasons." She found her voice and switched her brain back on.

"Sure. Reputation management, right? Well, in my book, if you get the basics right and you're honest with people, you don't go far wrong."

"Yeah, I'd agree with that." Ruby wasn't sure why she was eager to please Fred, especially when she didn't want this job in the first place.

"You need boots on, Reputation Ruby. Follow me, please."

Ruby fought the sudden thought that Fred commanding the situation was kind of a turn-on.

"Try these." Fred chucked a pair of wellies in Ruby's direction when they went inside the metal shed. They hit the floor and toppled over, sending a cloud of dust into the air. Ruby slipped off a heel, balanced on one foot, and wished she'd packed a pair of thick socks.

"You'd better sit before you fall over again." Fred gestured to the wooden bench. "Here." She pulled a tarpaulin over the dried mud.

Ruby slipped the rubber against her calf. Her fingernails caught against dry cement and set her teeth on edge. She forced her left heel into the damp boot and twisted her right into the second. As she took a step, Fred burst with a deep laugh.

"What?" She turned to face her, wishing her new wellies came with a platform heel to give her a couple of extra inches to rise above Fred's taut chest. Even in a hi-vis vest, she looked ripped.

"Those are far too big for you. What size are you anyway?"

Fred's laugh had simmered to a chuckle now, but Ruby still hated to be made fun of.

"A five."

"Well, those are an eight. The smallest we do on-site." Fred's face softened, and she looked embarrassed. "I should know better. I'm sorry. They only stock men's sizes as standard."

"They're fine, honestly." Already feeling tiny, Ruby didn't want to make any more of a fuss. "Will I be okay with these?"

"You'll be safer than in those heels you turned up in, that's a dead cert. But be careful. Stay on the flat surfaces, and don't climb anything. Straight to your meeting and then back on civvy street for you, where the pavements are less risky." Fred's chuckle resumed.

Ruby's frown burrowed deeper across her forehead. "Where will I be seeing Adrienne then?"

"We'll be under a gazebo for now. I'm not sure why the big wigs are heading down, to be honest, but they like to show their faces every now and again."

Ruby stood a little taller. The big wigs she could handle. Within ten minutes she'd have them eating out of her hand and giving her an expense account and all access. This site manager, she couldn't work out. She looked amazing and was bossing her career, but something about her attitude stunk.

Clients usually fell at her feet. This morning, she'd been the one to fall at the first hurdle. She shrugged off the feeling of failure and put it down to the northern weather. But every cloud had a silver lining, she thought, when she saw Adrienne rock up in a sparkling, blue Porsche.

Blisters formed as the baggy wellies rubbed at her ankles, but she forced her frown into the widest, most professional smile she could muster. This job might deliver more than broken skin, but she was determined that the grey weather and miserable boss wouldn't break her spirit.

CHAPTER FOUR

"GET THAT TRUCK OFF my site," Fred shouted towards the lads gathered at the entrance.

A hard hat popped above the crowd. "You all right, boss?"

"Those lads haven't had a safety briefing. They can drop off at the gate then turn around." Fred tutted. "If they're staying, they can join the briefing at ten a.m. We've got some posh visitors, so they'll have to behave themselves. The last thing I need is untrained jobbers floating around when cabins are landing out of the sky."

Fred already had enough on her plate looking after the new marketing woman. Across the yard, Ruby leaned against the shed with her cinnamon hair falling to her shoulders. She looked out of place here, but in a bar, Fred would have thought about asking her out. The idea fluttered in her stomach, before rapidly turning to bile, and the bitter memory of rejection rose in her throat.

Ruby's skirt rode up. *Who wears a skirt to a building site?* She smiled and dipped her head, the vision of Ruby's thigh lingering in her mind. She shook her head. She was as bad as the lads, ogling over every female to grace the place with their presence.

"Right then, folks. Under the gazebo for this morning's safety briefing." She clapped her hands, drawing everyone's attention. Her heart stammered as all eyes fell on her. "You'll have all read the manuals. If you've not yet completed your induction, then stay behind after class."

The assembled crew mumbled.

"I'm afraid I have some VIPs to attend to this morning, so I'll be leaving you in the very capable hands of my deputy." She turned to her right. "Champ, can you carry on with the safety checklist, please? Everyone, lend Champ your ears, otherwise you may lose an eye or a finger."

There was a ripple of laughter, as if they all had a story to share of someone who'd met a nasty end on a building site. Fred turned away as Champ started talking. She had paperwork to file in the shed before the cabins were delivered. She'd forgotten about the visit from Adrienne and the high-ups, and she needed to gather herself to put on a show for them, which didn't come easy. She was much happier laying down bricks than playing up to the bosses.

She snuck a look back at the little crowd under the gazebo. Ruby had nestled between Adrienne and another suit that Fred didn't recognise. She wondered whether Ruby preferred the boardroom to the mess room. No matter. She was used to the marketing people coming and going. They rarely stayed long enough for the boys to take down the naughty posters from the snack shop.

"Boss, the cranes are on-site," Champ said over the crackling radio.

Fred held the button down to speak into the receiver. "Roger that. What's the ETA on the cabins?"

"Twenty minutes."

"Marvellous. See you out there." She caught Ruby's eye and smiled.

"You okay there, boss?" One of the new boys had crept up beside her.

She shrugged off the embarrassment of being caught staring at the new exec on-site. Respect was hard-earned for a fresh site manager. "Waiting for the cranes, Billy. Sit tight, and they'll be here soon."

"Who's the new girl?"

So he had spotted who she was looking at. "PR. She might not last long, the poor lass. She turned up in heels."

He tutted. "She'll learn."

Only if she's given the chance. Fred remembered all the

mistakes she'd made as an apprentice. But she'd at least been a labourer, not a fancy-pants office bod here to make everything look pretty.

"Good to see you, Fred," Adrienne said.

"Morning." She stepped back as Adrienne brushed imaginary soot off her collar in a gesture she now recognised as flirting. "Don't worry about cleaning me up. There's no point fighting the filth on a building site."

"I guess so. You're always so dirty, you and the boys."

Fred looked away, fighting the urge to snap back. "What brings you lot here today? Is there a press conference I missed in the diary?"

"No, not yet. Although I have brought the new PR to meet you. She'll put this place back on the map." Adrienne flashed a wicked grin. "Be kind with her; she's not as robust as your usual crew hands."

"We've met. She arrived this morning like a walking hazard. I should've chucked her off the site." Fred stuck her chin out to make the point.

"But you didn't?"

"I gave her some safety boots."

"You darling thing. Took pity on her, did you?" Adrienne smirked. "I like her. If her reputation is anything to go by, I think she'll be good for pre-sales. So keep her on your good side, please. I don't want to have to smooth things over like the last time."

"If you insist on sending me people who know nothing about keeping themselves or others safe, then what am I supposed to do?"

"Train them. Or get one of your crew to do it for you."

Adrienne touched Fred's sleeve, and she drew away. Her body no longer belonged to anyone else. Whether her heart did was another question. Either way, Adrienne wasn't the one. She just wasn't sure if she'd ever trust anyone enough to *be* the one.

***

Fred shrugged off her coat as she entered the bar, the cold air following through the door.

"Hello, love. The usual?" Trevor, the landlord, met her with the same warmth as the fire blazing in the hearth. "Good to see you knocking off at a reasonable time."

"I thought I'd sneak in for one before my tea."

"Your dad's in the skittle alley." He waved towards a narrow door, beyond which lay an old games room, now defunct.

"I'll leave him be for now, Trev." She cradled her cold beer and dipped her head, in no mood for conversation. Her mind swirled with second guesses, going over each decision she'd made that day. If she carried on like this, she wouldn't make it to the end of this project without driving herself mad.

"You look lost in thought, our Winifred."

She looked up to Stanley's kind eyes. He pulled a stool beside her and tipped his half empty pint glass in her direction.

"Hello, my old friend," she said.

"Not so much of the old, you."

Stan had three decades on her, and his eyes creased in new places since they'd last seen each other. She nudged his elbow. "It's good to see you, Wise Stan." She'd coined the term as his sixteen-year-old apprentice. He'd taken Fred under his wing, teaching her everything he knew in the trade. She narrowed her eyes. "It's funny I should see you tonight."

"Why's that, young one?"

The timbre of his smooth, deep voice calmed her, as it had done all those years ago, hanging from joists and scaling four-storey buildings. "You know I'm in charge on that new project at Boot Street?"

He smiled in his knowing way. "Quite right too. It's about time they promoted you."

"I'm not sure I'm ready for it." Her words fell flat onto the bar.

Stan stilled his pint in mid-swig. "Who says? If you're letting your demons eat away at your confidence, then you need to have a word. If you've got into overthinking everything, then you're in a battle against yourself that you'll never win." He finished his drink in one gulp and gestured for another. "If, on the other hand, someone has tapped you on the shoulder and told you that you might not be delivering the goods, then that's another story entirely." He paused. "Which one is it, Fred? Are you firing yourself before you've even got going?"

She sighed. "I guess so. I keep going over everything. I can't seem to make a decision. What if I'm no good?"

"The lads respect you, and the bosses believe in you. That's all you need. Get on with it, and the job will be half done before you know it."

She grinned. Stan always knew how to build her up in ways no one else had ever done. Her mum and dad believed in her. They encouraged her to be whatever she wanted. But it had taken Stan to show her what she was capable of.

"Let me tell you something." He nodded in thanks as Trevor swapped his empty glass with a full pint. "When you stumbled into my building site as a scrap of a thing, I was convinced you'd be gone by the end of the day. Your hair was all over the place, your mother had to practically force you through the gates, and you couldn't look the yard hand in the eye, never mind me."

Fred dropped her gaze. She didn't like to be reminded of the mess her life had been when she was a teenager. If it hadn't been for her mum, who knows where she'd be now. "Is this supposed to make me feel better?" She screwed her face up, hoping he'd move on.

"What I'm saying is that you kept coming back, day after day. You took on every job that needed doing. You learned the ropes. By that second week, I was impressed." He laid his hand on hers. "By the end of that first year, I'd come to rely on you. You were my right hand."

The silence rested between them, as if he wanted her to think about that. "Fred, you weren't even eighteen, and you'd proven yourself on that site. You worked hard, you looked out for the others, and you cared about whether the job was done well. People look to you because of that. Because you're fair. You call a spade a spade. That's leadership."

Fred took a long breath. She was used to Stan's pep talks, but they weren't often this personal. She faltered, forming her next words in her mind. "Do you really think I can do it?" Dread pooled in the pit of her stomach.

"I know it. The bosses know it too, otherwise they'd have sacked you already." His belly shook with laughter. "Now get on with it and stop second-guessing yourself."

"Thanks. I couldn't do it without you."

"Nonsense. It's been years since you've needed me."

She gulped down the last of her beer, swallowing the doubt that had been festering in her ribs since she'd taken the job. Maybe Stan was right. Maybe she could lead a hundred men on a construction-site if she wanted to. If only she could believe in herself as much as he did. And if she didn't, she'd have to fake it until she did.

CHAPTER FIVE

"Trix, I told you I'm going to give it a week, and if it doesn't get any better, you'll have to find me another gig," Ruby said, pinning the phone to her ear.

"Don't be unreasonable; a week isn't long enough."

Ruby shrugged off the accusation and took a breath, ready to defend herself.

"I can't tell DJ that you're coming off the project already. He'll flip his lid. He's trying to impress some old school friend or something. These are big clients, and it needs to be a success. Can't you work your magic and win this boss over?"

"She's a nightmare. She treats me like I'm an idiot." It wasn't truly that. Ruby hated feeling like she wasn't making a difference, and so far, she'd done nothing but get in the way.

"It's early days. You'll find your groove with this one, I have no doubt. And for bonus points, you're so much closer to home. Why don't you knock off early today and visit your sister for the weekend?"

"I guess I could. It'd be nice to see the sea for a change." Ruby recalled the ball of dirty clothes she'd left in her hotel room. "I could do my washing at least."

"See? It's a win-win. I bet Mel would love to see you," Trix said. "DJ's on the other line. I'll call you on Monday to see how you're doing. Enjoy the seaside for me." She sent an over-dramatic kissing sound down the line before hanging up.

The door to the cabin screeched open to reveal Fred carrying a cardboard box. "Knock, knock."

"Hey, can I help you with something?" Ruby tried her best to sound professional but dreaded another telling off.

"I come bearing gifts."

"Really?"

"No need to sound so surprised." Fred stepped back and looked at her boots. "I didn't give you a very warm welcome the other day. You caught me on a rough morning, and you didn't deserve the end of my tether."

Ruby smirked at Fred's turn of phrase, letting her guard down an inch. She nodded at the box between Fred's firm biceps. "Is that for me?"

Fred shuffled forward. "Yeah, sorry." She dropped it on the table and stepped back. "It's nothing really. I only wanted you to be comfortable." She cleared her throat. "Safe and comfortable."

Ruby picked at the packing tape with her painted nails, careful not to chip the polish.

"Here." Fred took a knife from her tool belt and flicked the blade. "I'll do it."

Ruby caught her scent, a blend of cologne and fresh rain.

Fred flipped open the parcel and brought out another, which Ruby recognised as a shoe box.

"My own boots?" She grinned. "You found size fives?" She met Fred's gaze, mirroring the joy on her face.

"I pulled some strings." Fred shrugged and fiddled with a thread on her vest.

"Thank you. This is brilliant." She pressed the back of her hand to her cheek, knowing it was glowing. "I feel..." She wasn't sure what it was, this tightness growing in her chest.

"You can't be walking around this place with wellies hanging off your feet. I'd have faced an inspection." Fred dove back into the box. "There's a safety vest too, so you've got one of your own. Pop your name inside, then it won't grow legs."

The moment between them had passed. Ruby took the neon vest and tucked it into her bag. "Thanks again, Fred."

"I'll see you Monday then." Fred walked towards the door

then looked back over her shoulder. "Are you up to anything this weekend?"

The question was stilted, like she'd had to remind herself to be polite.

Ruby weighed up her options. "Yeah, I thought I'd visit my sister back home."

"Home?" Fred turned around.

"In North Wales. She still lives up there."

Fred raised her eyebrow. "I thought you were from down south?"

"Nope. I grew up on the Llyn Peninsula."

"Ah, I can hear it now, in your voice. Gorgeous place. We used to holiday in Wales every year. I've fond memories of that place. Lucky girl." Fred stiffened, looking awkward again. "I'll leave you to it. Have a good one."

Ruby shook her head as the door clipped back into its latch. Fred's gift had surprised her. Maybe she'd stick with this job after all. She picked up her phone and searched for trains to her hometown. "Fifty minutes." She smiled before dialling her childhood telephone number. "Mel? It's Ruby."

By the end of the day, she stood at the porch of her family home, staring at the naked branches of the wintering wisteria. The wind howled across the garden as it wrapped its way around the imposing Georgian house.

"Welcome home." Her sister's figure filled in the doorway, and Ruby leaned in to give her a big squeeze. "What are you doing all the way up here?"

"I'm working in Manchester."

"Wow, little sister, that's a big change for you. Aren't you missing the bar and your exes?"

"My exes?" Ruby arched her eyebrow at the strange question. Why would she miss her exes? They were a distant memory and usually so fleeting she barely had time to tell Melissa about them.

"No, silly. Your *axes*."

"That makes more sense. Yes, I'm bereft. I haven't thrown in a week, and my muscles are wasting away." Ruby laughed for the first time in a few days. The sea air and a friendly hug was already doing her the world of good.

"Let's get in for a cuppa. It's freezing out here."

Ruby followed her sister across the threshold, shaking off a fleeting memory of tripping when she was six and bruising her knees on the cold flagstones. She closed the door behind her, trapping the cold air inside, and shivered.

"The fire's roaring, so get yourself warm. I'll put the kettle on."

Ruby made her way to the large living room, noticing her sister's latest changes to the house. Her mum's old chair had finally been removed, and there was a new sheepskin rug against the hearth. The ageing Labrador raised his head to acknowledge her, but he was too ancient to move.

"Too lazy to say hello, Douglas?" Ruby scratched his head anyway.

"How long will you be in Manchester?" Melissa set down two mugs of steaming tea.

"I'm not sure if I'm staying yet."

"Is it a quick job then?"

"No, it's a big property development. But I'm not sure I fit in with the team." Once she said it out loud, she doubted herself even more. Fred hadn't exactly welcomed her with open and firm, ripped arms. But she had just made an effort with the new boots.

Melissa's brow furrowed, clearly trying to work out what Ruby was holding back. They'd chosen such different paths growing up. The eldest staying put in the gentrified coastal town they'd called home when they weren't at boarding school, while Ruby had spread her wings at the first opportunity.

"You'll find your way. You always do."

Ruby rose from her chair and approached the tall window. Thick, grey clouds gathered at the horizon, threatening to engulf the shoreline. A few scattered rooftops stood between her and the deep green of Tremadoc Bay. She'd been so quick to run away from all the space and beauty that home offered. All for the promise of a swift promotion and a heady nightlife.

"Do you have a travel mug? I might take my drink outside for a stroll."

"Are you sure? It's almost dark."

"Yeah, I won't be long." Moments later, she pulled on her sister's wellies and stomped to the edge of her parents' garden, sinking into the salty ground.

"What's going on with you?" Melissa's tone hardened like the whip of the sea breeze.

She faltered, thinking for a moment of brushing off the question with her usual swagger and wondering if she could spin a half-truth. Her shoulders sagged, giving her away. "I'm feeling a bit out of place on this job. There's something about it. It's like I can't rely on my usual..."

"Charms?"

"Yeah, I guess." She hated to admit it, but Melissa was right. There was something else eating at her. "I feel weird being this close to home."

London had been her sanctuary for so long, she was out of step. She'd forgotten the genuine friendliness and the humility of those around her. "People are so nice. It's a bit strange."

"Stick around, dear sister, and you might find you like it." Melissa touched her shoulder, breaking her downward stare. "It might be time to start some adventures closer to home, closer to people who love you."

Ruby considered the vision of the future that her sister was painting, here against the blank canvas of the grey sky. For some reason, Fred appeared in her imagination. "Maybe you're right. I've been wanting to do something that makes a difference for so long. I don't just want to flog things. I want to do something meaningful."

"Of course you do. But you could do whatever you want." Mel looked up at the darkening sky. "What *do* you want?"

"I don't know." Ruby huffed. Successes came easy, but they didn't always bring satisfaction. She'd always had more to prove.

"What's this new project anyway?"

"It's a street of derelict terraced houses built back-to-back, like in the old days. The developer wants to keep the old frontages but demolish the inside and rebuild with bright, open family spaces."

"Sounds pretty amazing. Like breathing new life into old family homes." Melissa strolled down a sodden path towards a cliff edge. "Imagine the lives that those houses have started. All the families they've cherished in their four walls."

The vision of families in the rows of back-to-back houses filled Ruby with hope. Suddenly, she saw the potential stories she could tell, the treasure trove of past lives she could explore, and the future warmth and love that new homes could create. Excitement bubbled in her stomach, and she reached for her phone, taking notes as fast as her thumbs could type.

"Got some ideas?"

"Loads of them. This is amazing."

A wide smile stretched across Mel's cheeks, illuminated in the bright light of the phone screen.

"I'm glad I came home. Thank you."

"You're always welcome, little sister. We'd better head back; it's almost pitch black. The light falls ever so quickly out here. What do you fancy for dinner?"

With a blink, the grey sky had turned to ink, like a blackboard had been pulled down from the sky. Ruby's eyes adjusted to the lack of light, and she smiled at the feathers of clouds hanging in the sea air.

She stepped a little lighter on the way back to the house, knowing she could make a go of it back in Manchester. She vowed to start looking for a place to stay so she could say goodbye to that cheap hotel room and rehearsed the pitch that she'd make to Fred first thing on Monday.

A sticky start wasn't going to put her off. She wasn't always sure of herself, but she could bring all her ideas and charm to this new job. Maybe it could work out. She'd certainly turned a corner with Fred earlier today, so it wasn't all bad. Sure, she missed her London life, but it was time for a change of pace.

CHAPTER SIX

A WEEK HAD PASSED since Ruby's return from home on the peninsula. The mirror betrayed her nerves but, determined to make this a brand-new day, she tapped some colour into her cheeks. Her phone buzzed, and she rummaged in her deep bag. A text from the local reporter flashed on her home screen.

Hi Ruby. ETA five minutes. Look forward to meeting you.

Her phone wasn't the only thing buzzing. The thrill of hosting the press never failed her, and she strode across the building site as fast as her new size fives would take her. "Hello, Jonah." She tipped her chin up and flashed him a winning smile.

"You must be Ruby." He pointed at the crew behind him. "This is Gavin and Seth. They're camera and sound today."

"Good to see you all. Let's get you hard hats and boots." A warm glow rose inside. She almost sounded like she knew what she was doing. "Follow me."

Once kitted out, she led the team to the far end of the terraces beyond the demolition zone. Cracked with weather and age, they presided tall over the run-down street. "These houses haven't changed much in a whole century," she said with a flourish, hoping her new media friends would share her excitement.

"Can we get any higher, do you think?" Jonah scratched his chin, surveying the skyline. "It'd be great to capture the symmetry of these rooftops on camera."

Ruby's belly rolled. It was a great coup to get the television news to Boot Street, and she'd practically begged the director to send them, but she wasn't sure about that request. "We'd agreed a wide shot at street level. The reflection off the cobbles is looking lovely, don't you think?" She clutched at straws, knowing full well if the crew wanted an aerial shot, they'd get it.

"Could we order a drone in?" Gavin asked.

"No go. It'd take too long," Jonah said.

"How about climbing up there?" Seth, who'd so far been silent, pointed towards the flat roof of an end terrace.

Ruby scanned the empty street. Fred wasn't around, and there was no one else to check with. Seth hauled his camera over his shoulder and set off towards the house. Ruby jogged to keep up, her mind racing with questions. "I should check with the site office before we go in there."

"We haven't got much time," Jonah said. "I've got to be at a school fête in Didsbury by ten o'clock. It's an empty house, isn't it?"

"I'll call someone." Her phone almost slipped from her hand, and she struggled to scroll to Fred's name. "Voicemail." She hung up, not wanting to bother her unless it was really necessary.

Seth leaned on the front door, and Ruby hoped it was locked, giving her a fighting chance to stall their progress. "Hang on, let me —"

The door swung back on its hinges, and Seth disappeared inside.

"Good work, chaps," Jonah said, his voice booming across the cobbles. "See, Ruby? We can nip up there and be done in fifteen minutes."

She stiffened, fixed her smile, and followed him through the front door, before being engulfed by the damp lack of sunlight. She flicked a switch in vain. "No power. Guys, I really think we'd better go outside where it's safer." Part of her wanted to put her foot down and march them out of there, but a little voice inside reminded her that tonight's TV coverage would be gold if they could get a view of the street. She heard stomping footsteps up the narrow, wooden staircase.

"Jonah, I've found a way to the roof you saw."

"On my way."

Ruby panicked. "Folks, could you let me go first? I really need to check out where we're heading." But it was too late, so she followed, resigned to getting in and out as quickly as possible without causing any trouble. She hadn't been this far into the houses before. She climbed the steep stairs, skimming her fingertips across the peeling lime plaster.

As she emerged into the back bedroom, the crew had already made their way out of a large window and onto the flat roof. Seth was setting up his camera, while Gavin twiddled buttons on a portable sound desk. She climbed out to join them.

"Ruby, give us some space while we run through a couple of takes." Jonah breezed past, and she almost fell back through the window.

"I'm not sure we should be on this roof without any type of harness."

Everyone ignored her. She bit back her irritation, not wanting to rock the boat with the local TV crew.

Jonah muttered his weather spiel, reciting place names and predictions. Ruby took in the view. It was pretty cool. If she leaned over and squinted through the gaps in the rooftops, greater Manchester sprawled as far as she could see. The terraced peaks looked like an industrial mountain range. At the site's entrance, a collection of yellow vests marched around like a game of Pac Man. Down the street, cranes pierced the silver sky. She followed them higher and higher until her neck ached.

A yellow vest broke from the crowd and moved rapidly towards them. She looked back at Gavin, head down, wearing huge tin-like earphones.

"Almost there, Jonah," Seth said. "Let's have a final run through before we go. In three, two, one."

Gavin concentrated on the sound instruments, and Ruby held her breath, worried he could hear the rise and fall of her lungs.

"Good morning, everyone, from the old Boot Street estate in Greater Manchester. It's good to have you with us. As you can see, this part of town is undergoing a major transformation– Can we try that again, Seth?" Jonah screwed his face up. "I didn't like it."

A siren blasted, sending Ruby into the air with fright.

"What the hell are you doing up there?" Fred shouted from the street. "I'm coming up."

Ruby swallowed the fear in her throat, and it didn't take long before Fred climbed through the window, her face thunderous.

"Can I ask what you lot are doing on a roof with no safety equipment in the middle of a live building site?"

"Fred, I'm sorry. The crew wanted to get a high shot of the terraces for tonight's weather. It'll look so beautiful on camera. I thought it would be okay to come up."

"Get down, please," Fred said tightly. "You've no business being here, and it's a violation of all our site rules. You should be accompanied, and you should all have a harness." She looked directly at Ruby. "I don't know why you thought this would be acceptable, but it isn't. Not on my watch."

Jonah took a few steps closer to Fred. "Now listen–"

"Please, sir. I'm Fred Caffrey, and I'm in charge of this site, Mr?"

"Jonah. Jonah Meredith. You may know me from channel six."

"No, Mr Meredith, I do not. I'd like you and your assistants to come through this window and climb down the stairs. You will regroup on the street outside. You may wish to know that the structure of these buildings has been condemned. They're due to be demolished on Monday."

Humiliation burned Ruby's cheeks. She'd wanted to impress the TV crew so she could win some great press coverage for the project, and the last thing she'd wanted was to disappoint Fred even more.

Seth grew fidgety. "We're going live in seven minutes, Jonah. We'd better get a wriggle on."

Jonah pinched his brow. "This is ridiculous."

But he followed Ruby back into the house and down the stairs.

"Fred, I'm so sorry," Ruby said.

"Save it. We can talk later." Fred marched them outside and pointed to a spot in the middle of the road. "This will be safe. I'll watch you from here."

Ruby willed the cobbles to unzip and bury her beneath them. Not only couldn't she organise a media opportunity, she had to be supervised by the boss herself. It could only be worse if Jonah had stomped his feet and walked off without doing the weather report, but it was too close to the live segment for him to find another backdrop now.

Fred stood to one side, her heavyset frame growing even more dominant. Ruby shrank even further into herself.

When the forecast was finished, Seth counted Jonah down, and they all visibly relaxed.

"Right then, boss, we'll be out of your hair." Jonah flipped his floppy fringe over to one side. With the weather in the can, he'd clearly already moved onto the next piece.

Fred nodded and held her radio to her chin without breaking eye contact with Jonah. "Champ, can you send Tim down on a buggy to escort some visitors off-site. Immediately, please, to location five."

The radio buzzed. "Okay, boss."

"They'll be a couple of minutes."

Every passing moment stretched as slowly and painfully as the last.

"Shall we walk?" Ruby ventured, knowing as soon as the words popped from her lips that she was pushing her luck.

"No. I'd like to ensure our guests are safely returned to the gate." Fred glowered in Jonah's direction but not before flashing Ruby a cold stare.

When the buggy arrived, Fred touched Ruby's sleeve. "You'd better stay with me for a debrief."

As she waved them off with pleasantries, worry settled in her gut. She pondered what flavour of telling off she was about to get.

"Ruby, I appreciate your hard work, but you can't have random people wandering all over the place. It's dangerous."

Fred was being reasonable, and Ruby knew it. But there was a part of her that wanted to fight back. "I did try to stop them, but they marched on."

"It's your job to stop them. You shouldn't even have been all the way up here without someone else. If something had happened, it's my neck on the line."

That was it. It dawned on Ruby that Fred wasn't angry with her but fearful that something might go wrong on her watch. She shoved her hands in her pockets. "I'm sorry. I hadn't thought of it like that. I didn't really have time to."

Fred sighed. "Next time, call someone in for back up. Champ or one of the other guys can help."

"I've been an idiot, haven't I?"

Fred looked at her and took a long breath. Ruby braced herself for another dressing down.

"It's okay. Don't beat yourself up. But learn for next time, won't you?" Fred walked on without waiting. "Follow me back, so I know you're safe too," she said over her shoulder.

"Yep. Definitely," Ruby said, grateful for the second chance. She hated the idea of disappointing Fred now that they'd built some sort of rapport. She let out the breath she'd been holding in. This job had her wound so tight that she wasn't sure whether she could keep it up. Maybe she should talk to Trix again about another contract.

But when she thought about moving on, the image of Fred striding down the street came to mind. She shook her head. It's not like she'd miss getting told off every day. But the cock of Fred's head and the warmth of her smile lingered in her mind. She looked up to the distance Fred had created between them and jogged to keep up. Why was she struggling to impress someone who quite clearly had no time for her?

CHAPTER SEVEN

FRED SLAMMED THE DOOR, shaking the flimsy walls of her office. She pulled off her hard hat and threw it onto the desk. "For fuck's sake," she said, regretting losing her temper with Ruby. She hadn't meant to come down so hard, but the sight of three strangers practically dangling off a rooftop had made her blood boil. Everything she was working so hard for could come tumbling down in an instant if there was a serious accident on-site, and Ruby was putting them all at risk.

She scraped off her boots and wriggled her toes. It felt good to release them from their steel toe-capped prison. Outside, the sky turned sapphire and Fred welcomed the sun setting on another day against the timeline. She needed a drink. Something to wash away the stresses of having to keep everyone in line. She pulled on her coat to head home, flicked the light, and made her way to security.

"Good night, Rattle." She'd given the new guard his nickname because of the heavy set of keys dangling at his waist.

He stood taller as Fred approached. "Night, boss. Have a good one."

She couldn't face her local tonight. It would mean pleasantries she didn't have the energy for, so she headed for the backlit welcome of the pub across the road.

The double doors to the Jolly Anchor creaked open and two canoodling lovebirds tumbled out. She tutted, her impatience clinging to her like the smell of sweat. Inside, she recoiled from the stench of stale beer. A few regulars gathered at the bar, but she spotted a space between the pumps. "Pint of pale ale, please."

She cut short the woman's eye contact, not wanting to prolong the small talk. With a cold pint, she sat in a booth and reached for her phone to numb the day away.

A shadow moved across the table. "Mind if I join you?"

Ruby held a bulbous wine glass between her delicate fingers. She wore an awkward smile, but somehow still looked fresh as the morning, her lips painted red and her nut-brown eyes sparkling.

"Could we chat about earlier? It won't take long."

She installed herself opposite Fred before she had the chance to object.

"Did you follow me here?" Fred raised her eyebrow.

"No," Ruby said. "It's the local. I needed a drink after this morning."

"Yeah, me too." Fred sighed. "I'm not sure I've got the energy to go over today's chaos, to be honest. I came here to relax and forget about it all."

"That's what I wanted to talk about. I've been going over what happened. I'm sorry things got away from me." She fiddled with a beer mat. "I know I was stupid, but I felt like a complete joke in front of that TV crew."

Fred clenched her jaw, biting down on the anger rising in her throat. "I see." She stared at the foam top of her amber beer. "I'm still pretty wound up by the whole thing, Ruby. I'm not sure the pub is the right place for us to have another debrief."

Ruby held her hand up. "I don't want that. I really was trying to do the right thing, and I made a mistake. It hasn't been easy starting here. I feel..."

Fred glanced up to her adorable face, her eyebrows furrowed with confusion, and her shoulders hunched up to her ears. She gulped at her pint, unsure what to do. "I'm sorry." She wasn't certain why she was apologising, but she wanted to make Ruby feel better. Somehow, it made her feel better too. "Okay, I might've come down a bit hard. It's my fault, really, if protocols aren't followed, and you shouldn't have been gallivanting around on your own."

She searched Ruby's face for signs of understanding. Maybe even remorse. "I hope we can put it behind us."

"Yeah, I'd like that. I honestly didn't want to let you down." She pouted. "Can we start again?"

Fred clinked her glass to Ruby's. "In the spirit of moving on, let's talk about something else." She scratched her earlobe, searching for a neutral topic they could settle on. "How're you getting on in your new place? Where did you find in the end?"

"It's temporary. Nothing special for now."

Ruby bit her lip, sending a flutter across Fred's tummy.

"I've been keeping an eye out for something better, but there's nothing local. I didn't really want a long commute, but I guess I'll have to look further into Manchester," Ruby said.

"It's a cool city. You'll love it. Great nightlife." Fred drained her pint. "Not as good as London, I guess."

"That depends. London doesn't always deliver on its promises." Ruby nodded to the bar. "Can I buy you another drink?"

Fred hesitated. "I should get home." She clocked the disappointment on Ruby's face, and the desire to make her happy peaked. "Go on then. I'll have the same again."

Ruby returned with two more drinks and a broad smile. "So, Fred, where is home?"

She frowned, weighing up how much to divulge. "I live on the outskirts of the city with my mum and dad." She paused, trying to stem the urge to explain herself. "My dad got sick, and I moved home to help. My younger brothers are still there, hanging around like gone-off cheese in the fridge. The older two have flown the nest."

"Sounds hectic, but lovely."

Ruby tilted her head, revealing the length of her smooth, kissable neck. Fred shook the vision from her head and studied the woodgrain in their table. "It's chaos most of the time. I come to work for a rest."

Ruby chuckled. "Surely you get away with murder as the only

girl in a house full of brothers?"

Fred cringed. "Well, I wasn't much of a girl, so I kept up with the boys. I lived in cut-off jeans and trainers for my entire childhood. The only dress I owned was for my first Holy Communion, and even that day I changed into shorts and roller blades for the after-party." They laughed in unison, and Fred revelled in the joy radiating from Ruby. "How about you?"

"Mixed bag, really. There's me and my sister. She lives at home in Abersoch. Mum and Dad retired to Spain a few years ago, and we see them every now and again. I moved away at eighteen when I went to university and didn't really look back."

"How come you don't have a thick Welsh accent? There's a hint of it, but only if I listen really hard."

"Ah, I blame boarding school and moving around all over the place. I'm a bit of a nomad really. I blend in wherever I land."

"Yeah?" Fred couldn't imagine moving from place to place with nowhere to really call home. "But you lived in London before you came here?"

"London is where my little flat is. But if the agency sends me to Dubai for three months, then off I go."

Fred admired her sense of adventure. It was a far cry from living back in your childhood bedroom, even if that was with good intention.

"I pretty much moved straight to London after university." Ruby ran her finger around the rim of her glass then licked away a spot of wine. "There were a couple of jobs, but the lure of the big smoke was irresistible and before I knew it, I was tied into one of the huge agencies. I've been hopping on and off contracts for about a decade."

"Didn't you miss home? It's so lovely there." Fred frowned, hating herself a little bit for sounding so parochial. Of course, Ruby wouldn't miss Wales when she had the whole world at her feet.

"It's gorgeous. When I went back last weekend, it was so quiet and grounding. But I outgrew the town and needed to get away when I did. Maybe one day I'll go back, but there's not much for me there now."

"I don't suppose there are lots of glamorous PR accounts begging for your attention on the Llyn Peninsula?"

"Maybe not." Ruby shrugged and gave her a mischievous smile. "There aren't that many glamorous accounts here either."

"Hey, are you accusing me of running a dull construction project?" Fred touched Ruby's arm, sending a pulse of connection through her.

"Not at all, boss." Ruby winked. "It's far from boring. But I don't feel that glam in my boots and oversized yellow vest!"

"I think you carry off that vest just fine." Fred gulped, realising what she'd said.

"Really? I don't fill them out as well as you. But then I spend most of the time exercising my brain rather than my biceps."

Fred shrugged, trying not to look at Ruby's body though she didn't miss Ruby doing the same to her.

"I mean, not that you don't exercise your brain too. Sorry, I didn't mean that. I spend too much time exercising my mouth."

Fred laughed. "It's okay. I took it as a compliment." She flexed her guns, mocking herself.

The intensity of Ruby's gaze was too much. Fred dropped her hands in her lap and rubbed at the callouses on her palms.

"I've actually been giving this job a lot of thought," Ruby said after a short silence.

"Yeah? What're you thinking?" Fred sighed, relieved to be back on firm ground where she could talk about work for a while.

"I've been fretting over how to bring this project to life. Seeing as we're not going to be launching any sales for months, I need something with a shelf life. A kind of hook to capture people's imagination and bring them with us for the long haul."

Fred nodded, uncertain where this was heading but willing to give Ruby the space she needed to explain. "Go on."

"Let's go back in time."

Fred rested her chin in her hand. "What do you mean?"

"I want to delve into the stories of the families who lived in our streets of terraced houses when they were brand new, when the industrial revolution wasn't a chapter in a stuffy old textbook, but a time that people were living through." Ruby's eyes flared with energy. "I want to tell the stories of the people who grew up here, who chased each other in and out of the back yards. Of people who fell in love kissing their sweethearts in the alleys."

Fred choked on her mouthful of beer. "Sorry," she said, getting her breath. "What's this got to do with our development?"

"Does it not make sense?" Ruby looked heartbroken.

"No, I get it." She absolutely did *not* get it. "Tell me more."

"I want to tell the stories of the past, so people will want to buy the homes of their future. It'll inspire a whole new generation to build their families right here." Ruby sat back with her chest puffed out, obviously delighted with her pitch.

Fred grinned. "I like it." She liked happy, proud Ruby. And she did appreciate the idea, even though she struggled to keep up with Ruby's runaway train of thought. The woman was a whirlwind. But there was something about her energy that made Fred want to gather her things and launch headfirst into the tornado to know more. "I really like the idea." Fred raised her glass. "To the past and the future."

Ruby clinked her wine glass against Fred's beer jug. "And the present. Let's not forget enjoying the present."

Maybe Fred was enjoying the present a bit too much. Ruby had made her forget the day's troubles and relax into the comfort of their conversation. Aside from the physical relationship she'd enjoyed with Adrienne, it'd been such a long time since Fred had really spent time with another woman. She'd almost forgotten the barriers that she put up to protect herself from the banter and ridicule that often came her way at work and at home.

She pushed away the thought that there might be something more between them. That maybe she was attracted to Ruby in a way that had burned her the last time. She met Ruby's gaze and forced herself to dwell in it. It felt good to be seen by someone, but the eye contact made her blink away, almost fearful of what might come next. It was probably nothing anyway. Ruby was friendly with everyone. Fred wasn't that special, was she?

CHAPTER EIGHT

"WILL YOU HELP ME?"

"Ruby, this isn't a great time." Fred scanned the room as the last of her crew exited the morning briefing.

"I brought you this." She thrust a takeaway coffee into Fred's ungloved hand. "Flat white, no syrup."

"Sweet enough, am I?"

"Something like that." Ruby scratched at her neck as the heat breached her collar. "I have tonnes of ideas." She held a bulging notepad up to Fred's face.

"Okay, you win." Fred grinned. "But you'll have to walk with me. I need to check in with the demolition guys."

"Absolutely." Ruby zipped up her oversized coat and followed Fred to the door. "I've been thinking about going to the records office and looking up all the people who used to live here."

"Good idea. Go for it."

Ruby sensed Fred was trying to get rid of her but persisted. "I figured we could find the details of at least one or two families who still have living relatives. They might be willing to talk to us." Ruby blinked into the cold wind, wishing Fred would give her a few more words of encouragement. "Would you come with me? You know more about the local area than I do."

"When? I can't take a day off-site and go swanning about."

Her harsh words were softened by a chuckle that Ruby was fast learning was a Fred specialty. "I'm one step ahead of you. We can go on Saturday."

Fred stopped in her tracks and turned to Ruby. She frowned, biting her cheek as if she were trying to work out a hard maths question. "You want us to go out to the records office on Saturday?"

"I was hoping we could go together. I'd appreciate your help." It was no biggie. It's not like she was asking Fred out on a hot date or anything. "I could go myself."

"What makes me think a silent room full of dusty records isn't your idea of fun?"

"I don't know. What does make you think that? I've done my fair share of serious research, and I spent a lot of time in the university library."

"And the university bar, I bet."

"It's thirsty work." Ruby squirmed under Fred's intense scrutiny. "But I'm serious about this. I want to do it properly."

"I get that. I'll think about it. I might have to shuffle a few things on Saturday to make it work."

Ruby bounced with excitement. If she could get a bit of traction with this idea, everything else would fall into place.

"My two favourite people," Adrienne said, her shrill voice cutting across the yard.

They both took a step back, making Ruby realise how close she'd been to Fred.

"Adrienne," Fred said.

Ruby sensed a tension that hadn't been there a few moments ago.

"Time for another visit?" Fred asked. "We can't keep you away these days."

"I like to keep on top of things. You know that." She raised her eyebrow, but Fred had turned away from them both, already making strides.

"Fred, we have a meeting scheduled. See you in the office in an hour?" Adrienne called after her, placing her hands on her slim hips.

"At your command." Fred waved her hand in a casual salute.

Ruby fought back a giggle. Fred sure knew how to brush people off. At least she wasn't on the receiving end this time.

Adrienne turned towards her. "How're you getting on? When can I see a launch plan?"

"Soon. It's almost there." Ruby plastered on the widest smile she could to hide the white lie. "Fred and I were talking about some ideas. We're onto something."

"Intriguing." Adrienne frowned, and her gaze drifted towards Fred's silhouette, shrinking away from them both. "Don't distract our site manager too much. She has a big job to do."

Adrienne's comment lodged in Ruby's mind. She didn't want to get in the way, but she couldn't do her job without spending time with Fred. She needed to get under the skin of Boot Street, nothing more than that.

The day on-site passed without incident, and Ruby returned to her shared flat. The door knocked and swung open with such a force that it rebounded. "Trix!"

"I'm here." Trix wrapped her in a hug and landed two air kisses on her cheeks. "God, it's taken me ages."

"It's Manchester, not the North Pole."

"Euston was a nightmare. Then there was a delay at some shire or other. And then there were endless green fields for miles. I thought I was going to nod off and miss my stop. I had a rough night."

Ruby rolled her eyes and pulled Trix up the stairs towards the kitchen. "Come, quickly. We can grab a cuppa, and you can catch me up on all the news."

Trix wrinkled her nose. "Why are you still living here, Ruby? Can't you get yourself a flat sorted?"

"I'm trying, but it's horrible out there. The decent places are snapped up before they're even viewed."

"Sounds like London."

"Sort of, but for half the price." Ruby flicked the kettle on and brushed at leftover crumbs on the worktop. "I hate living in someone else's space, but I can't get a break."

"What's she like? The flatmate?"

"The 'landlady,' as she likes to be known, is pretty harmless." Ruby cupped her hand at her cheek. "But boring as shit," she whispered.

Trix laughed. "She's not here, is she?"

"God, no. If she was, I'd have taken you straight out." Ruby stirred two sugars into Trix's tea and set it in front of her. "Come on, sit down and spill."

"There's not much to tell you really. DJ is in Spain on the reshoot of that commercial. Everyone's enjoying the quiet time."

"Is that why you could sneak up here?" Ruby winked.

"Absolutely. You don't think he'd have let me out of London? While the cat's away..." They both giggled. "I did have a proper reason to come though."

Ruby's jaw tightened. "And here I was thinking it was a social visit."

"It is." Trix put her arms around Ruby and squeezed. "I've missed you like crazy."

She avoided eye contact. Trix was gorgeous, and Ruby had often thought that if she hadn't been straight, they would've made a perfect match. "I've missed you too. I've got no friends up here."

"That can't be true. My little social butterfly must have a crowd of northern cool kids following her around by now."

Trix gave her a playful dig in the ribs, but the assumption that she'd already made this place her own troubled her. Why hadn't she hit the bars and made some new mates? "It's a bigger change than you think. I'm starting over. I miss the flat in London and the bar downstairs."

"You miss the hook ups, more like."

"No. Although I have suffered a serious dry spell since you banished me north."

"I didn't banish you, Ruby." Trix looked hurt at the suggestion. "I gave you this contract because I knew that you could make diamonds from brick dust. Once you've done it, you can return to London with some serious BDE."

"Big dick energy?" Ruby pursed her lips in disgust.

"Big dyke energy, more like." Their heads bumped together as they laughed. "Talking of which, what's all this about a dry spell?"

"It's been a busy time, and I can hardly bring anyone back here with landlady Lou breathing down my neck, can I?" Ruby sighed. It was more than that. She'd been a fish out of water here, and her run-ins with Fred hadn't helped matters. Ruby jumped as the front door slammed shut. "It's Lou. She's back early. Quick, let's go into my room." She held a finger to her lips to keep Trix from saying anything inappropriate.

"Hi there," Ruby said as they disappeared into her bedroom. "I'm getting ready to go out."

"Right you are. I'll leave you to it," Lou said as the door clicked shut.

"Wow. You really are reliving the student dream here."

Ruby looked around the cramped room and saw the piles of clothes and dirty mugs through Trix's eyes. She flipped the duvet to cover the bed and cleared her throat. "Sorry, I haven't had anyone back here, and it's been a full-on week at work. Here." She sat on the bed and gestured to the space next to her.

Trix settled against her. "Sorry I sent you up here on your own."

"So you should be, you cow." Ruby leaned against Trix's shoulders.

"Is it awfully lonely?"

Ruby bit her lip while she thought about it. So far, she'd had some embarrassing moments and some pretty low ones. "No, it's getting better. I think I've made up with the site manager now, and she's cool really. Especially when she stops worrying about everything."

"She? That's unusual for a development this size. She must be a pretty big deal."

"I guess so. She doesn't come across like that though. She's kind of humble. Understated."

Trix drew back and looked Ruby straight in the face. "Wait.

You've got that weird voice and dreamy look. The one you have when you're into someone. Do you like her?"

"What? No." Ruby wriggled on the bed and wished she was sat somewhere that didn't creak beneath her. "I'm simply saying I had a breakthrough with her at the pub the other night. Before that, she thought I was a bit of a loser."

"You've been to the pub together already? I thought you were in a lonely dry spell?"

"It wasn't a date or anything like that. It was a drink after work. And we'd had a really rough day. It was the day I almost shot the weather forecast on the roof, and she thought I was crazy."

"Why? That was a genius idea," Trix said and arched her eyebrows.

"I know. It was also perfectly adequate at ground level in the end."

"So she was okay with it, eventually?"

"Once she'd given everyone a good telling off, we got past it." Ruby sipped her tea. "Why all the questions about the bloody weather?"

Trix took a deep breath. "Well, that's sort of why I came up here."

"The weather forecast? Have we had a complaint?"

"No, it's not about the weather. Let me finish." Trix turned again, creating a tidal wave across the sprung mattress. "I've got a client who wants to do something extraordinary for a charity. You know the type: Monday to Friday, they're screwing people for every penny they earn but on a Saturday, they like to show their nice side."

"Go on. I can feel me getting embroiled in this somehow."

"That sixth sense never fails you, does it?" Trix bopped her nose. "I was thinking we could run an abseil off that derelict factory at the edge of Boot Street. My client gets the kudos, and your client gets to talk up the new houses. It's a win-win."

The vision of Fred stomping across the cobbles to shut down yet another of her escapades flooded Ruby's mind. "Fred won't allow it. She'll say it's frivolous and not worth the risk."

"Well, bugger Fred. I've already had it agreed by the board." Trix held her mug up in a victory toast. "My client has made a nice little donation to the company in exchange for their cooperation. So it's out of Fred's hands, I'm afraid. She'll have to live with it."

Ruby swallowed. "She won't like it."

"She sounds like a bit of a diva. Are you sure she's a good match for you? I thought you preferred to wear the trousers?"

Ruby stopped short of Trix's trap. "Nice try. She's not a match of any sort. She's the client, and I need to keep her happy if I'm to get any kind of publicity for this sodding account that you've thrust me onto." She hopped off the bed and slurped the dregs of her tea. "Get ready. I'm taking you to the pub. We can figure out this blasted abseil there."

The thought of juggling the competing demands of Trix and Fred made Ruby's head spin. It was lovely to have her best friend by her side, and she'd jump at the chance to work together again. But diving off tall buildings wasn't going to go down well in the cabin, no matter how much higher up Trix had gone to seal the deal.

Ruby shrugged. It wasn't her problem. So why was she twisted up with worry? They hardly knew each other. Why was she bothered about winding Fred up again or letting her down?

CHAPTER NINE

"TOMMY, LEAVE IT, PLEASE." Fred wrestled the saw from her brother's pale hand and placed it back on the workbench.

"But you never let me have a go."

"Stop whining. You're old enough to get your own tools." Brian stretched his long legs on the couch.

"Don't make me regret letting you two in here this morning."

"Don't blame me. I brought you tea and toast." Brian folded his arms across the bulk of his chest in protest.

"You carried a mug and a plate through the back yard. Mum made both, you cheeky git." She threw a cushion, and he caught it.

"Can I do this bit?" Tommy asked.

Unable to take the whining puppy act, she offered him the handle of a carving tool. "Careful then. I don't need a hospital trip. I'm trying to get this finished before I go out."

"Where are you off to? You're not coming to the football with us?" Brian straightened on the battered old couch. "You'll miss out on pie and pints with Dad."

"I know." Fred studied the movement of Tommy's blade across the walnut. He had a raw skill when he calmed down long enough to focus. "I promised someone at work that I'd go to the record office in town to do a bit of research."

"You're going to a stuffy old library for the day instead of watching United play at home?"

They stared at her, wide-eyed.

"Research for what?" Tommy asked, taking his blade from the surface of the wood.

"I'm not sure really. Something about the people that used to live in the old back-to-backs that I'm working on at Boot Street."

"Jensen's cousin used to live up there. He was telling me the other day at the pub," Brian said, flicking a kernel from the edge of the sofa.

Tommy jumped as the knife caught his skin and it split around the knuckle. "Ow, fuck."

"I told you to be careful, Tom. Mum will kill me if you chop your finger off before your mocks next week."

"Don't remind me. I'm shitting myself."

"You'll be grand." Fred passed him a plaster from the first aid kit she kept on the shelf.

"Safety first." Brian grinned.

"Too right. You don't want an infection getting in through a cut like that. Go and wash it," Fred said.

"But I want to stay."

"Tommy, go and wash your bloody hands, you idiot."

Brian's word was always final for Tommy. He flounced out of the shed, leaving the door swinging against its flimsy hinges.

"What were you saying about Mr J? Did he grow up in the back-to-backs?" Fred pulled the shed door to shut out the wind.

"His cousins did or something. That's what he said the other night." Brian shifted his weight, creating a plume of dust. "What's all this research about then? You going back to school or something to finish those exams?"

She flashed him a death stare reserved for her brothers, but he shrugged it off with a hearty laugh. "No, I told you. I'm helping someone at work look into the history of the houses. It's going to help us create the back story and eventually sell some properties."

"Sell the houses? Who's got you chasing your tail on this? Not one of the guys on-site, surely?"

"I can't imagine any of them going to the library on their weekend, can you?"

"Exactly. Which is why I'm baffled as to why you are. Dad'll miss you at the footie."

"I know." Her heart contracted ever so slightly, the months of worrying after her dad's health pulsing like a memory. "But I promised Ruby." Fred turned away, kicking herself.

"Oh, it's a girl. You should've said. Understood." Brian tapped the side of his nose in a disturbing show of camaraderie.

"It's not like that. She's a colleague running the marketing side of things. To be honest, it's all beyond me. I turn up to have my photo taken every now and again."

"Yeah, I bet you do."

"That's enough. You're making something out of nothing here." Heat rose to her cheeks.

"You getting a bit warm in here, sister? Shall I swing that door back open and get some air?"

"Get out, you idiot. Tell Mum thanks for the tea." She shooed him away with a filthy rag, ignoring his laughter.

"I will tell Mum, don't you worry." He strode off up the garden path.

"Brian, I'm warning you," Fred shouted after him, but it was no use because he probably couldn't hear her above the racket coming from the kitchen.

Fred stilled herself in the shed for a moment, slowing her thoughts in the silence. Brian was wrong. There was nothing to tell about her and Ruby. They were just friends. Not even that: merely colleagues. She didn't like to let people down, and she'd said she'd go with her. That's all.

An hour later, Fred pulled over to search for the number that Ruby had scribbled on a scrap of paper. The chronology of the houses confused her, with buildings carved up into three or four flats and the space between them built on over the years.

A post van appeared in her mirror, and she started in pursuit of the driver. "Hey, do you know where sixty-seven is, by any chance?"

"Down that alley and 'round the back. There's a few of them, but you'll find it."

"Thank you." She waved and sent the chap on his way before

climbing through a neglected and overgrown front garden. She stepped over strewn beer bottles and burger wrappers which clung to the boundary wall. How did Ruby end up in a place like this? It was a far cry from her high standards. She always looked great, glamorous even, in a casual way.

She tutted, annoyed that her thoughts had drifted again to Ruby's flawless appearance. Maybe this morning was a mistake. She should've said no and kept her distance. They had to work together, and nothing good ever came from getting involved with a colleague. She'd learned that lesson the hard way.

Fred marched on, following the path to the rear, and drew the collar of her heavy coat around her. The temperature had plummeted overnight, and she'd woken up with a cold nose. A battered old door came into view, and she knocked on it.

Ruby's towel-covered head popped out of a first-floor window. "It's on the latch. Come on up."

She disappeared, leaving Fred to make her own way into the maisonettes. She climbed a flight of stairs and reached another door marked with the letter A. It opened without warning.

"Sorry, I'm running a bit late," Ruby said, short of breath, wearing just a towel.

Her damp hair had sprung into ringlets, creating the cutest frame of her perfect cheeks.

Fred cleared her throat and drew her gaze away from Ruby's glistening, naked collarbone. "Don't worry, we're not in a rush." She concentrated as hard as she could on the blue hallway carpet.

"I was working on something for next week, and time ran away from me. Please, take a seat while I finish getting ready. I won't be long," Ruby said when they reached the kitchen. "Would you like a drink?"

Fred swallowed, not sure if she could take much more of Ruby's bare skin on show. "No. You get going." When Ruby had gone, Fred let out the long breath she'd been holding onto. *Jesus, I should be at the footie.* She took in the space. It was a shabby old flat, showing signs of wear and tear in all the wrong places. She crouched at a loose socket on the plasterboard.

"I'm sorry about this place," Ruby called from another room, her voice carrying through the paper-thin wall. "I'm really not planning on being here long but finding a flat of my own is a bit of a nightmare."

Fred wiggled a cupboard door, hanging from its hinges. "So, this is the stopgap?"

"God, yeah. It's not the nicest place, is it?"

Fred thought of her own family home, rough around its edges but worn with love and laughter. She grabbed her rucksack, pulled a screwdriver from her pencil case, and lifted the cupboard door back into place before tightening the screw into the hinge.

"What are you doing?" Ruby stood in the doorframe, fully dressed, her damp hair falling at the nape of her neck.

"Fixing the hinge. The whole thing was falling off." Fred raised her eyebrow.

"You're a strange one, Fred Caffrey." Ruby shook her head, sending a spray of water to her shoulders. She put her hands on her hips, drawing Fred's attention to the curves beneath the tight jeans she'd put on.

"Am I? It needed mending, that's all."

"Not many people carry a screwdriver around and start fixing things in random flats."

"Well, I do. And it's not random, it's yours." As soon as the words left her mouth, Fred regretted them. Her tone was too soft, too sentimental. "Let's go."

"Ready when you are." Ruby grinned.

Fred marched out and led the way back to the car. "Excuse the mess." She lifted a pair of work boots out of the footwell and brushed mud off the seat.

"Don't worry. I'm used to going home with dirt all over me these days."

"I guess so." Fred focused on the road ahead, grateful not to have to maintain eye contact. Ruby's just-out-of-the-shower appearance was a major distraction. "What were your previous clients like?"

"Corporate. Stuffy. More about money than making a difference." Ruby folded her arms. "I'd been begging my boss for a more worthwhile project for ages. We work for artists, big charities, and social enterprises. But none of that came my way. Trix said I was too valuable to lose to the pro bono and low budget clients."

"Is that what you wanted? To work for charities?"

"I guess I've always wanted to. But once you're on the big client circuit, it's hard to step off."

"It must come with some perks though." Fred signalled left into the city and headed towards the archives.

"If you mean dining with strangers and going to bed alone in a cold hotel room."

"I hadn't thought of it like that." Fred pulled into a space on the street, got out, and flashed her credit card at the parking meter. "Here we are."

"Have you been here before?" Ruby asked.

"I've been to the old library with my brothers when we were little. We got thrown out because they made too much noise." Fred shook her head in shame. "But no, I've never been to the archives before."

"I'm excited. Are you?"

Fred couldn't help but get caught up in Ruby's anticipation. "Yeah, I am."

Ruby took the stone steps up to the entrance two at a time, dragging Fred along with her enthusiasm.

"You move fast in those heels," Fred said.

"They might not suit your building site, but they're perfect for a Saturday at the library." Ruby winked.

As they crossed the threshold, it occurred to Fred that she hadn't been swept up in someone else's joy for such a long time.

She'd been open to the idea, but it simply hadn't come her way.

Beyond the entrance porch, a heavy set of double doors stood tall to greet them. She held the handle, gesturing to Ruby to go in.

"After you."

"Such a gentleman," Ruby said and gave her a playful wink.

Fred's chest swelled. It would be her pleasure to hold any door open for Ruby. *Slow down.* They had a job to do. Trouble was, the more time they spent together, the less it felt like work. Echoes of her brothers teasing her rang in her ears. Why had she given up her Saturday for Ruby's extra-curricular activity? Not sure of the answer, Fred continued through the archives, grateful for the hushed corridors to untangle her thoughts. At this rate, she'd need a lot more peace and quiet to silence her racing mind.

CHAPTER TEN

RUBY BLEW A DUST cloud from the box file and ran her finger over the yellowing label. "Newspaper clippings from the *Northern Star* and *Chronicle* from 1904 to 1924." Inside, reams of microfiche held the secrets of the past.

"The houses were originally built for the mill workers in the 1800s. We might need to go further back than this." Fred lifted another box down from the shelves.

"But we're not going to find anyone still alive from two centuries ago." Ruby scratched her head. She wasn't sure where to start now they were here. "If we could find some records from say, eighty years ago, we might have a fighting chance of getting in touch with them."

"What about the births, deaths, and marriages? Or we could find out who was christened at the church. They'd be local, surely."

"In those days, definitely. Good plan." Ruby snuck a look at Fred. Thank goodness she'd agreed to come. The scale of this place was overwhelming. Shelves upon shelves of books, paper, and artefacts stretched right up to the ceiling. But it all seemed much more manageable with Fred by her side.

Within a few minutes, they had tracked down the parish records and seated themselves at a microfiche table.

"I guess most people have better things to do with their Saturdays." Ruby spread her coat and bag across two chairs since they had the place to themselves.

"I expect so." Fred fed the machine and flicked a switch.

The strange mechanism burst to life with a back light, revealing the white scrawl of someone's handwriting against a black, shadowy background.

"Wow, it's all there." Ruby gripped Fred's forearm, and she tensed beneath the soft wool of her sweater. Ruby released her quickly. "Let me get my phone."

"There must be an easier way to do this. Isn't all this online nowadays?"

Fred had a point. She probably could have joined some website and found all she needed to. But somehow, smelling the age of these documents, seeing the scratches of their past lives, and feeling their fragile texture brought cheer with it. "It's not the same though, is it? There's nothing like getting your head stuck in a book."

Fred shook her head, but a smile flickered on her lips. Ruby stopped to take in her calm stature at the desk. She commanded every space she occupied. On-site, she was confident and everywhere at once. Here, stripped of her safety gear and winter layers, she was more approachable but no less imposing. She stalled, studying the shape of Fred's jaw. Ruby thought of the makeup she'd slapped on to go to a library. But Fred's face was naked to the world. Bold and fearless in her own skin. It intrigued her, that level of inner peace.

"What is it?" Fred asked.

"Nothing. I wanted to take some pictures or scribble some names down."

Fred leafed through a few more records. "This is interesting." She pointed at a single name. "Jensen. That's my neighbour's family."

"Really?" Ruby leaned over to get a closer look.

"His relatives lived on our street."

"Wow, do you think he'd be willing to talk to me? Maybe put me in touch with them? That might be a good place to start." She bounced on her seat.

"I could ask him. He's a kind old guy; I'm sure he would help."

For a second, Ruby leaned against Fred's firm frame, thanking her with the weight of her body. "That's brilliant. Jensen." She wrote the name in her notebook. "Let's keep looking." She contemplated the neglected fragments of the past, and then sneezed, an embarrassing squeak that threw a veil of dust between them.

"Bless you," Fred said, looking up from the records.

"Sorry. I think the dust mites are getting up my nose." She rubbed her fingers together to reduce the itchy burn across her skin.

"I guess I'm more used to it than you are." Fred stretched, her body tight and long in the chair.

It stirred something in Ruby to see the shape of her so relaxed. She blinked in the low light, and her mind wandered to what they could get up to in dark corners of this lonely library.

After a couple of hours, the lack of daylight and decades of dust had grown oppressive, and Ruby rubbed at her sore eyes. "I think we should take a break. I have enough leads to follow up for now."

Fred glanced at her watch. "How about lunch?" She hesitated. "Sorry, you probably have plans already."

"No, I don't. I'd love to have lunch with you." In truth, she wasn't ready for their time together to be over yet. "There's a rooftop bar across the road. Fancy it?"

"Why not?"

"Unless you'd rather find somewhere more casual?" Ruby asked.

"No. The roof place is good with me. I'm more comfortable with craft ale than canapés, but I'm sure they have something on draft." Fred grinned and graciously packed away her things.

A few minutes later they were settled into a booth looking out over the city. Fred shifted against the black leather.

"This isn't really your kind of place, is it?" Ruby asked, already knowing the answer.

"I like it." Fred smiled. "I like it, with you." She dropped her gaze and frowned, rubbing the back of her neck like it was sore.

"You don't have to lie to make me feel better." Ruby gulped her expensive wine. Even she'd been shocked when the price had been for a glass and not the whole bottle.

"It's not my usual kind of place, no. I'm usually covered in mud, and they wouldn't let me past the entrance. But this afternoon, with a day off and good company, I'm up for it."

"Okay. I believe you." Ruby took a deep breath, her nerves fluttering. "I'm glad you're in a good mood, because I did need to talk to you about something."

Fred's eyebrows furrowed.

"It's a work thing." Ruby hurried on, not wanting to prolong the agony. "I told you my boss, Trix, is in town."

Fred sipped her beer and nodded.

"She wants to run a charity abseil off the old factory."

"You want what?" Fred's eyebrows shot up even higher than usual.

"Not me. Trix. It's not as bad as it sounds." Ruby dug her nails into her thighs, wishing she hadn't ruined their pleasant afternoon with Trix's outlandish request.

"I'm not letting you throw people off buildings. Not for some silly PR stunt."

Ruby sighed. She wasn't even offended anymore by Fred's disdain. Part of her agreed. "Let me get Trix to explain it to you."

"I don't need anyone to elaborate on such a foolish idea, Ruby. The site is under my control, and I don't want any shenanigans. What is it with you and bloody heights?"

They both looked out of the window, towering tens of stories above the city's pavements. Ruby couldn't help but laugh.

"It's not funny," Fred said, but her shoulders softened and her lips twitched upwards. "Listen, I don't want to piss on your chips. But a load of amateur do-gooders falling off a tall building is an accident waiting to happen. It fills me with fear if I'm honest."

"Me too." Ruby reached across to touch Fred's hand, hesitated and pulled back. "I told Trix, but she said the board had done a deal and already given it the green light."

A dark shadow passed over Fred's eyes, and her face filled with fury. "Is that right?"

Ruby regretted letting that detail slip. She hadn't meant to anger her. "I don't know whether I've got the wrong end of the stick. Maybe this should wait until Monday when we're in the office."

"Maybe it should have, but you brought it up."

Ruby recoiled, hating herself for ruining what could have been a lovely afternoon. "I'm sorry. I didn't mean to annoy you."

Silence hung between their sips.

"It's okay," Fred said. "We'll get to it Monday. I can't wait to meet your boss." She rolled her eyes and raised her glass. "For now, let's enjoy our drinks and order some food. You're paying."

Ruby allowed herself a weak smile, grateful not to have completely alienated her only friend in the city. "Deal. I'll grab us some menus."

They'd enjoyed a lovely, if unexpected, morning. Why did she have to ruin it by winding Fred up so much about the abseil? Her stomach churned for the hundredth time. Could she make it right without blowing up the deal Trix had already stitched up? A few months earlier, she would have given it her best shot. Anything for the client. But sat in this booth, across from Fred, she found herself on wobblier ground than ever. Why did Fred mess with her head so much?

CHAPTER ELEVEN

"THE FAMOUS FRED CAFFREY. Good to meet you at last." Trix extended her hand.

Fred rubbed the remnants of a sand delivery onto her cargo pants and returned the handshake.

"A firm handshake to match your reputation, Fred. I'm Trix Palmer, one of the directors at Liquid Communications."

Fred bit her tongue before an insulting remark tipped out.

Trix leaned in further. "Are you the strong, silent type, Fred?"

Ruby stepped forward. "Fred's busy. She hasn't really got time for lots of chit-chat."

Fred laughed, enjoying Ruby's discomfort at the tension between them. "Welcome on-site, Trix. It's nice to meet you. I've heard something about you from our Ruby here."

"Our Ruby." Trix pulled Ruby by the waist into a warm hug.

Fred tried to ignore the pang of jealousy in her ribs. "She's filled me in on your plan." She'd spent Sunday mulling it over. If the board had already agreed to such nonsense, there was little point in fighting it. She could waste her energy trying to overturn the decision or just let the wretched thing happen under her supervision. "I'm willing to allow it. But you need to stick to my rules at all times and follow the express wishes of me and my staff. Do you understand?"

Trix smiled. "Absolutely."

Ruby shuffled from one foot to another, turning into Fred's space. "Are you sure you're okay with this?"

"No. I'm certainly not okay with this, and if you'd have come to me first with this proposal, I would have given you an itemised list of safety concerns." She glanced at Trix. "As you've sadly circumvented my authority, I had to work through the weekend to mitigate my concerns." Fred stifled a sigh. She didn't want Ruby to feel guilty about this. This stupid mess had come from the corporate team, not her. It was the latest in a long line of decrees thrown from on high that she simply had to make work, whatever the consequences.

She loved this company but the longer she worked here, the more she questioned whether she'd gained any kind of authority over anything except more paperwork.

"Trix, it was good to meet you." Fred nodded. "Ruby, can I borrow you for a minute?"

"Of course."

They walked across to the cabin, and Fred opened the door to show her in. "We have the development director on-site today," she said. "Hugo Garre. He's married to the architect, Delphine. He can be demanding."

"I can do...demanding," Ruby said, with a flirtatious glint in her eye.

Fred laughed, warmth spreading through her chest. "I'm sure you can. But he's a particular kind of director."

"Why hasn't he been on-site before now?"

"He's had a spell in hospital."

"Oh." Ruby's compassion etched on her furrowed brow.

"He was in Turkey for some cosmetic work," Fred said, hurrying to put her straight. "Hair transplant. Something like that, I can't remember. Reinventing old buildings aren't the only renovations he's interested in." She chuckled, and Ruby did too. "I wanted to give you the heads up—"

"No pun intended."

"Quite..." Fred stopped another laugh. "In case you want to bring him into any of your media work, you'll need to work with his assistant to manage his diary and give him a proper briefing."

"I get you."

"He's not as flexible as I am. And your charms will be lost on him."

Ruby arched her eyebrow. "My charms are working on you then?"

"I didn't admit to that." She raised her hands in mock protest. This conversation was taking a turn she hadn't expected.

"When does he arrive? Should I try and get some time for an introduction?"

"He's coming down from Aberdeen with Adrienne." Fred straightened, wanting to reinstate the professional tone to the meeting. "Hugo's assistant is Jay Jackson. Drop him an email."

"Got you. See you later?"

"Sure." Fred watched Ruby exit the cabin, taking the energy with her and leaving the air still and cold.

At the end of a long day, Fred made the familiar journey home. It was only Monday, and she was already flagging, so she skipped the chaos around the table and took her plate out to the shed. It was freezing in there, but she tapped on the oil heater and kept her coat on.

"Fred, you've got a visitor," Brian shouted down the garden.

"Who is it?" She retreated into the sofa, wishing she could disappear for a few hours.

"It's me," Adrienne said from behind the shed door. "Can I come in?"

Fred's heart sank even further, knowing that whatever conversation came next, it would be uncomfortable. "I'm coming." She opened the door, her cheeks flushed with cold.

"Thanks," she said and entered the shed.

"Why are you here?"

"You've been avoiding me at work, and I think we should talk. I tried to catch you before you left, but you were already gone." Adrienne pulled the fingers of her gloves off one by one.

"So you followed me home?" Fred's heart raced, not knowing what was coming and how to control it.

"I didn't follow you home. I know where you live, Fred. Or have you forgotten all the times I dropped you off?"

Fred held her breath. She hadn't forgotten, but she'd done her best to push it to the back of her mind. She didn't want to live in the past. The past was for ghosts like the ones she and Ruby had been chasing in the archives.

"Am I disturbing your supper?" Adrienne asked.

"It's tea." Fred knew she was being petty but now more than ever, she was conscious of the gulf of difference between them.

Adrienne laughed. "You're not going to let it go, are you?"

"We work together. I think we should keep it professional."

"I miss you," Adrienne said. "At work. In my bed."

"In your hotel bed, Adrienne. That's the only place I was welcome if you remember." It was no use. She clenched her fist, desperate not to lose control. "I wasn't good enough for you to bring home or introduce to your colleagues as your actual girlfriend. I was your fuck buddy whenever you were in town."

Adrienne swallowed and opened her mouth, but nothing came out.

Fred stared. "No. You can't deny it."

"I'm sorry."

"Are you? Because it's been six months, and you've barely been near me until we started on-site." Fred took a step closer to her, knocking over a tin mug which clattered to the floor. Blood rushed to her temples. "And now you're back in town more often, and you're bored. So, you thought we could hook up again."

"It's not that. I'm not like you. I'm not comfortable in my own skin, and I can't brazen it out," she whispered. "I don't want to be different."

"You think I like standing out?" Fred asked, rubbing the back of her neck. "I want to be one of the gang too. But we are who we are. We have to take up our own space, even if it's uncomfortable sometimes."

"You're braver than I am. Look at how you've made it to the top in such a toxic macho environment. People respect you for who you are, not the veneer of who you pretend to be."

"Don't try and make me feel sorry for you. You're not a veneer. You're on the board, for Christ's sake. You have everything. You don't want the high-up folks to know that, deep down, you want to have frantic, desperate sex with people like me."

With scarcely inches between them and their breath visible in the cold air, Fred couldn't deny that she was still deeply attracted to Adrienne. Their gaze locked for a moment too long, and Adrienne leaned in, touching her lips to Fred's.

A bolt of desire shot through Fred's abdomen, and her body softened for a second before every muscle recoiled and she broke away. "And now you have the balls to come to my house and stroll into my shed, for what? To say you're sorry so you can take me to some cute boutique hotel for a few hours? No, thanks."

"I really hurt you, didn't I?"

Could that really be shame on Adrienne's face? Fred doubted it. She turned towards the backlit windows of her family home and thought of the conversation bouncing off the walls between her parents and siblings. "Don't give yourself the credit. I'm not hurt by you. I don't feel anything about what we did. I don't like you disturbing my family in the evening. If you want to talk to me about work, it can wait until the morning."

Tears pooled in Adrienne's eyes. "I shouldn't have come. I'm sorry." She turned and walked away.

Fred watched her exit and close the back gate behind her. She slumped onto the sofa with a sigh, the last remnants of her energy spent on her outburst. She hadn't meant to be so dismissive of Adrienne. She'd enjoyed their time together. But she hated the feeling of being hidden in a relationship, like a dirty secret. She wanted someone to be proud of her. Adrienne had crystallised that yearning, releasing it from deep within. She wanted to be someone's *someone*. And she wouldn't settle for anything less.

CHAPTER TWELVE

"I FOUND THE PERFECT place. You're going to love it." Trix dragged Ruby by the hand through the narrow streets of Manchester.

Shadows of the past stood at each corner, with tall, industrial buildings brooding over the city's modern life. Steam-powered revolution echoed off the façades like flashbacks. Ruby stopped, pulling Trix back a few steps to crane her neck towards the sky. Red brick upon red brick piled high, standing firm against the rapid pace of modern life.

"It's kind of beautiful here." She pointed to gargoyles perched on the precipice. "I wonder who lived in these buildings when they were new and sparkly?"

"Are you falling in love with this northern outpost?" Trix scrambled on. "Quickly, we're going to be late, you soppy thing."

"Where exactly are you taking me?" Ruby had been quizzing her since they left her flat to get the metro into town, but Trix wouldn't give it up.

"You'll see." Trix checked her phone. "It's along here, to the left."

Ruby followed, trusting her best friend to entertain her for the next few hours. A traditional pub sat among a sea of glass-fronted monstrosities, each begging for the attention of passersby with their bold architectural fashion statements. The pub simply remained, staking its claim to the space, daring its corporate neighbours to come on in. She imagined Fred sat at the bar, cradling a pint, comfortable in her own skin.

"I wanted to cheer you up about being here. I know you've not quite settled in the right place to live yet and haven't found your tribe. So here we are: something to remind you of home." Trix waved her arm with a flourish at a battered red door, rusting in all the right places.

"An old door?"

"You should know better than that, Ruby. It's what's behind the door that counts...if you're brave enough to enter." Trix smirked.

Ruby's heart fluttered with excitement. If Trix wasn't teasing, this would be the perfect stress reliever. "Are you kidding? You found axes?"

"Not any old axes, darling. Manchester's finest." She squealed with delight. "Come on."

Ruby skipped behind her friend, her palms itching with anticipation.

Inside, the panelled wall threatened to splinter her bare skin if she stood too close. A sleeveless bear of a man stood at a makeshift reception desk, barely raising his triple chin to welcome them in.

"Have you been before?" he asked.

"Not here. But we've thrown before." Ruby stepped forward.

"No smoking, no drinking, no funny business. The bar's available after your session. Looks like you've paid up front, so enjoy yourselves."

"We will." Ruby gathered her axes. She balanced the weight of the handle in her hands. "Thanks for this, Trix. It's funny, I've really missed it these past few weeks."

"I thought you would."

They passed the next hour in virtual silence, with Ruby focused on the distance between blade and board, ignoring Trix's attempts to start a conversation.

When the hour was up, they made their way through to the bar.

"I'll get these." Ruby's vocal cords sprung back to life with a renewed energy pulsing through her veins. "What are you having?"

"Gin and tonic. A nice one, none of the basic crap."

"Of course. Coming up." Ruby went to the bar and brought the drinks to their table in the nook. "That was amazing. I'll definitely be back."

"Good for you. Maybe you should bring Fred next time."

"Yeah, she might like it."

"She might like you." Trix winked.

"She doesn't. Not in that way." Ruby leaned back, unwilling to accept what Trix was suggesting.

"I've seen the way she looks at you. Don't tell me you haven't noticed." Trix sipped her drink, cupping the bulbous glass in her petite hand. "I'd bet my bonus you've got the hots for her too. Not that you'll admit it to me or yourself."

Ruby nudged her arm. Most of the time she didn't mind her playful jibes at her love life, or lack of it. But tonight's stung. "I can admit it. I do like her now I've gotten to know her."

"As in, fancy the cargo pants off her?"

Ruby gulped. The more she got to know Fred, the more she wanted to get to know. But that wasn't the same as being attracted to someone. Was it? She didn't really have the answer. She hadn't had much time for dating back in London. The odd one-nighter didn't really count for much in her book. "Why do you always have to bring the drama? She's nice. She's fit. I wouldn't say no if it fell in my lap."

"If *she* fell in your lap!" Trix snorted.

"Stop it! It's not like anything is going to happen."

"Why not?"

"We work together, for starters. She's practically my boss."

"I'm your boss. Don't forget it." Trix gave her a look of fake incredulity.

"You know exactly what I mean. She's the client." Ruby fidgeted on the bench. The more she thought about it, the more uncomfortable she grew. "It's hot in here."

"It's you. You're hot under the collar for the new dollar."

"You're unbelievable. Isn't there a clause or something in my contract which says no messing around with clients?"

"If there is, I'll find it and destroy it in the name of love... and lust." Trix belly laughed.

"I don't know where this came from, but can you pop it safely back in the box and never speak of it again, please?" Ruby held her hand up to close the conversation.

"Fine, I need to pee anyway. I'll get another round in on the way back. Same again?"

"Go on then." Ruby wilted against the chair as Trix crossed the bar. She hadn't been expecting the onslaught of questions about her feelings for Fred. Under the microscope, maybe something was brewing between them. They were getting on now they'd gotten over Ruby's initial calamities. Fred was stunning. More than that, she was kind and generous, which were beautiful qualities in anyone. But Trix was making something out of nothing. Ruby had a job to do and a home in London to get back to. The sooner she got on with it, the better. Fred's company along the way was just a bonus.

***

A week later, Ruby picked the edge of her clipboard and rubbed the sharp seam between her fingers. The sting of it distracted her from the rooftop goings-on.

Another rope was thrown off the side of the building. It strained against the carabiner, and Ruby clenched her jaw, as if her molars were solely responsible for its safe descent. This hadn't been a great idea in the first place, but the growing unease of something going badly wrong was bubbling in her gut like acid.

"Great, you're here," Trix bellowed across the roof of the factory, with her hands on her hips, creating a silhouette against the winter sun. "It's a beautiful day to jump off a building."

"No one's jumping off." Ruby echoed Fred's warning tone and closed the distance between them. "Abseiling isn't jumping."

"Don't be so uptight. You know what I mean." Trix hugged her. "Fred's not here yet, so you don't have to be on your best behaviour." She winked.

On another day, Ruby would've jumped into the ball pit of their banter. Today, she was so jittery, everything set her teeth on edge. "I'm sorry. I'm worried that something will go wrong."

"It won't. The safety guys have done their checks, and we've had a run through." Trix waved her hands in small, jazzy circles. "Enjoy it. The press will be here soon, and they'll want to see the real Ruby."

Who even was that? Before she'd moved north, organising an abseiling stunt would've been her dream day at the office. Now, she couldn't stomach the thought of letting Fred down.

She tiptoed to the edge of the roof. It was a gorgeous day, she had to give Trix that. She held her breath, and the crisp air cupped her cheeks. Closing her eyes, she silenced the hubbub around her, turning away from the clanking of chains and the hum of instructions.

"Are you ready?" Fred's alto voice pierced the stillness.

She opened her eyes and couldn't help but smile at the interruption, before she stepped towards Fred, willing her into her personal space. "Not really. But Trix is all over it."

"I can see that." She folded her arms. "You're in charge of stuff like this, Ruby. At least while you're on my site. Do you want me to put her in her place?"

Ruby squirmed under her attention. "She's fine. I'd rather she took the lead. It was her idea."

"Another overstep in my opinion." Fred looked across to the harnessing area. "What's the running order?"

"Twenty people throwing themselves off the side of the factory for charity. It starts once the safety guy has done his abseil and given the all-clear."

"I can't believe I let you talk me into this." Fred frowned.

Her brooding discomfort simmered blatantly at the surface. Ruby swallowed. She looked hotter than ever. Ruby imagined the firmness of Fred's muscles under her jacket and the feel of her skin beneath the fibres.

"You all right? You look weird."

She coughed, caught in the act of indulging her latest Fred-inspired fantasy. This was getting ridiculous; if she couldn't focus on the job, she'd end up losing it. But Trix's questioning had opened a Pandora's Box that had been slumbering in her subconscious. Now her darkest thoughts were very much alive and kicking in her knickers every time she was around Fred. "Sorry, I was thinking about the press area. Did you want to speak to them when they arrive? It'd be good for the development if you did." She did her best to get the conversation back on track, but Fred's presence was sending her sideways.

"If I must. I thought Adrienne might want to talk to the press today."

"She's back in Aberdeen."

Fred whipped round, her face full of confusion. "How do you know?"

"She messaged me to say." Ruby took a breath. She didn't want to dwell on why Fred was so interested.

Fred took her radio from her waist band, giving Ruby a glimpse of her boxers and a sliver of skin. "Champ, can you meet me on the factory roof, please? I've got to talk to the bloody papers, and I'd rather have you here to keep an eye on this nonsense." She flashed Ruby a grin, as if to say she didn't really mean it.

The radio sounded with Champ's reply. Fred walked away, and Ruby fought the urge to follow. She didn't want to be seen trailing Fred around like a puppy. She scanned the rooftop, but no one was paying any notice to her. She'd gone from standing out like a sore thumb around the building site to blending into the background. Finally fitting in was a huge relief.

Within a few minutes, Champ was at her side. "Right then, I'm all yours."

"I need to supervise the media, so can you stay with Trix and make sure she doesn't break the rules?"

"You're sounding more like the boss-lady every day, Ruby. She must be rubbing off on you."

"I doubt that." She smiled at the image though.

If they could get through this farcical day, she'd be able to get back on with what she was here to do...*if* she could stay focused. But seeing Fred every day was making that harder than ever.

CHAPTER THIRTEEN

FRED IGNORED HER RADIO. Champ had control of things this morning. She had hoped to observe proceedings from a distance, but she'd had to show her face. She could hardly let something as crazy as a charity abseil happen while she wasn't on the bridge. Even though the last thing she wanted to do was scrape her tired bones away from the comforting dent in her mattress.

The showdown with Adrienne had bothered her more than she realised at the time. She'd tossed and turned every night since, going over each word exchanged, like analysing a game of chess. It hadn't been calculated. The whole thing had come from nowhere when she'd turned up unannounced. Fred hadn't even known she'd harboured such ferocious anger. But when Adrienne had started to act as if they could pick up where they left off, it was like ripping off a bandage to see the gangrenous wound of rejection that had been festering all along.

She took a long breath of cold air deep into her lungs, hoping to cleanse the negative thoughts from her body. She needed a release from all this. To truly move on with her life. It was hard when Adrienne's name jumped into her inbox every morning. Her job title was scrawled all over the cabin, and half the time she could turn up like a building inspector.

Time spent in Ruby's company had been a welcome distraction. But since Trix had appeared, they'd had fewer opportunities to see each other.

Ruby was hunched over a clipboard, phone in hand, furiously scribbling something. A camera framed her to the right, and a boom mic hovered above her head. Fred usually hated the fuss that film crews brought onto the site, but something about the scene warmed her. Was it Ruby? Why was she so bloody good to be around? She was annoying as hell, created nothing but hazards, and had no respect for the rules. But still, Fred couldn't stop staring.

"Right then, boss. All clear. We're about to lower the first willing victim," Champ said over the airwave.

"Got that, Champ." Fred hoped no one would be a victim today—not on her watch. She edged closer to the precipice where she could make out a figure stepping backwards. He wore a harness with loops around his legs. His red face popped out from beneath a black helmet, and she couldn't see whether he was terrified or excited with his bulging eyes and wild grin, but he was nodding like his life depended on it. He leaned backwards into the air until the rope stretched taut under his weight.

Fred's breath rattled through her ribs, as her unspoken plea for it to hold up was granted. The man began to walk backwards, descending with each step until he was out of sight.

Fred blew into her clammy hands. Ruby made her way back across the roof.

"That's one down," Ruby said. "Let's hope it doesn't take all morning, hey?"

Fred had forgotten this was eating into all their weekends. She grunted, wanting the whole thing to be over and done with.

"I wondered if you fancied doing something afterwards?"

"What kind of thing? You've got form, Ruby Lewis, for leading me astray on Saturday afternoons." She smiled, recalling their time at the bar after their visit to the archives.

"Well, you're not far from the mark there." Ruby blushed. "I've been in touch with the family we found in the records. I spoke to Mrs Jensen. They said we could go and see them."

"We?" She prepared herself for another Ruby escapade.

"I explained that you were a neighbour of their cousin, George." She scuffed her boots against the tar on the roof. "They seemed to warm up. I think they'd be more comfortable with you there."

Fred kept her eye on the progressing abseil. Victim number two was being strapped into the jumping off point.

"Go on then. What have you arranged?" Fred took it for granted that Ruby would have already shackled them into touring across the city. "No doubt I'll have to drive you."

"I said we'd be there at two. They'll have the kettle on. They sound ever so nice." She stepped a little closer. "Thanks."

Fred shrugged under her thick coat and vest. "Let's get this over with first."

The final descent done, and everything packed away, they snaked across the city in the Saturday traffic. "I guess this is where people moved to from the back-to-backs?" Ruby asked, her head tilted towards the car window, her bare neck on show.

"I suppose so. I don't know if the terraces were cleared like they were in other cities, but people certainly drifted away to nicer areas. Boot Street was abandoned before we came along."

Ruby turned and flashed the warmest smile Fred had seen in a while. "You're really making a difference here, aren't you?"

Fred thought about it. "We both are." The moment seemed to bring them together like the right ends of a magnet. She pulled over at number fifty and cut the engine. Silence filled the car, and Fred welcomed the stillness of sitting in Ruby's presence.

"Let's go. I can't wait to meet them." Ruby opened the door, letting in a rush of wintry air. "I don't know how we managed to stay on that roof for so long. It's freezing."

"I know. I hope they've got the heating on."

They approached a glazed front door with leaded panes criss-crossing the glass, holding it all together. Fred stood back as a shadow moved towards them.

"Yes?" The tiny woman kept the chain on.

Fred smiled widely and tried to look as friendly as possible.

"It's Ruby. We spoke on the phone the other day," she said softly.

"Oh, yes, I remember. Come on through." The chain rattled

against the door before it was fully opened to allow them into the passage. "I thought you were coming tomorrow."

"I'm sorry. Is now not a good time?"

"Don't be silly. It's no trouble at all. Take a seat, and I'll put the kettle on." She gestured to a floral sofa against the back wall of her living room. "Would you like tea or coffee? Mind you, I've only got instant. No fancy stuff, I'm afraid."

"Your standard tea for me, please. That'd be lovely," Fred said.

"Me too." Ruby stood at her side.

When Mrs Jensen left the room, they both exhaled, relaxing into each other.

"Let's sit, we're taking up too much space." Fred took one end of the sofa, expecting Ruby to take the other but she sat next to her, their thighs briefly resting against one another. Fred's pulse raced at the touch, but she gathered herself in time for Mrs Jensen's return with a tray.

"Don't get up," she said as Fred made to help her. "I've got it." She rested the tea pot and cups on the table. "Now, Ruby, isn't it? Tell me more about what you wanted to speak to me about."

"We're both working at the old back-to-backs at Boot Street, where your family used to live. Fred is the site manager."

"Fred?" Mrs Jensen narrowed her eyes. "That's a funny name for a lass."

"It's short for Winifred."

"Is it?" Ruby looked surprised.

Fred grew conscious of her audience of two. "Yeah, I was named after my grandmother. But it didn't really suit me, so everyone calls me Fred." She wriggled against the soft cushion. "Trust me, it's much easier to be a builder called Fred than one called Winifred."

"I can imagine." Mrs Jensen chuckled as she poured tea into some fancy teacups. "So if you're in charge, what do you do there, Ruby?"

"I'm helping to promote the new houses. I want to tell the story of the families who grew up there so that we can inspire new families to make Boot Street their home."

Mrs Jensen raised her grey, whispery eyebrows. "You want people to move back in there? It's been a mess for years."

"Not anymore. We're clearing it right now and starting on the first homes in a couple of weeks," Fred said.

"Here, drink up."

Fred took a cup from her host and tried to keep it from wobbling off its saucer.

"What's all this got to do with me, my dears?" Mrs Jensen smiled, creases deepening in the corners of her eyes.

"Well, your family were there, weren't they? I saw your name in the archives, and Fred's neighbour is a cousin of yours."

"Yes. We were there. I was eleven when we moved away. My dad got a job across the other side of Manchester, and we moved onto an estate. It was wonderful." She stared out of the window for a moment, lost in her own thought. "At Boot Street, we had no heating, no inside toilet, no space to ourselves. In the new house, we had carpets and eventually a fridge and a washing machine. It was the modern world."

"What do you remember about the street where you were born?"

"It was grubby. We'd come in with dust on our faces and under our fingernails." She picked at a frayed thread on her skirt, the creases reappearing at her eyes. "But we were together. All the kids would scramble through each other's back yards. We knew everyone. I'd be in and out of their houses. If my mum wasn't in, someone else's would feed me. It was a little village, really. Right in the middle of the city."

"Would you come back and have a look around? If we were to have, say, a little tea party? Would you bring anyone you know from back then?" Ruby leaned forward on her seat, almost bouncing.

"A tea party?" Fred asked, not sure where the idea had come from.

"We can pin it down later." Ruby waved away the detail that

Fred craved. "Would you come though and see what we're doing with the old street?"

There was a pause between them. Mrs Jensen blew into her steaming cup of tea and took a tentative sip. "Yes, I'd like that. But you'd have to get a taxi to pick me up, because I'm not sure I'd make it there on my own."

"Of course. That would be a pleasure," Ruby said.

Fred couldn't help but catch the enthusiasm radiating beside her. Mrs Jensen stood slowly, taking time to regain her balance against the arm of the chair. She opened the top of an oak bureau, revealing a smooth velvet writing desk, perfect except for the signs of age.

"Here it is." She drew a leather-bound address book out and leafed through its yellowed pages. "You'll want to look up Ambrose and Florence Walsh. Cousins. I think they still live together. She never married, and he's a widow. They're older than me. I'm sure you'll be able to talk to them about the old back-to-backs."

She wrote their details on a tidy square of paper and passed it to Ruby.

"Thank you. This is fantastic." Ruby held her hands together.

Pride rippled across Fred's chest, and it made her sit up a little and take notice. She wasn't sure why Ruby's happiness was so contagious, but she moved closer. She rested her hand on her arm and mirrored Ruby's wide grin, suddenly wishing they were alone so she could enjoy this moment without scrutiny.

Aware of Mrs Jensen in the chair opposite, Fred withdrew and retreated to her sidekick status. It had been a fleeting vulnerability. She could've taken it, opened up to Ruby and let her in. But distance was for the best. They worked together, and nothing but drama would follow, she told herself again. But this time, it rang in her ears like a lie.

CHAPTER FOURTEEN

Ruby flinched as the coffee burned her lip. Distracted, she brought her phone closer and flicked through the pictures of the flat she'd seen for rent. It wasn't far out of town. She'd ask Fred about the area, and maybe she'd check it out. She emailed the agent to book a viewing.

She leaned against the wall, wondering how long this contract was going to last. She could launch the pre-sales in six months and pass it onto someone else. Otherwise, she'd be stuck on the job until the topping out, which could be a couple of years yet. The dread that she'd felt about moving to Manchester had mellowed considerably. She thought about Fred and the friendship they'd forged in the rubble of this old street. It warmed her heart to think about the history she was unearthing, one story at a time, and she no longer felt compelled to run away from it all.

A shadow approached in her peripheral vision, and Ruby stepped out of their path. She knew from the dark glasses and swagger that it was Hugo Garre brushing past her into the boardroom. Even though Fred had given her fair warning, she couldn't help but scowl in his direction. He was solidly built, carrying extra weight in the wrong places, and overflowed with self-importance.

"Move," he said, barely acknowledging the people around him.

Ruby smirked. She'd seen the size of some people's ego in the PR business, but his was another level of narcissism. Fred followed behind, rolling her eyes and shielding herself with a clipboard. She winked at Ruby, pulling at the string of desire which had been weaving itself between them.

"Hey," Fred whispered. "Have you looked up the Walsh family yet?"

"Not yet. I've been a bit bogged down with finding somewhere to live."

"Maybe I can help. I'll put the word out and see if anything comes up."

Fred's eyes shone with a deep kindness that made Ruby want to bathe in them. A queue of people filing into the boardroom broke the spell. Ruby followed them in and took a seat reserved for observers. A throng of people gathered, all wearing two-piece suits. It was a contrast to the usual horde of safety vests and jeans.

"Shall we make a start?" Hugo asked.

Beside him, Adrienne took a seat, her hair perfectly coiffed.

Fred seemed to hesitate and then moved away from Adrienne to the opposite side. As she edged her seat closer to the table, she knocked a coffee all over the place.

"Tracy, get a cloth." Hugo looked unimpressed. "We have a full agenda to get through, so let's formally open the meeting of the Boot Street Steering Group. We are quorate with two directors, the scheme architect, and the site manager present."

Ruby zoned out there and then, wondering why she'd offered to come along in the first place. The room grew hot and stifling, and the exchanges dragged on, with detail that Ruby didn't understand. She'd almost nodded off when raised voices brought her back into the room.

"I told you that wasn't possible last month." Fred's eyes blazed.

"You did no such thing." Hugo stared. "This isn't a negotiation, Caffrey. The site manager is in charge of the trades, not in charge of the whole scheme. This is my vision, and I won't have it diluted into some god-awful, run of the mill house-build."

There was a collective pause, while everyone waited on Fred's reaction to Hugo's dismissal. Ruby stood, lending Fred her physical support, even if she had no idea what their argument was about. Her chest flushed with rage on Fred's behalf. How dare he speak to her like that?

Fred held an excruciating silence for quite a while. "I request that the chair of the board reflect on his comments, and I suggest an adjournment of the meeting while each party can gather further information." She tilted her head. "I also ask that I be referred to by my first name on this site."

Ruby's rage melted into pride. Fred had slam-dunked Hugo with as much grace as she could muster given that she had brick dust in her hair and a smudge on her cheek. She caught Fred's eye and smirked. A secret between them. Just for them.

Adrienne started to pack up, and Ruby took that as her signal to leave. She made her way to the cabin and waited inside.

A few minutes later, the door swung open, and Fred's heavy boots hit the carpet tiles.

"Jesus, Ruby. What are you doing sat in here in the dark?"

"Sorry. I just wanted to make sure you were okay, after all that."

"I'm used to Hugo. He likes to have a little dance at the first few meetings to get a sense of who's alpha on a site. He'll calm down," Fred said, but she still looked flustered.

"You sure? It seemed pretty harsh to me." Ruby stepped closer. "I've been in some tough boardrooms, but Hugo was a condescending bastard."

Fred laughed, filling the room with her ease and restoring the balance. "You're right. Trouble is, he's got the money and the power around here." Fred brushed a thread off Ruby's shoulder. "Thankfully, I get to work with some nice people who even things up."

They lingered together, each daring the other to move first. Ruby's pulse thundered in her ears as she saw what might happen next if she just leaned a few inches forward and took Fred's lips against her own.

They both jumped as the cabin door opened again, and Adrienne stepped over the threshold.

"Fred, what the fuck was all that?" She didn't acknowledge

Ruby's presence. "Are you trying to make life hard for yourself? Because you did a good job of humiliating your board director just then."

"I humiliated him?" Fred's eyes grew wide at the accusation, and her body stiffened again, as if she was fighting to control her impulses. "That's right, Adrienne. You see what you want to see."

"That was unprofessional."

"I thought that was about as professional as it could get, considering he basically called me chief lackey. I may not have all the letters after my name, but it's my name on the boards outside. It's my name that's in court if something goes wrong. So, I *am* in charge here. Those proposals were not costed, and without the budget, they weren't safe."

"You're a fool if you think he's going to let you get away with that."

Adrienne stepped into Fred's space. They froze and Adrienne's lips parted. It looked like foreplay.

"It wouldn't be the first time you've taken me for a fool." Fred choked on the last word, as if her heart was about to spill down her chin.

Ruby bit down on the shock of it, her pulse beating through her chest. She wanted to cross the cabin, pull Fred into her arms and protect her from the attack.

But there was something between Fred and Adrienne that didn't add up. This wasn't just about the meeting room. Something much deeper was being said, and Ruby had no idea how to translate it through the silence. Could she smell the burned embers of scorched desire?

Her head swam. How had she not picked up on this before? Why hadn't Fred said anything? She shrugged off the sense of betrayal which hung loosely about her shoulders. Fred didn't owe her any kind of explanation for this. They were colleagues, nothing more.

But she'd felt a connection, something more than functional.

She left the cabin, not wishing to intrude any longer on the weird intimacy. Across the yard, the loss enveloped her in the dusky light, and a heavy sadness weighed on her chest. This winter was dragging on, and she wondered how long this damned contract was going to last.

CHAPTER FIFTEEN

"I DON'T KNOW, STAN. She treated me like a fucking kid today." Fred slammed her pint onto the bar, sending a wave of beer over the top of the glass.

"Hey, watch your manners there." Trevor tutted and wiped down the oak with a cloth.

"Sorry," Fred said quickly.

Stan shook his head, remaining silent.

"I'm not a kid anymore."

"No. You weren't much of a kid when you started, to be honest. An old head on young shoulders, you." He rested his hand on her arm. "Adrienne didn't mean it, love. She thinks the world of you."

Fred huffed.

"I can't say anything for that Hugo. He's always been up himself."

"Too right. He's had it in for me since I was put on this job. I was lucky he went off to Turkey to have his surgery, otherwise I would've had weeks of hell already."

"Had his what done?"

Fred smirked. "He had a hair transplant, and he couldn't show his face until it had started to heal or something."

Stan spluttered on his beer, and Fred slapped him on the back. "The daft bugger."

"I wouldn't mind if he was daft, but he's conniving with it. He wants me off the site so he can bring in his own lads—the ones that keep quiet and don't argue with him." Fred's smile faded as she thought about losing her job. She'd worked her whole life to get here, and she wasn't about to throw in the towel for some stroppy director.

"Lucky for you it's not Hugo that pulls all the strings at that place, and we both know Adrienne wouldn't see you off the job. She's much closer to the big boss than anyone realises."

Fred swallowed. "A few months ago I would have said the same thing, but I'm not so sure now."

"What makes you say that?"

"I've pissed her off." Fred sagged. "Actually, she's pissed me off. But I've made it worse this past week. I've told her a few truths about her behaviour."

"Is it all off between you two then?"

She wondered if Stan would take their secret to his grave. He'd been the only one at work who'd known about their relationship.

"It has been for a while. I'm not sure it ever really started."

"I thought you were in deep for a while there."

"Maybe I was. Trouble is, she was swimming safe in the shallow end."

"Well, plenty more—"

"Don't say it. I'm not interested in plenty more." Fred pushed the image of Ruby from her mind, but she kept sliding back into focus like a viewfinder.

"What's that look?" Stan asked.

Could he read her thoughts? She hesitated. Most people wouldn't spill their love life to an old guy in his seventies. But Stan had offered his wisdom lovingly and willingly at every pivotal moment in her life so far, and she trusted him more than anyone.

"There's something, isn't there? Or someone. Who's it getting under your thick skin?"

Fred shuffled, her back stiff from overthinking. "Jesus, you don't give up, do you?"

"Not when it comes to you." He raised his glass. "Now, come on, out with it."

"Her name's Ruby. She's the new PR person."

"Christ, you know how to pick 'em."

"Oh, thanks." She sulked into her own tankard.

He nudged her in the ribs. "Keep going now you've started."

"There's something about her. I don't know." Fred scratched her neck, crawling with awkwardness. "She's got me all tied up in this business looking for old people who used to live on the street. She's so into it. It's dead sweet."

"Sweet, is it?" Stan raised his eyebrows like it was the last thing he expected her to say.

"I mean...kind. She's kind."

He stroked the white stubble on his chin. "Sounds like a good match."

"We're not a match. I didn't mean it like that. I'm enjoying having her around. Makes a refreshing change from all the smelly lads. Between the building site and that house full of brothers, I don't get much female company."

"Can't argue with that. So, what's next?"

"Next?"

"With Ruby the PR lass?"

"Nothing." Fred shut down. "The absolute last thing I need is to get wrapped up in anything with someone at work. Not after what happened, you know?" And especially Ruby. That would be impossible. She was frivolous, she didn't think before she acted. "Ruby would do my head in, really. She's like a pinball, always dashing from one crazy idea to the next. You'd have hated having her around."

"Well, we didn't get as tied up in all the promotions as you have to now. We built a little sales office, decked out the showroom, and the rest was someone else's job."

"Feels like everything's my job at the moment." Fred waved across the bar for a refill. "It's draining."

"You'll sort it. You always do."

"Thanks." She draped an arm around him. His frame had shrunk a little since they last embraced, and she shuddered at the thought of her Stan fading away, day by day, year by year.

***

"No way," Fred said, making for the door.

Ruby stood in her way. "It won't take long. Five minutes, max."

"What makes you think I would want to stand on stage in a room full of cocktail dresses and bow ties?" Heat flushed her cheeks, and she struggled not to raise her voice.

"I know this will be out of your comfort zone, but you'll be amazing, and people will really warm to you."

"Ask Adrienne to come down for it. Or get Hugo."

"Hugo is already speaking."

"Of course he is. He'd love to stand in the spotlight now that he won't blind everyone with his bald spot."

Ruby laughed.

"It's not funny. I'm not laughing. This is a non-negotiable for me." Fred stared hard, unable to take her eyes from the upturn of Ruby's lips. "There's no way I'm going to be Hugo's warm-up act, not after last week."

"But it'll be fun. A chance to dress up and let your hair down for the night with us all."

"I don't have the hair to let down." Fred attempted to exit again. "This is where you and I differ, Reputation Ruby. I don't care about the glitz and glamour. I care about the plan, the budget, and the near-miss log."

Ruby stuck out her bottom lip, and Fred's stomach flipped. She wanted to scoop her up right there and give her what she wanted. "What is it all about, anyway?"

"It's a charity dinner for the investors. And a chance to warm up the pre-sales." She bounced on her toes. "It's my first proper opportunity to make my mark on this project. I'd love a female speaker on the line-up, and you'd be the star."

"You're making it worse."

"I mean, you'd need to be you. Nothing else. Just your humble, authentic self. People love you."

Ruby's declaration touched Fred's heart. That's all Fred ever wanted to be: herself. Especially when Adrienne had wanted to hide her from the world. "What would I need to do?"

"Tell your story. How you started here and how you've grown with the company. That's it." Ruby touched her sleeve, and Fred almost melted. "I'll help you write something, if you like. And we can put it on the auto cue."

Fred paused. "Don't give me those eyes. You're like an excited puppy. I can't say no, can I?"

Ruby screeched, grabbing Fred's hands and enclosing them in her own soft palms. Her skin was like silk compared to Fred's calluses.

"Thank you. This is going to be brilliant."

"I think that depends on your perspective." Fred sighed, anxiety already gnawing at her gut.

Ruby tapped notes into her phone, her flushed cheekbones and full lips illuminated by the backlit screen.

Fred looked away before she fell further under Ruby's spell. "I have to check on a load of steel."

Charity dinners and speeches were so far away from Fred's world but once again, she found herself orbiting Ruby's galaxy like a wayward lump of rock. The heat of Ruby's sun was drawing her so close, she was afraid she might burn up into nothing.

CHAPTER SIXTEEN

"You look beautiful," said Trix.

"Thank you." Ruby blew her a kiss. "Not too much?"

"Fuck, no. It's a charity ball. Maximum sparkle, in my opinion." She did a twirl in Ruby's kitchen. "How do I look?"

"Perfect. Here's the cab." Ruby swallowed her nerves and nodded at the window.

As they reached the city, the glazed towers climbed, almost touching the sky. Ruby fiddled with her hem. "Thanks for coming back up for this, Trix. I needed an extra hand."

"You had this in the bag way before I got here. And I need no excuse for a spray tan, you know that." Trix leaned in for a quick hug. "Plus, I'm getting used to that train ride. I think the trolley guy fancies me."

"You're a nightmare." Ruby grinned, happy to have her friend by her side. "I am nervous though. I hope Fred's okay."

"Why are you worried about Fred?"

"Because I forced her into making a speech," Ruby said.

"Fred strikes me as a person who wouldn't be bullied into anything she didn't want to do. So dial down the guilt. She'll pull it off."

"I hope so." Raindrops raced across the windowpane, making Ruby think of how fast things were moving. Maybe she'd been too quick to put Fred on stage. It wasn't really her kind of thing, and she didn't want her to look silly, especially in front of the board.

The taxi pulled into the hotel's underground car park.

"Come on, we have an hour before everyone starts to arrive." Ruby jumped from the cab, keen to see everything in its place in the ballroom. They entered a glass elevator through a huge foyer, and she pressed the button for the ballroom on the fourteenth floor.

"This place is amazing." Trix craned her neck.

"It's another one of Delphine's schemes before she started to specialise in residential."

"God, you sound like you've swallowed the brochure."

When the lift came to a stop, Ruby stepped into the ballroom and took a breath. Everything looked precisely as she'd planned. The perfect temperature of lighting bathed the entire room, enough to see your neighbours but not their pores. Midnight-black cloths dressed each of the thirty tables, adorned with rose gold cutlery and crystal. Ruby put her hand to her heart, proud that she'd played a part in creating something so beautiful.

"I'm going to powder my nose and have a little look around," Trix said, leaving her side. Ruby's nerves settled a touch before the drapes gathered, and Fred emerged from the unending fabric.

"Hey, you."

Ruby's heart stopped for a brief second. Enough to make her cough. "Wow, you look so good." Her words came without warning. She breathed in the vision of Fred in a black tuxedo, so snug it looked like it was hand-stitched and custom-fit. Ruby was used to seeing Fred in loose cargos and baggy fleeces, but this outfit revealed every inch of her carved muscles. Each strand of hair framing her makeup-free face, her skin flawless and glowing.

Fred blushed and looked away, revealing the edge of her collarbone beneath a crisp white shirt. "You look stunning."

Ruby brushed at her own dress, picking off imaginary lint, suddenly aware of the pinch around her toes. "I'm regretting the heels already. Wouldn't get away with these on-site."

"No. Those are definitely not safe for a building site."

When Fred examined her heels, Ruby felt her gaze climb her legs, leaving a trail of heat burning in her pelvis.

"Do you mind if we run through my lines again?"

The spell broke, and Ruby came back into the room. "Of course.

But it's not a script. You don't need to know it word for word."

"Yeah, but I don't want to let you down."

"Ruby!" someone called from behind the stage.

"Sounds like someone needs you. This can wait." Fred bowed.

Ruby crossed the velvet carpet and almost collided with an oncoming Trix.

"Thank goodness. The sound guy has blown a fuse or something. You need to come up here."

They rushed backstage and into the sound booth.

"What's happening?"

"We're having a little technical issue with the footage you supplied," he said.

"What? I thought it was a blown fuse?" She looked between Trix and the sound guy.

"No. I can't get the audio to stream from your file."

"But it was working in the run-through?"

"Yeah."

The guy's monosyllabic responses were pushing Ruby's buttons in the worst way possible. "What can I do?"

"You got another copy somewhere?" He bit down on his pen.

"Oh, sure let me grab my laptop from my pocket. Oh, wait, I'm wearing my cocktail dress and it wouldn't fit." She grabbed her phone. "Fred? Can you come backstage?"

Within moments, Fred was at her side in all her suited glory, making it hard for Ruby to focus. "I need to get a copy of the showreel from the marketing suite. Is there a chance anyone is on-site?"

"Only security, and they won't be able to leave their posts to bring it here. But I can go over there in a taxi and fetch it."

Ruby almost dropped to her knees with gratitude.

"Do we have time?"

Fred checked her watch, flashing her cuffed wrist and another tempting body part that Ruby would like to press her lips to.

"I think so. You might miss the canapés."

"You should've led with that. Any excuse to skip the small talk."
Fred turned to go. "So, what am I looking for?"

"There are loads of little computer memory sticks next to the
brochures in the cupboard in the marketing suite. Grab a few, to
be safe."

"What brochures?" Fred looked blank, like Ruby had given her
an advanced axe-throwing technique to practice.

Trix stepped in. "Both of you go. Fred can get you on-site, and
you can find the exact stuff you need. Jesus, stop dallying. I can
handle it here."

"Got it. I'm all yours." Fred held out a hand.

It was the adrenaline rush that Ruby hadn't needed, but she
couldn't deny the thrill of having Fred at her command.

Ten minutes later, Fred led the way into the yard.

Rattle dropped his paper at the security gate. "Evening, you
two. Looking a bit flash tonight."

"Charity ball. We're on a bit of a mission," Fred said.

"Come on, we don't have long." Ruby ran to keep up behind.

"Wait. You can't come across here in those shoes."

"Fred, are you going to get all health and safety on me, right
now? Really? We're on a deadline." Ruby scoffed and attempted
to push past her.

"I mean it. Get some boots out of the gatehouse."

"You've got to be kidding me. What about your shoes?"

"They're flat and safe enough for a trip to the marketing suite.
But those heels would get me fired."

"What?" She held the skirt of her dress and looked at her feet.

"Unless you want me to carry you over the yard," Rattle said
from the gate.

"That's enough, thank you."

Fred shut down the banter, but it left Ruby with a stirring
thought of being carried across her strapping shoulder. "You're
unbelievable." Ruby grunted as she swapped her delicate heels for
a pair of filthy wellies.

"And you have no respect for the rules."

"Come on, we don't have time for this nonsense." Ruby pulled Fred with one hand and hoisted up her dress with the other.

At the door, Fred fumbled with her keys. "It's here somewhere."

Ruby picked out the key in the bunch. "It's this one." Her hands rested in Fred's for a moment, and the physical contact sent a shiver through Ruby. She withdrew and ran to fetch the memory sticks. She turned back briefly and saw Fred's silhouette against the floodlit yard. If it was possible, she looked even more handsome than she had in the ballroom. She stood all alone, just for Ruby's delight. Her mind raced with temptation, and she filled her lungs with air to steady her heartbeat. Ruby held Fred's gaze, desperate to convey everything she wanted to do to her.

She strode across the room and pulled Fred towards her.

"What are you doing?" Fred asked.

"I don't know. But if I don't kiss you right now, I'm going to explode." Ruby met her lips, heat rising between them.

Fred pulled away. "This is unexpected."

"Is it?" Ruby panted, her lust tipping into fear. "I'm sorry. You just look fucking awesome tonight."

Fred smiled and studied her shoes. "Ditto." She scanned the floor, as if she was weighing up the risks of their current situation. "Okay, you win. Let's do this."

She wrapped her arms around Ruby's waist and gave her a delicious, hungry kiss. The connection pulsed through Ruby's veins, and she fought the impulse to unbutton Fred's shirt there and then in the shadows of the suite. Instead, she slowed, tasting their kiss and its softness, the lingering familiarity that Fred had, like they'd been waiting for this moment for their whole lives.

Eventually, she broke away. "Wow. That was amazing."

"Yeah, it really was." Fred grinned. "We need to get back to the party. They'll be waiting for you."

Ruby couldn't bear the distance between them, but she nodded. Fred stroked her cheek with the edge of her finger, and the tremor between her legs shook once more. *Get a grip.* She remembered the massive event she was in charge of across town. "You're right." She looked into Fred's eyes, patting down the edge of her collar. "Can we do this again?"

A flicker of uncertainty passed over Fred's face before she nodded. "Yes, I think we should." Fred kissed her cheek.

Ruby's feet left the floor. Or she imagined they did. Her body floated with desire while her brain tried its best to get in gear. She had work to do, but her attraction to Fred had revealed itself in the most tangible way possible. She hadn't seen it coming but when it did, it was like a bullet train. Rapid, impressive, and foreign to her. She'd heard of first kisses like that, but she'd never experienced one. Now she had, she wondered whether she could ever be satisfied with anything less.

CHAPTER SEVENTEEN

BACK IN THE CAB, Fred struggled to breathe. Her palms were clammy, and she squinted at the brake lights in front, the red glow radiating in and out. She counted in her head, calming the urge to pull Ruby to her chest and peel the silk dress from her.

The driver cleared his throat, interrupting her thoughts as if he could read her sordid mind, and she began to panic. She'd had no intention of kissing Ruby but in the dark, hazy moment, she had burned to explore her mouth, taste her lips, and drink in her scent.

She stole a glance across the backseat, where the glow of the street light caressed Ruby's bare collar as she stared out of the window. Fred absorbed every inch of her flawless complexion, a calm beauty against the city rushing past. Her heartbeat stuttered, taking it all in. It was like she'd never seen such gentle elegance, the kind she wanted to curl into and fall asleep.

She became aware of Ruby's little finger on the edge of her palm, and her touch, barely there, sent shockwaves through Fred. Her body recalled every moment of their kiss, the impulse to bring them together growing. She covered Ruby's hand with her own and stroked her silky skin.

The car pulled over at the hotel, and they exchanged a look which Fred took as a promise to get through this evening in one piece and pick up where they left off. Her pulse raced, pounding through the neck of her shirt.

"You okay?" Ruby asked.

"I think so," Fred said and opened the car door.

Trix welcomed them back among a line of guests entering the ballroom. "You made it. Everything go as planned?"

"Not exactly, but we've got the showreel." Ruby rushed in and headed for the stage.

"What does she mean, not exactly?" Trix asked Fred.

"I've no idea." She shrugged and backed away, worried that Trix could read the truth in every movement she made. "I should get ready for my speech." It was the last thing she needed, the scrutiny of two hundred people when she felt so exposed.

Fred made for the bar, eager for a drink to settle her nerves. She compromised on a vodka, not wanting to stand out from the posh crowd with a pint of beer in hand.

"Careful, you don't want to overdo it before your big speech."

She looked up to see Hugo and his oversized ego had sidled up beside her at the bar, cradling a flute of something white and fizzing.

"Thanks for the tip."

"When Ruby told me you'd be my opening act, I was quite surprised. You don't strike me as a natural public speaker."

Fred bristled, every word poking at her insecurities. "Well, I've been instructed to be myself. So that's what you'll get. No more, no less."

"That's disappointing, I thought you'd rise to the occasion." Hugo smirked, raising his glass in a mocking toast.

Fred turned towards him and squared her chest. "Why have you got such a problem with me?"

Something like annoyance flickered across Hugo's brow. "I don't. I like to keep you on your toes."

"Is that it?" She knew there was more, but he clearly wasn't going to admit it tonight. "Enjoy your evening."

"See you backstage for the finale." Hugo waved.

Fred walked towards the table plan to find her seat. Fatigue set into her bones as the adrenaline of the last hour wore off. She scanned the list of names, seeing her own next to the only other she dreaded. *Adrienne*.

Closing her eyes, she fought the urge to run, to walk out of the ballroom into the night and back home. But she couldn't let Ruby down. She'd promised to do this opening speech and didn't want to throw the running order into chaos. Ruby didn't deserve that.

So she dragged herself towards the table where Adrienne waited, immaculately dressed in a designer gown, her hair sculpted into a geometric shape on top of her head. She looked like something out of a modern art museum. "Didn't you approve this table plan?" Fred asked, slumping into the velvet chair.

"There was a last-minute change because some investor couldn't make it. So, I got bumped to your table, to help you get through the evening without spilling your soup down your tux."

"Very funny. I can cope without you babysitting me."

"Can you? Because Ruby didn't seem convinced."

"Don't try and wind me up with your bullshit." Fred turned away, wondering why Ruby had sat them together.

"Nice. You're really watching your manners there."

"Listen, we have to work together. It doesn't matter what we've been through in our personal lives. You're one of the directors, and I'm the site manager. Let's try to maintain those professional boundaries." Fred steadied her hand around her crystal tumbler.

"Have you been on some sort of HR course?" Adrienne laughed.

It was the kind of thing they'd have laughed at together a few months ago. "No. I'm trying to make this bearable for both of us. For everyone. If we can't get along, it'll be bad for the whole project."

Adrienne raised her eyebrows. "If you say so. I still haven't forgiven you for what you said to me the other night."

"I don't need your forgiveness. I need to move on with my life." The thought of Ruby's hand clasping her collar flooded her brain.

"What is it?"

"Huh?"

"You looked at me with a bizarre expression." Adrienne scowled.

"Sorry. I've got a lot on my mind. Hugo's been winding me up about making this speech tonight."

Adrienne relaxed. "You'll be fine. Be yourself."

"That's what I said."

"Ignore Hugo. He's got a chip on his shoulder. He's jealous because you've earned the respect of every single guy on-site. He barely knows their names, and they couldn't give a flying fuck about him."

Fred laughed, enjoying Adrienne's take on the source of Hugo's spite towards her. Maybe she was right. It would make a lot of sense for him to envy the respect Fred commanded on-site. "The bonkers thing is that if he worked with me, the crews would respect him."

"Yeah, well, that penny hasn't dropped, has it? He has the emotional intelligence of a house brick."

Fred's phone buzzed with a text from Ruby.

Can you meet me backstage for a quick mic fit?

Her breath stuck between her ribs. Ruby's name triggered electrical impulses through her nerve endings. She excused herself and half jogged between the tables, sneaking behind the velvet drapes at the side of the stage. As she headed for the rigging, she felt a tug and almost tripped. "What the fu–"

"Sh." Ruby held her steady and placed her finger on her lips.

"What are you doing?"

"I know we said we'd wait, but I wanted to do this." She pressed herself against Fred's chest and kissed her, this time with more force and a deeper hunger than before.

Fred held Ruby's slender frame, wanting to lift her, wrap her legs around her waist, and lean against the stage wall. She held back, cupping Ruby's face, cradling the softness of her cheeks between her hands and nipping her bottom lip with her teeth. "You're naughty, Ruby Lewis. If we get caught, we'll be in a lot of trouble."

"But you're the boss, aren't you?" Ruby winked, apparently blissfully unaware of the effect she had on Fred.

"There are bigger bosses here tonight than me." Fred stroked Ruby's lip with her thumb, dying to touch every part of her. "Which reminds me, why did you stick me on a table with Adrienne?"

"Because she asked me to. Why?"

Fred blew her cheeks out. "No reason. I thought we were splitting ourselves up so we could network." She should've explained the baggage she had with Adrienne. But now was not the time. "Where were we?" She leaned back in, biting her lip before nestling into Ruby's neck and linking a trail of kisses to her ear lobe.

"We don't have long. You do need a mic."

"You tease. Bringing me back here to leave me hanging?" Fred grazed Ruby's chest with her kisses.

"Trust me, I'm leaving us both hanging." Ruby giggled then met Fred's kiss. She opened her lips wider and flicked her tongue inside.

Fred groaned, her fever building. "How about we ditch this ball and find somewhere quieter?"

Ruby leaned back with a playful grin. "We'd both live to regret that. Now, you get your mic on. We'll eat, entertain some people, and pick this up later."

"You expect me to let that sound guy put his hand in my shirt after you've wound me up like this?"

"You want me to mic you up?" Ruby held her gaze while she untucked her shirt, caressing the bare skin above her hip.

Desire pulsed through Fred's thighs. "Don't tempt me."

"You ticklish? It's only a little wire. It goes in here..." She trailed a line with her finger, lifting Fred's shirt to reveal the outline of her sports bra. "All the way up here." Ruby brushed over her breast, lingering on the bare skin of her chest.

Fred kissed her fingers.

The sound of wheels against concrete disturbed them, and they broke from their embrace.

"I should get that mic on." Fred adjusted her shirt and flapped air beneath the cotton to cool herself down.

Ruby patted at her own dress, revealing the curves underneath the silk. Fred averted her gaze. The temptation was far too great. She nodded, turned back towards the rig, and walked away.

Tonight had taken quite the unexpected turn. The hunger for Ruby was powerful and something she wasn't sure she was in control of now that she'd acted on it. Maybe she didn't mind. They were both adults. Sure, it could make work a little uncomfortable, but if no one knew, there was no harm in having a little fun. And if there was one thing guaranteed with Ruby, it was excitement.

CHAPTER EIGHTEEN

RUBY STUDIED THE BLACK spots on her ceiling. It was obviously mould, but landlady Lou had skirted over the issue when she'd moved in.

Unable to sleep, she replayed every moment she'd shared with Fred that evening. God knows where she'd gotten the courage to go in for that first kiss. It was so unlike her to abandon her professionalism. But she and Fred had been growing more than a workplace friendship over the last few weeks. The heat between them threatened to scorch the very ground they were preserving if they weren't careful.

The second kiss had been far more calculated. She'd weighed up how much time she had between the starters and the speeches then decided to lure Fred behind the stage to make out. The result was thigh-trembling, and it took all of Ruby's self-control not to drop to her knees there and then and devour Fred.

She'd thought about it through the entire four-course meal. By the time Fred reached the podium to address the audience, Ruby's silk knickers were wet through. Knowing that an hour or so beforehand she'd had her hand up her shirt made her quiver with lust.

Fred had nailed her speech, of course. It was never in doubt. She'd given Hugo the middle finger by being her very best self. Every turn of her tale was genuine, and everyone in the room loved her. The pride that flowed over Ruby as Fred's time on stage came to its humble crescendo surprised her. She'd accepted the attraction, but the whirlwind of joy caught her unawares. She craved Fred's touch, but more than that, she yearned to see her succeed.

She turned over, willing the sleep to come so that her dreams could be filled with alternate and extended versions of the night's adventures. She trusted her mind to conjure the greatest fantasies, taking her further into Fred's embrace and deeper into her touch.

At some point she must have drifted off, because she awoke a few hours later with shards of light edging the blind at her window. Sweat gathered at the creases of her armpits and behind her knees. The sleep, when it came, had been fitful and disjointed. Ruby screwed her eyes shut, trying to piece together the fragments of ecstasy that had come to her in the night. The evidence of her pleasure pooled between her legs, and she reached below the sheets to touch herself, just as she'd craved Fred's touch the evening before.

Her breath slowed as she eased into her dream-like state, exploring her own body, imagining Fred on top of her. She arched under the rhythm of her fingers, thinking of how she'd bend and break at the will of Fred's strong hands.

The sound of her phone disturbed her pleasure.

I enjoyed last night. What are you up to today?

Ruby grinned. *I'm in bed, all alone, thinking about you.*

She held her breath for the next message, her centre pulsing with expectation.

Really? I'm in bed too...

The thought of calling Fred crossed Ruby's mind, but she wasn't sure she could pull it off, so she texted back.

I'm thinking about kissing you again.

The pause gifted Ruby time to touch herself, returning to the same source of pleasure she'd gathered. The image of Fred in her own bed, stroking her own skin brought Ruby to a peak of desire.

I'm thinking about more than kissing. When can I see you?

Ruby smiled at Fred's demand. Her bluntness was endearing.

How about tonight? I have an idea.

She rolled onto her side, spread her thighs, and brought herself to a delicious climax. Laying in her self-satisfied glow, she imagined all the fun she could have with Fred now they'd popped the cork of their attraction to each other. And she knew exactly where to start.

***

"This is a serious business." Ruby suppressed her smile, trying to mimic Fred's tone on the building site.

"Don't make fun of me, Ruby Lewis. You'll live to regret it." Fred stood with her hands on her hips, creases at her eyes.

"I hope so." Ruby giggled. "Now, this is a very dangerous place, can you assure me that you understand the risks?"

Fred's eyes twinkled. "Can you show me what to do? I need proper instruction."

"Of course. That'll be my pleasure." She lifted the handle of the first axe and stroked its oak shaft while she maintained eye contact with Fred, who shuffled adorably.

"You should keep your eyes on the blade. You're making me nervous." Fred reached for the axe.

"This is really getting to you, isn't it? Not being in control?" Ruby laughed, rubbing Fred's cheek with her thumb. "I'm pretty good at this. You'll see." She approached the throw, drew back, and flicked the axe with her wrist. It hit the target with a satisfying thunk.

"Very impressive." Fred bit her lip and looked like she wanted to bend Ruby over the bar there and then. "Is this your thing then?"

"Sort of. I live above an axe-throwing den back in London. It was one of the first. An underground kind of place. I started training with the owner."

"You can train in this?"

"You can train in anything..." The innuendo dripped from Ruby's lips, and she licked at the gloss she'd applied earlier.

"I bet you can." Fred rose to the challenge and put her arms around Ruby's waist.

"You need to earn your spurs here, soldier. Have a throw, and then we'll see if you deserve any attention." Ruby wriggled free and placed the axe in her palm. With her hands on Fred's hips, she guided her to the line. "Here, stand square." Ruby moved to face Fred and tipped her chin up. "Look at me." Her breath came faster in her chest, and she wondered if she could hold out much longer. All she wanted was to resume where they'd left off at the ball. "Now maintain your eye line all the way to the target. Lift your arm and give it a strong throw. It'll spin all by itself."

Fred raised her eyebrows. "I can throw, you know?"

Ruby took her place in the safe zone. "Okay. Let's see what you've got there, boss."

Fred released her axe, and it sliced the air, reaching the outer edge of the wooden target with a dink.

"Not bad for a virgin." Ruby winked, holding out another. "Practice makes perfect."

Fred smiled, like she was graciously humouring Ruby's foreplay. Her next throw was more decisive, her muscle responded to the weight of the axe, her eye judged the distance, and she hit closer to the target.

"Close. You don't take long, do you?"

"Take long?" Fred frowned.

"To weigh up what you're holding. To get the feel of something." Ruby put herself in Fred's way, hoping to be held by the same strong hands that had thrown the axes with such ease.

"I guess not." Fred kissed her.

It was a longing kiss that built as they stood wrapped together in the dim light of the axe alley.

"You taste amazing."

Ruby smiled, meeting her gaze as they continued to kiss. "You too. But you really are distracting me from my favourite hobby."

"I'm sorry." Fred paused, pushing a stray tuft of hair behind her ear. "Maybe this could be your second favourite hobby?"

Ruby melted as Fred traced a line of kisses along her jaw to her neck. The door swung open at the back of the room, and a gang of lads tumbled into the alley next to theirs.

Fred stepped away and picked up another axe. "Okay, how'd you really get into this?"

"I told you. I live above an axe-throwing place. I got to know the folks there, and they became a kind of substitute family. People to go home to when security finally kicked me out of the office." Ruby took a gulp of her lemonade. "Throwing axes around is a great stress-reliever."

Fred arched her eyebrow again. "I can think of other ways to blow off steam."

"No doubt. What with you being an expert on health and safety." They both collapsed into a fit of giggles. "Seriously, how do you work off all that pent-up energy from running the site?"

"Honestly? You won't laugh?"

"Scout's honour." Ruby held up three fingers and wiggled them, winking at Fred.

"I escape to the shed at the bottom of the garden." Fred fidgeted and looked embarrassed. "It's a bit cold now, but soon I'll start sowing some seeds ready to plant out in my neighbour's allotment. You know, Jensen, who put us onto the oldies we've been talking to."

"Yeah, good old Mr Jensen. Wow, that sounds so lovely. You have hidden depths, don't you?"

Fred shrugged and fiddled with the buttons on her shirt. "It's an excuse to get out of the house. It can be chaotic."

"Remind me, how come you still live at home? Haven't you built a housing development that you fancied the look of yet?"

Fred inspected the floorboards and stepped from one foot to another. "I moved out in my early twenties, but I came back a couple of years ago when my dad got sick. He got laid off and couldn't pay the bills."

"Oh, shit, I'm so sorry. I shouldn't have brought it up." Ruby wrung her hands together, and Fred reached to still them.

"It's okay, I don't mind talking about it. Dad had a stage three cancer diagnosis, but he's out of the woods for now. You know, as far as these things go. I wanted to hang around until I knew he and my mum were settled with everything. They've barely been able to wrap their heads around the benefits and pension coming in."

"I get that." Ruby looked at the floor to avoid probing any further.

"I've been looking for somewhere to buy for a while, but it hasn't been the right time or the right place."

"That makes two of us. My flat search is going nowhere. Places are snapped up so quickly, there's barely time for a viewing."

"I know. The market is crazy, and I'm not one for impulsive decisions. Especially for the biggest financial commitment I'll ever make."

Ruby cocked her head, taking in the cautious beauty standing in her way. "You really are a thinker, aren't you?"

"And what are you?"

"God, I don't know. A wanderer?" She wasn't sure she knew what she was.

She *was* certain that she wanted to escape somewhere quiet with Fred and pick up the kiss that had been so rudely interrupted, to find out whether there was more to come. Fred was slowly becoming a constant in her life up north. A constant source of wisdom, of care, and tenderness. Could it be more than a workplace fling? She had never really given in to anything more serious. But with Fred, it seemed like just about anything might be possible.

CHAPTER NINETEEN

FRED TIED HER BOOTLACE before leaving the cabin. The sound of crunching brick and earth moving reached her from across the site, where Champ supervised the demolition of the second line of terraces. They were bang on schedule, not that Fred was taking much note this morning. Her head swam with thoughts of Ruby wielding an axe so naturally it was like holding a power drill.

She shook her head, mystified at the depths the new PR exec had demonstrated in such a short time. Was there no end to the layers she could peel away? Half of her hoped not. She wanted to reveal many more physical and emotional depths to Ruby.

The other half feared that it would only lead to more heartache and rejection.

Fred returned to the cabin window to take in the morning. The crew moved like ants across the site, weaving in and out of cordons, all in unspoken sync with each other. She leaned against the glass, the sound of radios barely audible. She lifted her own to her mouth and pressed the button. "Champ, it's Fred."

"Hiya, boss. All okay?"

"I'm checking on that demolition. I've signed all the risk assessments. Are we on track for this afternoon?"

"Absolutely. It's going swimmingly."

Fred flinched at Champ's optimism. With a report like that, something was bound to go wrong. She looked over to the site plan on the wall, a gigantic sketch of what they were knocking down to make way for new life. Two of the old streets were almost ready for the new build to start. There was a third, which had stood still like a time capsule for almost fifty years. The town's historians had been interested in having a look. *"It'll be amazing for sales,"* Ruby had said when she'd heard about it. Her perfect smile had beamed with the excitement of it all, and Fred had drunk her enthusiasm like a fine wine.

The door opening disturbed her daydream, and she turned to see Hugo making himself at home.

"Nice of you to knock." Fred stood her ground, jutting her chin out.

"This is as much my site as it is yours." Hugo ran his finger across the papers on Fred's desk.

"It's my name on the boards."

"You're like a broken record, has anyone ever told you that?" He flashed a fake smile, baring his whitened teeth. "I only came in to ask whether we're going to hit next week's milestone."

"Of course," Fred said. She didn't answer to him, she answered to the board.

"Adrienne will be pleased." Hugo purred like he'd found Fred's soft spot. "Of course, you'd know how to please that particular director, wouldn't you?"

Fred stared down the question. The silence between them dense enough to snuff a match.

"Not going to take the bait?" Hugo folded his thick hands, waiting.

Fred pursed her lips. She could tell him to go fuck himself. Or she could take the higher ground. "I'm not sure what you're asking." She tilted her head and delivered her best confused frown.

"Sure, you keep it to yourself. It's the worst kept secret on-site."

Fred's heart raced. She'd wanted Adrienne to be open about their relationship while they were together. But now they were very much apart, she despised the thought of being gossiped about. She thought of Ruby and how she'd react.

"You wouldn't want anyone to talk, especially to the board. They might question your integrity."

"Are you threatening me?"

"Why would I?"

Fred could think of at least a hundred reasons. Jealousy. Pride. "I don't know. You don't exactly hide your contempt for me."

"Not true. We're finding our groove here, you and I."

"Are we finished? I have a staff meeting in five minutes." Fred stilled her hand, shaking with the rage she was fighting to keep a lid on.

"I'll leave you to it then. Wouldn't want to put off the heavy lifters."

The dig at Fred's labourers cut deeper than it should have. Fred was proud of her crew and of her origins as a labourer. "Fuck off then." There was something so patronising about Hugo's turn of phrase that she couldn't bite back the anger in time.

"Temper, temper. You need to keep that in check, otherwise Adrienne will be on your back. But then, you'll like that, won't you?" Hugo left, cackling like an unhinged hyena, and the door swung back into its catch with a bang.

"Bastard," Fred said, her mood crashing to the floor.

"Knock, knock."

"Come on in." Fred pushed Hugo's taunts to the back of her mind and mustered a welcome. She fixed a smile on her face and forced her shoulders down.

"You okay there? You look like you're in pain," Ruby said.

"Hugo has been winding me up."

"I saw him leave looking like he'd won the bingo."

Fred laughed at the image of Hugo hunched over a bingo card in a room full of pensioners. "Thanks," she said.

"What for?"

"Cheering me up." Fred touched Ruby's arm and wished she hadn't, because the urge to wrap herself around her was too strong. "You're the perfect antidote to his toxic masculinity."

"You're very welcome." Ruby pecked her cheek and winked. "I came in to ask about the history group visit."

"What visit?" Fred stood back. People like archaeologists and history nerds on-site only meant one thing: delay.

"The history group. They've asked if they can have a bit of a look around while they're here, and I thought it would make great TV. I can ask the local crew to come down and, you never know, they might syndicate it nationally. Especially if they find anything interesting."

"Ruby, you can't start poking around on a demolition-site. Everything is planned to the day, to the hour even. If I let a bunch of mud-movers have their fun in the sun, I could set the plan back by weeks."

Ruby's head dropped and guilt almost overcame Fred.

She tipped her chin. "I'm sorry. But we need to discuss this stuff before you go off and get carried away."

"I am discussing it, right now."

"Let's sit down, and you can tell me about it." Fred moved to the desk, and they took seats opposite one another. Grateful for the distance between them, Fred tried to reinstate the professional boundaries that she'd been crashing through over the past few days. "Now, what is all this?"

"Well, it's gathered some steam. Apparently, there are more of them than we thought, and some of them are keen on taking photos of the older houses and looking around before it all disappears." Ruby squirmed in her seat. "If we say no, they'll think we've got something to hide."

"We don't," Fred said. "We had the sign-off from the chief archaeologist before we started on-site. We're preserving most of the history here. There's nothing to see."

"I know you're frustrated. But hear me out. This would be a massive media opportunity and a great chance to build some relationships with the local community."

"There is no community here. It's been empty for decades. We're rebuilding the bloody houses."

Ruby patted the air. "Give me a second. The history group has already talked to the local press about it, so if we decline, they'll be all over it."

Fred shook her head, accepting defeat. "Christ, why didn't you lead with that?"

"I thought you'd be up for it. Or at least fine about it."

"Don't sulk."

"I'm not." Ruby huffed. "I'm trying to do my best here, and you're blocking my every move."

Fred took a breath. She was still riled by Hugo's remarks and didn't want to lose her temper with Ruby.

The radio beeped. "Boss, are you there?"

"Hold on, Ruby, I need to take this." Fred moved to the window. "What is it, Champ?"

"Do you know whose machinery this is on the lane? It's blocking the emergency route."

Fred's heart sank. She'd let the demolition contractors on-site this morning and trusted them to be off by now. "Look at the front. Is it Brownlow's?" Fred waited for Champ's response.

"Yeah, that's it, boss. What do you want me to do with it?"

"I'll come over." Fred grabbed her jacket from its hook and stormed out of the door. "Those sodding amateurs."

"Wait for me," Ruby said. "Are we finished talking then?"

Fred looked over her shoulder, willing herself to be calm. "Listen, you act before you think sometimes. This business is complex and comes with a fair amount of risk. And I don't mean that people will lose money or time. I mean people's lives are in danger when silly decisions are made." Fred was no longer talking about the history group.

Ruby's strides shortened to keep up. "I'm well aware of the risks, Fred. And you don't have to drag up every mistake I've made since I arrived," she said, clearly irritated.

The last of Fred's patience ebbed away as they turned into the blocked lane. "Champ, get me a forklift." It took a few moments for the crew to rally to her demand.

"Where do you want this, boss?" One of the new lads scratched the back of his neck.

"I'll take those." She took the keys from him and put the vehicle into drive. She approached the machinery which had clogged her emergency lane and positioned the forks, suddenly aware of her growing audience and the fact she hadn't operated a forklift for many months. "Out of the way," she said a bit too harshly, not wanting to injure anyone in the fog of her temper. She lifted the blockage, reversed to the end of the lane, found a skip, and deposited the Brownlow's abandoned equipment as if it was a bale of hay during harvest time. "No one leaves their junk where it can cause an accident, does everyone understand?" The question directed at the remaining crew was met with a host of nods and affirmative grunts. Fred climbed off the forklift and tramped back to the cabin.

She wanted to give in to Ruby's wishes, but there were so many moving parts on this building site, she didn't know which one to lock down first. Not to mention the rollercoaster of feelings she seemed stuck on since the night at the ball. If only something could stay still for long enough so she could get a grip on it, then she might be able to think clearly.

CHAPTER TWENTY

"ARE YOU SURE THIS isn't getting out of control?" Ruby asked, the phone slipping out of her grip. "Hold on, I'm putting you on speaker."

"I think it's a great idea," Trix said, sounding the two hundred miles away that was between them. "DJ is all over it. If you pull this off, he'll put you in for another award."

Ruby faced herself in the mirror, stretching the dark circles at her eyes. The truth was, she wasn't interested in winning more awards. She ached to make Fred happy.

"Are you still there?"

"Yes. I'm trying to fix my face. I look a state."

"What's wrong with you? This stuff is your bread and butter."

Ruby knew she could organise stunts like this one in her sleep. But Fred's reaction dissolved her confidence. Maybe she had overstepped.

"What's your plan?" Trix asked.

"Honestly? Do you mind if I come back down to London for a couple of days? I need to clear my head and see some friendly faces."

"Absolutely. I would love to have you for company. You want to stay with me and come into the office next week?"

"If that's okay, yeah. The sublet on my flat still has months to run. Can you book me a desk?"

"Of course. Listen, sort your train times, and let me know when you'll arrive. We can catch up properly then. Ta ta, beautiful."

Ruby grunted her goodbye and stared at the phone, hanging limply in her hand. How could she feel so distant from everyone?

Trix was such a long way away, and sometimes it felt like the connection between her and Fred was all in her head.

The doorbell rang, and she pushed her bedroom door closed. She didn't need company. She wanted to climb into bed and feel sorry for herself. Footsteps padded along the hallway, and there was a knock.

"It's me, Fred."

Ruby stiffened and scanned the room, cringing at the further evidence of her messy life. "Hang on a sec." She grabbed at the clothes strewn across the floor and scraped the board papers into a pile on her desk. "This is a surprise," she said, opening the door.

"Your flatmate let me in. Sorry, I don't mean to get in your way." Fred shuffled from one foot to another in her socks.

Fred's gaze lingered on the disgusting carpet, and Ruby wished she'd kept her boots on at the door. "Come on in." She stood aside and welcomed Fred into the bedroom.

"I thought you'd left in a rush, and I didn't want you to be mad with me."

Ruby melted. "I'm not. I'm angry with myself for not keeping you in the loop with all the history stuff." She closed the distance between them, dying to curl up into Fred's strong arms and fall into the bed. "I couldn't be mad with you."

"You looked pretty mad when you left." Fred's eyebrows furrowed, giving her the cutest curious look Ruby had ever seen.

She held up her hands in protest. "Okay, I was a bit ruffled by the whole thing because I don't want to disappoint you."

Fred stepped forward, leaving an inch between them. She was so close, the hush of her breath lingered at Ruby's earlobe.

"You don't disappoint me," Fred whispered.

Maybe this wasn't the time for talk. She was still pretty hurt that Fred had pulled the shutters down on her ideas, but here, filling this tiny room, Ruby could do nothing but submit to the moment. She tipped her chin to meet Fred's gaze, bathing in her wide pupils. Fred stroked Ruby's cheek, sending shivers across her shoulder blades. "I didn't want this to happen here. Not the first time."

"I know." Fred pulled her in, their bodies meeting. She kissed her forehead. "It doesn't matter where we are. It's just you and me."

"And Lou downstairs." They bumped heads giggling.

Fred put her finger to her lips. "Sh..."

Ruby sighed, revealing more of her neck, silently begging for more. Fred was right. She wanted this closeness, right here, right now.

"Shall we do this?" Fred asked.

"God, yes." Ruby moved first, kissing her hard as a wave of desire crashed against her chest. She leaned into the envelope of Fred's embrace.

They pawed at each other's clothes, peeling them off layer by layer. Fred sat, stretched her limbs off the bed, and drew Ruby between her legs. Every moment had led to this. Every time they'd caught each other's eye across the yard, every joke they'd shared. It had all led here, to this connection, which she delighted in.

Ruby trembled. Maybe it was the chill of the air, or maybe it was the thrill of what was coming as she took in Fred's firmness, the smooth lines of her limbs, the velvet of her skin.

Fred wrapped Ruby tighter in her arms and took Ruby's nipple in her mouth, driving a bolt of electricity through her nerves. A fire raged inside, flames spreading through her legs and reaching her chest. Fred touched the inside of her thigh, and her strong, rugged fingers brushed against Ruby's most sensitive skin. For all her front, she might need Fred to lift her up to new heights that she couldn't reach all by herself. Ruby arched her back, begging Fred for more.

It was enough of a signal for Fred to take charge. She flipped her like a doll onto her back, and they laughed together through another hungry kiss.

Fred broke away to take a breath and put her palm to Ruby's cheek. "What do you want?" she asked, her deep voice cracking.

Ruby couldn't gather the strength in her voice. "You. All of you."

Fred laid a path of kisses across Ruby's breasts and down her stomach. She paused, placing her tongue gently along her thighs before taking her inside her mouth. Ruby curved, wanting to give Fred more than she had, yearning to be closer. Every movement sent another thrill, and Ruby pulsed again and again under Fred's control, each flick releasing another level of delight.

She opened her eyes and leaned up on one elbow, wanting to consume the moment with all her senses. The sight of Fred taking her was almost too much. Her pleasure built until she was almost breathless, almost blind with indulgence. Fred went deeper and faster. Ruby gave herself up, released her muscles, and accepted the glorious climax Fred gifted her.

Time stopped and they lay together, the blood pounding in Ruby's ears until she lost count of the moments that passed.

"I need to tell you something," Ruby said, breathless from her exertion.

"Sounds ominous." Fred stroked the inside of her upper arm.

"It's not bad. I have to go back to London for a few days."

"When?"

"Tomorrow. I fixed it with Trix."

Fred edged away, and Ruby missed her body as soon as they parted.

"How long will you be gone for?" Fred kissed the tip of her nose, her touch sending ripples of desire back through Ruby's core.

"Not long. I don't want to leave now..."

"Now we've done this?" Fred's eyes scanned Ruby's face for what looked like reassurance.

Ruby wasn't sure she could give it. A couple of hours ago, she was ready to scurry back to London for some respite and a well-needed boost from Trix. She stared into the deep pools of Fred's pupils and lost herself and all her doubts. "I like that we've done this." She smiled, burying herself in the warmth of Fred's neck.

"Why do you need to go back? I'll miss you." Fred hooked her leg around Ruby's hip, her skin warming on contact.

"I felt off after we spoke in the cabin. I thought maybe going to see Trix would be good for the creative juices. Bit of a boost for the old confidence levels too."

"I upset you, didn't I? Flying off the handle about the history thing."

"Yeah, a little. It's not your fault." Ruby nestled further into Fred, seeking shelter from the exposure she felt. "I wanted to do something special."

Fred tilted her chin, holding her gaze until she couldn't bear it. "I think we could do anything we put our minds to, you and me."

"You think?" Ruby wasn't convinced, the bruise of her ideas being rejected still smarting even after Fred had tried to kiss it better. "Why don't you come to London with me? It'll be fun."

"What and leave the site to run itself?" Fred guffawed, as if Ruby had suggested popping to the moon for tea.

"Just for the weekend? Come back on Monday morning." Ruby faltered, wondering if she'd moved too fast. "Sunday night, even. If you're worried about it. Or forget it, it doesn't matter."

A pause hung between the sheets.

Fred sank back into the pillow. "Okay, you win. You can drag me south for the weekend. But what's the plan? Where are you staying?"

She hadn't thought about that. Doubling down at Trix's didn't seem appropriate now, and she wasn't ready to share Fred with other people yet. "I'll sort it."

"Okay, Ms Fix It. You'll have me all to yourself for the weekend. What will you do with me?"

Ruby could think of plenty she'd like to do with her newly naked site manager. Tonight had been a real turnaround. She'd gone from awful to orgasms in a short hop from the door. She laid back, ignoring the black mould on the ceiling and leaning into Fred's strong embrace. She felt safe in her arms, like nothing could touch them while they were together. Maybe Fred was right. Maybe they could achieve anything if they worked together. Ruby had been a lone wolf for such a long time, maybe she was ready to partner up and see what she could achieve as part of a couple. The idea sat for a moment before Ruby got distracted by the kisses being planted like a climbing rose up her chest.

For now, work was the last thing she wanted to think about.

CHAPTER TWENTY-ONE

FRED SLUNG HER RUCKSACK across her shoulders and did another little dance to dodge a wheelie case wielded by a fellow tourist. "Those things are lethal."

"Stay close, Fred. I don't want to lose you in the big city."

"I've lived in Manchester my whole life. I think I'll survive."

"People are friendlier up there. Here, no one would make eye contact with you lying in a ditch."

Ruby laughed her loud, world-warming laugh. The one that Fred had found so abrasive the first time they met. Now it rose above the hum of Euston station, a foghorn in the threatening riptide of the crowd. They hopped in a cab to Bank. So far, so familiar. London wasn't too scary.

"I can't wait to take you up to this place, you'll love it. The office isn't too far away."

"Tell me where we're heading." She put her hand over Ruby's on the back seat of the car.

"It's a surprise." Ruby leaned in, and their lips touched.

Fred sneaked a look at the rearview mirror to the driver's eyes on the road. The temptation to devour Ruby there and then was almost overwhelming.

"Quick lunch, then we'll get cosy at the hotel."

"That better be a promise." Fred rested her head against Ruby's, breathing in the heat of her desire. She knew the flames would be quick to reignite later, when they had a place to themselves. She was grateful, at least, that Ruby hadn't flinched at any hint of public affection. That was more than she'd ever had with Adrienne.

A few minutes later, she was being drawn by the hand past a

line of people. Most looked like tourists waiting for something to happen. A digital clock blinked with a wait time of an hour.

"We're skipping the queue?" she asked.

"Oh, yeah. I bagged us VIP access." Ruby strode confidently through the marble foyer and called one of the six elevators adorned in chrome. "I worked on the launch of this place, and I still have some privileges."

"A face like yours? Who could say no?"

Ruby squeezed her hand and shrugged off the compliment. They emerged from the elevator to an indoor oasis. The glazed atrium stretched out in all directions, filled with both tumbling and tall plants as far as Fred could see. She breathed in, a rush of oxygen filling her lungs, straight from the life-giving breath of each leaf.

Beyond the green canopy, she could make out the London skyline. She didn't recognise much, except the gherkin building and the general criss-cross of the city. She caught a glimpse of the Shard, poking through the ground level, with its sharp needle piercing the grey blanket of sky. At its feet, the dirty brown River Thames flowed by.

"I wish it was a nicer day for you. It's glorious up here when the sun's shining." Ruby's shoulders sagged as if she was disappointed that the city wasn't putting on its best show.

"Hey," Fred whispered, "the view's great. I intend to spend most of the day indoors anyway." They strolled hand in hand and climbed the steps up to the restaurant. She craned her neck to appreciate the architectural brilliance of the huge garden in the sky. "All jokes aside, this place is pretty cool, even on a dull day."

"I knew you'd like it." Ruby looked pleased as punch. "Booking for two, please. Under the name Lewis," she said at the desk.

They followed the waiter to an intimate table at the apex, a perfect spot, suspended above the skyline and surrounded by the lush green of the tropical house below.

"You know I thought a weekend in London would be more about

filthy tube stations and dodging black cabs," Fred said, squeezing Ruby's hand. Somehow, she'd brought her to a sanctuary, an architectural masterpiece, and one of the most peaceful spaces she'd ever been. "You surprise me sometimes."

"What do you mean?" Ruby tilted her head in a way that sent a rush through Fred's body.

"I assume stuff about you, and you blast straight through with something unexpected."

"Well, that's me. Keeping you on your toes." She winked.

"I don't think it's that." Fred shook her head, trying to wrap her mind around what was happening.

"What do you mean? You look serious." Ruby squinted.

"I'm not sure. I'm glad to be here with you, unravelling the layers." She interlaced their fingers across the table. The thought of being so publicly connected in a vast room full of people, suspended above one of the biggest cities in the world, was enough to make Fred's nerves tingle. She thought about all the times she'd begged Adrienne for attention. All the times she had been hidden, ignored, betrayed even, in front of an audience. This was so different. Ruby was proud to sit here, together, without a sliver of doubt.

The waiter delivered two glasses of prosecco, each with a strawberry garnish.

Ruby raised her flute. "You can have a beer afterwards. But the meal came with a welcome drink, so here you go."

Fred laughed. "I drink other things, you know!"

"Do you? Because I've only ever seen you with a pint glass in your hand." Ruby chuckled and tipped her glass in a toast. "London looks good on you, Fred."

She smiled at the compliment and dipped her head a touch in humility. She wasn't often out of workwear, so anyone noticing her appearance was a rare occurrence. She touched the collar of her shirt, checking it was still in place. "You look good everywhere you go," she said, almost under her breath so the table opposite wouldn't hear them.

Her words vibrated across the table and had a visible effect on Ruby, who twisted in her seat and held her finger to her lips. "Sh, you're turning me on, and we're in the middle of a restaurant."

"That's unfortunate. What could we do about that?" Fred scanned the room to check no one was listening in. "Maybe you need to call the hotel and see when our room will be ready."

"Fred." Ruby wriggled and shot her a look.

Under the table, she slid her bare foot along the inside of Fred's thigh. *Jesus, this woman will drive me mad.* Her progress was stalled by the arrival of the waiter, so they hastily made their choices and he disappeared.

"Seriously though, London suits you." Ruby picked up where she'd left off, without the tempting footsie.

"Yeah? It'll be the shirt. You're used to seeing me in scruffs." Fred gulped down the contents of the tiny flute and ordered a beer from a nearby waiter. "Don't get ideas though, you'll not catch me down here much. Too long and my nose starts bleeding."

"Really? You never thought about moving anywhere else?" Ruby did the irresistible head tilt.

"Too much to miss back home. How about you? What brought you down here?"

"Not enough back home." She picked at the tight thread of the tablecloth, inspecting its weakest link.

Fred hesitated, unsure whether to poke at the embers of Ruby's backstory. "That's sad. Why'd you really move away?"

Ruby fiddled with the cutlery and took a deep breath. "My mum and dad had their own things going on. They were running successful businesses at home and abroad. My sister was making a life, happy in her space. She always felt settled back in Wales."

A silence fell between them like a cloak. Fred leaned forward to lift it. "You didn't?"

"It was home, sure, at weekends and school holidays. I guess I didn't know what I wanted, but I knew I wanted more."

"More than growing up by the sea?" Fred couldn't quite wrap

her head around anyone wanting to move away from that. She loved the mindful power of the ocean.

"More than a tiny community was going to offer. More energy. More speed." Ruby wrung her hands, appearing to grasp for words that wouldn't come. "Everything. I wanted everything."

"Sounds big. Still want all that?"

"I don't know." She frowned.

Fred almost jumped to console her. "I didn't mean to make you feel bad."

"You haven't. Honestly, you're right. I wanted something so vast. I wanted the whole world. But if I think hard, I haven't really ever been content...until these past few weeks."

"Well, you know what they say. Happiness is a chug of hot tea in the morning and a rowdy mess room."

"People don't say that, Fred. You guys say it in our mess room."

They laughed, throwing their heads back in unison, enjoying their in-joke. The laughter faded, and Fred wasn't sure why she'd turned that moment into a quip. Ruby had revealed herself, and Fred had taken a comic wrecking ball through it to avoid her own exposure. She'd been a coward not to see it through.

She put her hand through her hair and snuck a good look at Ruby, checking she was okay. It was too late to circle back and reopen the vulnerability she'd shared. Maybe they'd get there again. Maybe even today. Whatever happened, they had a whole weekend together to figure this stuff out.

Fred breathed to the pit of her stomach. She'd spent her whole life surrounded by chimney pots and brick dust. She had no idea that a beautifully clean air pocket could exist in the smoky heart of the capital. It gave her hope that she'd upturn more surprises and that more gifts might come her way with Ruby by her side.

CHAPTER TWENTY-TWO

A DAWN DIFFUSED BY the hotel's linen drapes caressed the shape of Fred. Ruby edged closer, unable to resist the cut of her hip. She stroked her skin, and Fred stirred, gifting Ruby an unfiltered morning sigh. She opened her eyes, slowly coming to, and they locked into each other's gaze. "Hey, you," Ruby whispered, careful not to shatter the magical moment.

Fred returned a dreamy smile and tempted her closer for a lingering, sleepy kiss. A kiss that still tasted of midnight. Ruby drew their bodies together like a tightening vice. The ache in her core grew as they rocked in unison.

Fred stroked her hair, her grip betraying her need, and Ruby gave in, arching her back and allowing Fred to kiss her breasts. She moaned, her breath faster with each beautiful passing moment.

"Good morning, you," Fred said.

Ruby giggled, laid back onto the marshmallow of a pillow and relinquished the tiny thread of control she'd held moments ago. Now Fred had fully awoken, she looked ready to take Ruby by any means. "It's good to see you," Ruby grinned playfully at the echo of their morning routine at the site cabin.

"It's good to feel you." Fred leaned into Ruby's centre.

"I can't argue with that." Ruby moved to the beat of Fred's touch, her need building with every advance, as if she were consumed by her craving. She took Fred's lips to her own, devouring them with affection. As her climax built, Fred anticipated her demand, moving in time with her body, reaching the summit of her desire, edging to the verge of orgasm. Ruby lost track of all thought as the passion whipped through her body. Her thighs quivered, and she froze in mid-air, hoping the moment would last forever.

The orgasm, gathered and grown from its ebb and flow, crashed against her like a wave on a cliff. She opened her eyes to see Fred mirror her want. She drifted into a gorgeous haze before the reality of the morning dawned with the arrival of room service. Fred slipped from beneath the sheets to deliver the tray to the bed.

"Only the best," she said, uncovering the silver platter of fruit and pastries.

"This looks delicious." Ruby beamed. "But I have an appetite for something else." She tugged at Fred's oversized robe.

"How can I possibly satisfy you?" Fred let the robe fall to the floor and climbed back onto the bed.

"I can think of so many ways." Ruby reached between her thighs and stroked the dewy softness. For all Fred's tough exterior, she purred like a kitten under Ruby's caress. "Lie down on the bed."

"Are you in charge this morning?"

"What made you think you were ever in charge?"

Fred chuckled. "So true. I am completely under your spell, Ruby Lewis. You know it too."

Ruby smiled, replacing her fingers with her lips. "I told you, I'm famished this morning." She took Fred's centre in her mouth, grazing her clit with her tongue.

Fred moaned as Ruby kissed her and skimmed her pulsing centre with her thumb.

"Harder," Fred said, gasping for breath.

She pressed and released, building intensity to discover the tipping point of Fred's desire.

"Yes," Fred whispered.

Ruby clasped against her lips, so close to orgasm herself she had to focus on Fred's need.

Fred clutched a handful of her hair. "Please."

And with that, Ruby gave her everything she wanted. The simplicity of Fred's request, succumbing to Ruby's control of her body, was enough to abandon her reign. With one hand, she reached between her own legs and brought them both to the peak of their pleasure.

Fed, watered, and radiant, they finally left the cocoon of their hotel room and headed for the civilised bustle of the nearby coffee house.

"She's dragged you all the way down here then?" Trix arched her eyebrow.

"We fancied a break from work. You don't have to enjoy this so much." Ruby squirmed as she tried to explain how she and Fred had ended up in a London hotel room together.

"I didn't need much persuading." Fred scratched her ear.

She looked a bit uncomfortable, but humoured Trix's interrogation, and Ruby loved her for it. Despite being uptight sometimes at work, she knew when to go with the flow.

"Well, it's nice to have you down south for a while. We're not too bad, you know?"

"I know." Fred shot Ruby a look, reminding her that they'd been naked a few hours ago.

"Ruby doesn't count as a Londoner, because she's actually Welsh," Trix said.

"Sort of. My parents weren't Welsh. They landed in a lovely place and got lucky." Ruby huffed and looked away from Fred's confused expression. "It's complicated."

"Where do you feel like you're from?" Fred asked.

Ruby wriggled, awkward in her own skin. "I don't know. I was born in a hospital in Cambridge. I grew up in Abersoch. Now I live in London."

"You live in Manchester." Trix laughed and spun her around. "Let's get those coffees. You look like you need to wake up. Heavy night?" She winked.

"You have no idea," Ruby whispered out of Fred's earshot. She desperately wanted to fill Trix in with all the steamy details of her overnight stay. But for now, she'd enjoy the company of her oldest friend and her newest.

"Seriously, Fred, how are you enjoying the city?" Trix asked.

"I like it more than I expected. Ruby has treated me to some amazing sights."

Ruby almost choked on thin air, picturing them rolling between their hotel sheets.

"We've been to the sky garden place and down the river. It's been really cool." Fred gave Ruby's hand a squeeze.

She held still, not wanting to recoil from the innocent affection.

Trix grinned, exhaled a high-pitched squeak and made jazz hands. "It's nice to see you two together. I knew there was a spark of something back in Manchester."

"Yeah?" Ruby smiled through clenched teeth. She didn't want Trix to reveal all the details.

Trix pursed her lips. "I know when Ruby is crushing on someone." She giggled and leaned into Fred. Fred towered above her slim frame.

Ruby melted under Fred's gaze, wanting to be anywhere as long as they were alone and barely clothed. "Stop it, Trix. We don't need your twisted take on the situation."

"It's fascinating though. I'd like to hear all about Ruby's crush on me." Fred winked and smiled, obviously enjoying Ruby's awkwardness.

Two lattes and a black coffee arrived, interrupting Trix's dissection of their relationship status. Ruby sighed with relief, blowing foam across her steaming coffee.

"While you're here, there's something I want to talk to you about." Trix turned towards Fred and gave her a hard stare. "The next press opportunity, the one with the cute little history group. It could be a bit of a coup for the developers. Ruby would no doubt work her wonders, and the press would be eating up the story. I mean, who doesn't love a few pensioners cooing over new shiny things?"

Fred frowned. "You know, I'm enjoying my coffee with you two lovely people. I don't expect to be lobbied about this stuff on my day off."

"The board are all over this, Fred. You'd be getting in the way if you block it." Trix held her steely eye contact.

Fred's shoulders stiffened, and the tension became palpable.

"Can we leave this until Monday? Fred can hop on a video call with us both while we work out the details?" Ruby gripped her thighs, wishing for an end to the moment.

"No, let's have all this out now if you're both convinced." Fred's expression softened, her eyes twinkling. "I don't want it hanging over the rest of the weekend."

"I think the more we can make of the development's past, the stronger the sales will be. People are investing in their futures and the city's heritage. It's golden." Trix inspected her painted nails, looking completely oblivious to Fred's discomfort. "And Ruby can weave gold from garden string. If anyone can pull this off, it's our little PR gem here."

The clattering of the cafe filled the void in their conversation. Chair legs screeched across the floor, cutlery scraped across plates, and the hum of conversation grew louder against Ruby's ears.

Fred shook her head. "You two make quite the team when you want to gang up on someone—"

"We're not ganging up. I did not want to talk about this right now," Ruby said with her hands up pleading her innocence. She threw a filthy look in Trix's direction, silently willing her to leave the topic be.

"It's okay, I get it. It's a strong opportunity. Like you said, if we pull out, it'll look like we have something to hide. Let's do it." Fred raised her mug in assent. "There's one condition: I sign off on all the details. No one moves on that site without my say so."

Ruby could have kissed her there and then. "You trust me with this?"

"Yes." Fred frowned. "But we work together on it."

"Absolutely. This is going to be brilliant, I promise," Ruby said, the blush of excitement creeping up her neck. She put her hand on Fred's knee and leaned in, smiling. It couldn't get any better than knowing Fred supported her.

"Well, that's sorted then." Trix had the final word, but the conversation continued silently across the table. Ruby couldn't wait to get Fred somewhere suitable to rip apart that shirt she was wearing and peel away the layers beneath.

Fred's eyes burned with the same intensity, and the world around Ruby faded.

"Guys?" Trix pierced their bubble, intruding on the moment.

"Sorry. Where were we?"

"Well, I was right here with you two practically drooling on the table."

She laughed with them, and Fred attempted to hide her embarrassment with another gulp of hot coffee.

An hour or so passed, and Trix said her goodbyes, leaving them at the South Bank. Ruby hooked her arm through Fred's. "Let's stroll."

"Sounds good."

"I'm sorry Trix was a bit intense about the work stuff."

Fred stopped and turned to face her. "It's fine. We'll do the thing. But for now, let me enjoy being with you." She cupped her chin and bent down to meet her lips. "I've been wanting to do that all morning."

Ruby's toes almost left the ground. She'd imagined it, the feeling of floating. But there was something so physical about her attraction that she could almost believe that Fred's magnetic draw would raise her off the floor.

Now that they'd lifted the lid on their relationship, she wasn't sure she could pack her desire into a neat little box when they got back to work. Would it mess everything up? She hoped not. The last thing she needed was to screw this contract up. But maybe some things were more important than work. Perhaps she'd uncovered more than just job satisfaction with Fred.

CHAPTER TWENTY-THREE

"YOU WANT TO VISIT my old haunts?" Ruby's eyes widened as if Fred had suggested a trip to the local cemetery.

"What's wrong with that? I want to know a bit more about the place you lived." Fred gripped her waist, easing Ruby into the snug of her arm. The truth was she couldn't get enough, and Ruby was fast becoming an addiction. She wanted to absorb every fact about her.

"Okay. How about a little axe-throwing at my old joint?"

This time it was Fred's turn to raise her eyebrow. "I've already proven my ineptitude at that particular task."

"Not true! You were strong. It's your aim that could use a little work." Ruby nudged her in the ribs playfully and wriggled out of reach before Fred could do anything about it.

"Hey, you promised to be nice about that."

"I made no such promise. I'm serious when it comes to axes. You've either got it or you haven't." The twinkle in Ruby's eye betrayed her humour, but Fred was curious to see her old place.

"Fine. We'll go to your axe den. But the beer better be good."

"Oh, the beer's good. The whiskey is even better."

"That sounds promising." Fred wasn't sure she could stomach much more of London's fine wine. She had a thirst for somewhere more down to earth.

They took the underground for two stops and changed tracks. Fred followed Ruby's boots, staying in line in case she shoulder-barged someone on the escalator. She was used to Manchester's hustle for the tram or the bus, but the single-minded purpose with which Londoners seemed to move through the city was nothing to play with.

By the time they emerged from the sweaty tunnels to ground level, Fred was ready for fresh air. No such luck. The bar stood on a main road, passive exhaust fumes choking the oblivious pedestrians.

She stepped too far into the road and into a mouthful of abuse from an oncoming cyclist. "Shit, sorry mate." She tried to call after him, but he'd sped onto the next junction.

"Careful, I don't want to be taking you to the hospital on a Saturday night." Ruby grimaced.

"No. I can think of better things to do."

"Like going to a rough bar and throwing some steel?" Ruby did a ta-da motion outside the dingiest bar Fred had seen in a while.

"You live here?" She craned her neck to the upstairs flat.

"Up there." Ruby pointed. "It's nice. A sort of loft style. Without the space."

"So, just the wooden floors and draughty windows?"

"Yeah, kind of." They laughed.

"Still, at least it's a place of your own."

"True. Better than landlady Lou breathing down my neck." Ruby pulled at the door.

"The lights are on. Who's up there now?"

"Some chap called Steve. I didn't ask the agent that many questions. Sub-letting a London flat is one of the easiest things I've ever done." Ruby shrugged off the adulting. "Shall we?"

Fred ventured inside, ignoring the urge to oil the door's hinges.

"You see? It's a pretty normal bar."

"Ruby! You're back." A guy built like a beef stack came out from behind the bar to drag Ruby into a bear hug.

Fred registered a pang of jealousy and shook her head in disbelief. This woman had really got under her skin.

"Hi, James. This is Fred."

"Fred." He nodded his approval. "Cool name."

Fred shuffled. She didn't want to get into the origins of her name, but it sounded jarring out of James' mouth. Sometimes it felt too male, like she was trying to fit into a shape she didn't belong. The alternative was far worse. She could never be a Winifred. Not in a million years. "I was named after my grandmother."

"Well, she sounds cool too. Come over. What can I get you two to drink?" James returned to his position behind the bar, where his towering height seemed less obvious.

"The usual for me." Ruby winked.

"You're not throwing, are you?"

"What if I said I was?"

Was that flirtation in her tone? Fred couldn't settle on the status of the relationship between these two, but she'd never seen Ruby in this mode before.

"Calm down, fruitcake. You can have one. Speedy will have my ass if you're over the limit."

"Scout's honour." Ruby held up three of her perfectly formed digits.

Fred had a flashback of those same fingers tickling the crease of her thigh that morning. "Who's Speedy?" Fred asked, trying to break into the rhythm between Ruby and James.

"She owns this place." James looked over the shot glass he was filling. "She can be pretty strict, hey, Ruby?"

Ruby shrugged. "She's okay with me."

"Sure. Missy here gets away with murder."

James's voice had lost its edge, the innuendo replaced by a sort of brotherly playfulness. Fred was definitely picking up sibling vibes, and her irrational anxiety dialled down a few notches.

"She absolutely gets away with murder. I know that much firsthand," Fred said.

"Not true." Ruby swiped at Fred's elbow with mock violence and leaned in for a hug. "Fred's the site manager on the new development I'm working on in Manchester."

"Oh, I get it. She has you wrapped around her little finger up there, hey, Fred?" James asked. "I've seen it all before."

"Really?" The temperature on Fred's jealous streak rose a couple of degrees. Why did she have to be like this? Why was she so all-or-nothing about people she liked? So what if Ruby had a past? Maybe she even had a past with this guy. It wasn't a crime, and it wouldn't make a difference to the fun they were having in the present.

"Fred will have a beer. One of the American ones."

Fred's internal spiral was cut short by Ruby's mind-reading drink order. "How'd you know I'd go for that?"

"I can read you like a book, Fred Caffrey," Ruby said, trailing her fingers to count the buttons on Fred's shirt until she reached the opening at the top, where her chest was bare. Fred shivered at the caress and wondered how long they'd need to throw axes before they could get back to their hotel room.

"You're lucky. Speedy's got the night off, so I doubt she'll be in monitoring your booze tonight." James placed a full pint of amber ale in front of Fred.

"That's a shame. I wanted Fred to meet her." Ruby slouched. "How's the new tenant getting on upstairs?"

"Don't see much of him. He's not a thrower. And I'm not sure this place is his kind of watering hole."

"I get you. Well, it won't be long until the six months is up, and I'll be back to torment you."

Fred's stomach dropped. She knew that Ruby's contract wasn't permanent. She was aware somewhere in her rational brain that she wasn't going to make Manchester her permanent home. But to hear a throwaway line about her moving back to London made Fred feel like she herself had been thrown away.

"Go and sit. You're cluttering up my bar." James shooed them both away and turned to serve another couple.

Fred swallowed the dread rising in her throat.

"You okay? You look worried about something?"

Fred straightened her face. It crossed her mind to brush the whole thing off as if it wasn't a big deal. But it was. And if she'd learned anything from her last fleeting relationship it was that hiding your feelings stored up a shit tonne of resentment later down the line. "I'm sorry." Fred sat on a battered leather chair and set down her beer. "I hadn't really thought about you moving back here when you're done. It's made me a bit sad."

Ruby's eyes widened, and her lips twitched in an expression that could have been pity or regret. Fred wasn't sure.

"Christ, I am so sorry. I didn't mean it like that." She clapped her hands against her cheeks and then reached for Fred's fingers, holding them tight in her own. "I was making small talk with James. He's a good guy, but he likes the banter. It's funny, and we talk shit most of the time."

"But you're still coming back to London, aren't you? When you're done, that is." The finality of the words hit Fred in the chest.

Ruby stroked the back of her hand. "Nothing is set in stone. I like to buy open tickets."

"Don't talk in clichés, Ruby." Fred pulled her hand back. "I'm being honest. It took me by surprise." Fred sipped her beer and leaned into the lumpy chair. "I knew you would be going. I... Why are you only on the job for six months anyway? It's going to be at least two years til we're done."

"Because I'm in Manchester for the start-up phase until we've got some show homes, and then I'll pass the scheme to the sales team, and they crack on. It might be longer than six months."

"I don't know. I think I've got a bit too wrapped up in us this weekend. I sort of forgot that it was all temporary."

"Listen, let's not get bogged down in this seriousness. Let's enjoy ourselves here, tonight. Tomorrow will come. And the day after that. We don't know where all this is going. But I am open to it. Really, I am."

Ruby put her palm to Fred's cheek, and she leaned against it, wishing for more.

"Who knows where we'll end up?"

Fred yearned for more certainty than that. Couldn't they decide that they were good together and that was it? Deep down, she knew that life wasn't like that. She'd raced ahead a few chapters while Ruby was still enjoying the prologue. Maybe this would work out with Ruby. Maybe it wouldn't. It didn't all stand or fall on tonight. She needed to let go and enjoy herself.

But the thought of Ruby walking out of her life in six short months had spooked her. That was the only certain thing she had tonight.

CHAPTER TWENTY-FOUR

"AGAIN? YOU SPEND MORE time down here than you do in Aberdeen." Fred shuffled a pile of papers on her desk.

Adrienne brushed brick dust off the chair and sat down. "What can I say? Your site is particularly demanding of my attention."

Fred tutted. She wouldn't be drawn into Adrienne's nonsense. That was all in the past. And after the weekend she'd enjoyed with Ruby, she wanted to keep it that way. She held her silence, ignoring her radio hooked onto her belt. "Do you need something? The crew will be waiting for me to start the shift."

"I need next month's projections."

"Budget or milestones?"

"Both, in my inbox by Friday, if that's okay with you?"

"Since when do I answer to you on this build?" Fred bristled with defensiveness. Adrienne could come down here asking about pre-sales and promotions, but she was well out of her league when it came to construction.

Adrienne rose from the chair and stepped towards her. "I want to stay close to this project. It has huge social value, and it's important for our reputation," she whispered.

If Fred didn't know better, she'd think Adrienne was trying to be seductive.

The cabin door swung open, and Ruby rushed in with a gust of wind behind her. "Oh, sorry, I wasn't expecting you to be in here." She stamped the mud from her boots on the mat.

"Don't mind Adrienne; she was just leaving," Fred said.

"Was I indeed?" She tipped her head to the side. "I don't mind hanging with you two. Maybe we should do lunch today and catch up on plans."

"You know I don't have time for lunch." Fred popped on her hard hat and nodded to Ruby, hoping she'd recognise the warmth of her affection behind its brevity. She paused, looking back and forth between the women in her office. One ex-lover and one current. Maybe she shouldn't leave them alone.

"You okay, Fred? Have you lost something?" Adrienne asked, clearly reading her thoughts like an open book.

Beside her, Ruby's eyes flicked between them. The radio crackled once more, disturbing the growing tension. Fred decided it was easier to get one of them out of her office. "Ruby, did you need me for something?"

"I thought we might go over the location of the marquee."

"Oh, do tell," Adrienne said. "Marquees on a building site? Sounds like some sort of fancy event is in the offing. How about you and I really do squeeze in lunch today, and you can tell me all about it?"

Ruby stuttered, and Fred almost growled. Adrienne might not let this go. She looked determined to create a situation where one or both of them slipped up.

Fred stood her ground. "Fine. I'll go to lunch with you both. We can discuss it then." She unhooked her radio on the way out. "Champ? I'm on my way down. Will you gather the crew for me?"

"See you both at one o'clock. My treat," Adrienne said in a sing-song voice.

Two hours in the dirt flew by. Fred peeled off her vest and sniffed in the vague direction of her damp armpit. She debated whether she could go to lunch without a shower. Having one might give Adrienne the wrong idea that she was out to impress, so she wiped a smudge from her cheek and judged herself clean enough.

"Come on, you, we'll take one of the site cars," Adrienne said, popping her head around the door.

"You know they might not be that clean."

"I'm ten steps ahead of you. I asked Champ to get a lad to give one the once-over for me."

Fred tutted. "You know the crew have better things to do than be your personal valet." She pulled her jumper over her head, ruffling her hair before popping her hat back on for the trip across the yard.

Ruby and Adrienne didn't take a breath in the car, and she was glad she'd jumped in the driver's seat so she escaped the incessant small talk.

"I'd like to get a profile piece in one of the nationals next month. Maybe something for Delphine," Adrienne said.

"Sure, the architect's vision would be a good angle. Shall I line up something for you too? Maybe a photoshoot here and in Aberdeen."

"I like the sound of that. What are you thinking?"

"Something in the trade press. The different faces of construction and regeneration."

Ruby came to life in the back seat, and Fred averted her gaze, trying to concentrate on the road ahead. She was lucky she knew these roads like the back of her hand.

"You'd better include Sebastian and Hugo in your plans. Otherwise, we'll get accused of plotting against them like we're in some sort of coven, hey, Fred?"

Fred murmured her agreement. She'd had enough of Hugo to last a lifetime. and the idea of fuelling his ego with press interviews made her feel sick.

"Sebastian. He's the top guy, right?" Ruby asked.

"Right. He's the one with the connection to DJ. I think they go way back or something. To be honest, he has a whole black book of contacts that we tap into every now and again." Adrienne wiggled her fingers, catching Fred's eye in the rearview mirror.

"Here we are." Fred pulled over and parked the truck.

"Great, I'm hungry. Let's go eat." Adrienne got out, and Ruby followed.

Fred asked herself why she'd gotten herself at a table with them both. Not only did they drown each other out with their mutual enthusiasm for almost everything, she jumped out of her skin every time one of them mentioned anything personal. She should tell Ruby that she and Adrienne had a thing, and it was no big deal. But she could hardly do it across the main courses.

"What's with you?" Ruby asked when Adrienne disappeared for a bathroom trip.

"Nothing. I prefer to work through lunch."

Ruby looked disheartened.

"I mean, if I took lunch, I would've preferred it to be the two of us."

"You don't like Adrienne? She's nice."

"Sure. She's nice." Fred remained tight lipped while Adrienne squeezed back into her chair, her perfume arriving ahead of her.

"I don't know how you manage it, Ruby, but it's pretty rare for Fred to come out for lunch on a workday." Adrienne's eyes creased as she raised her glass. "You must have the magic touch with our site manager."

Fred cleared her throat.

"I guess I do," Ruby said, touching Fred's thigh under the table. She squirmed beneath Adrienne's scrutiny.

"So, what's next?"

"Fred's doing a podcast tomorrow at the local college."

Adrienne almost spat her wine out. "That *is* out of character. What's got into you?"

Fred shrugged.

Ruby leaned forward. "Her brother asked, and I said it would be an amazing opportunity to talk about the site. So I'm going along to film it."

Fred tied a knot in her napkin. It collapsed, so she repeated the process, pulling tighter at the white linen and disengaging from the conversation.

"You're so right." Adrienne laid her manicured hand on Ruby's bare arm. "Stuff like that is great for community relations. I knew we'd hit the jackpot with you."

Fred bolted upright as if her spine was charged. Was Adrienne flirting with Ruby now? This could not be happening. "I think we should get back to site." She raised her hand. "Could we get the bill, please?"

Fred got up from the table and started to gather her things.

"We're barely finished," Adrienne said but signed for the bill when the waiter returned.

Fred couldn't bear to watch these two women build a bond over chardonnay and cherry pickers. She'd been honest with Ruby. She wanted to spend every moment together, alone. Her ex-lover sitting across the table churned her stomach with worry. She had nothing to hide, but she'd hardly been upfront about her previous relationship either. It was niggling at her, the thought that Ruby might turn on her over this little omission. The sooner she could tell her, the better. But how?

CHAPTER TWENTY-FIVE

RUBY APPLIED A FRESH layer of balm to her lips. "I don't know why you didn't tell me about this before. It's perfect."

"Is it?" Fred threw a questioning look in her direction as they crossed the road together.

"It's a great story. A top female apprentice goes into college to inspire the next generation. It's PR gold."

"If you say so." Fred kept her head down.

"Don't be so humble about your successes. They're going to love you. Will Tommy be there?"

"I don't think so. He said something about having a mock exam."

"That's a shame, I would've liked to meet him." Ruby followed through revolving glass doors to the reception of the college.

"Not today, but soon." Fred flashed her smile before a bulky teenager shoulder-barged her.

"Sorry," he muttered on his way through.

Fred shrugged. "At least he was polite about his lack of spatial awareness."

Ruby giggled. "Come on, let's tell them we're here, and I'll get a couple of photos of you. Will you say a quick piece to camera?" She grabbed her phone.

"Is that really necessary?" Fred grimaced.

"If we're going to make the most of it, yes. Otherwise, it's you talking to a few adolescents."

"I guess so." Fred dragged her feet to the desk and announced their arrival. A few moments later, the inner doors swung open to a floppy-haired boy on the cusp of adulthood, all limbs and loose clothing.

"I'm Declan. Tom's sister, is it?"

"That's me, Fred Caffrey." She signalled to her left. "Ruby Lewis is our PR manager at Design Futures."

Compelled to explain herself, Ruby stepped forward. "Do you mind if I join you for the podcast recording? To take pictures and a few clips for the socials."

"Sure, whatever. If you tag us, we'll share."

She liked Declan. They spoke the same language. She winked at Fred and ducked in front to lead the way before doing a one-eighty and turning her phone towards Fred. "I'll get you walking down the corridor."

Fred rolled her eyes.

Declan led them through a padded room with a sound desk to a larger studio, where a small crowd gathered.

"This is the audience for today's recording. We've got a growing following of media students." He pulled out a chair for Fred and handed her a mic to clip on. "Take your seats, everyone, we're almost ready to start."

Fred stared at the mic and mouthed something unintelligible in Ruby's direction.

"Let me help you." Lifting the fabric of Fred's shirt reminded her of their kiss backstage at the charity ball. Her heart rate gathered speed, and she was sure the blush reached her cheeks.

"Don't enjoy it too much," Fred said.

"You ready then?" Declan asked.

Ruby grew conscious of the audience, and she took her own seat at the side of the platform, remaining in Fred's eye line.

"Thanks to Mikey for going through the logistics of today's recording. You all know the score. We'll start in a minute, and we'll be looking for a bit of background ambience as well as some questions from the floor."

Declan sounded pretty professional for someone who still struggled to get the pH balance of his face right.

"Any questions before we start, Fred?"

Her eyes widened, and she looked to Ruby. "No, I don't think so."

"Great." He counted his fingers down and fiddled with some buttons. "And we're on."

Ruby relished the unobstructed view of Fred's lean figure. It was rare not to have to avert her gaze in case someone caught her staring too hard.

"Welcome to Downtime, our campus podcast for all things post-college. This week in our careers special, we're talking to one of the first female construction managers in Greater Manchester, Fred Caffrey," Declan said in a pretty convincing radio voice. "Fred, you're working on the iconic Boot Street development, which is taking regeneration to the next level. But tell us all how you got into the building industry, and what it's like to be a woman at the top of your game?"

"Um, thanks for having me on. I'm really pleased to be here with you all." Fred looked anything but pleased. "I..."

Ruby willed her to find the words, but the silence stretched on. It was so true what they said about dead air on the radio: it was deafening. Fred froze, pressing her lips together until Ruby worried she'd never open her mouth again. She gave her a double thumbs-up and widened her smile.

Fred breathed a long, audible sigh, which would undoubtedly have to be edited out. "I didn't leave school in the best circumstances. I wasn't like you guys at the college. I didn't even make it to further qualifications." She shuffled in the chair before she held her natural pose and flawless strength, comfortable in her own skin. "The truth is I was bullied at school, and I left as soon as I could. It was a pretty desperate situation and for a while, I didn't know what I was going to do."

The room held its breath. Ruby leaned in.

"My mum saw an advert in the local paper for apprentices wanted at the new Design Futures scheme. They were a young firm at the time, but they were already shaking up the property industry."

"There must've been some stiff competition," Declan said.

"You know, I didn't really think about it at the time, but yeah, I guess there would've been. My mum took me down to the office, and I must've looked like a rabbit in the headlights."

The gracious audience laughed.

"How did you make your mark in the early days?"

Fred looked up, as if she was watching her memories of that time. "This one guy, Stan, really took me under his wing. He was my boss. Taught me everything I know and never, ever let any of the other lads talk down to me. He would say, 'You're here on your own merit.' That really stuck with me."

Declan nodded, scrolling his phone for the next question. "What's it like to be the boss now? Do you still command that same respect?"

Fred paused. "I think so."

Yes, she does. A reel of Fred taking charge ran through Ruby's mind, starting in the yard and ending in the bedroom. She coughed, drawing the attention of the panel.

"Yes. I work hard, and I've earned the respect of my crew." Fred shifted in her seat. "But it's entirely mutual. I respect them for their skills, for their effort, and for their loyalty."

"What would you say to those considering a career like yours? Perhaps in a male-dominated industry where they might need to put themselves out there to get noticed?"

"Do the work. Keep doing the work. Don't compare yourself to others around you. There will always be those who try and drag you down with negativity or humiliation even." Fred looked at Ruby and held her gaze. "You'll find the people who lift you up, who join you in your successes. People who make the working day unpredictable and maybe a little enjoyable." She dipped her head. "All you have to do is your best."

A hum of agreement rippled around the room, and Declan looked pleased with himself.

"Let's turn to questions from our audience now. Mikey, will you take the roving mic?"

Ruby fidgeted. Fred had smashed it, and she couldn't wait to tell her. She snuck a few extra photos and posted them straight to their social media accounts.

When the torrent of questions had finally dried up, and Fred had recorded a couple of extra lines for Declan to use in the trailers, they stood on the pavement outside the college gates.

"You were amazing. They loved you!" Ruby jumped on the spot, gripping Fred's arm in excitement.

"All right, don't make a big thing of it." Fred bit her lip as she smiled.

"But it *is* a big thing. You don't know how impressive you are. When you speak, and people see you, they love you." Ruby's stomach flipped. She didn't mean, love as in *love*. She meant Fred was loveable.

Fred walked off, leaving her working out her next sentence on the kerb.

"Come on. I deserve a drink after all that nonsense."

"Perfect." A drink would be good. That would also distract from Ruby dissecting what she really meant when she said that everyone loved Fred.

"Let's go further into town though. I don't want to get stuck for round two of question time in a student bar."

Ruby followed, panting from overthinking their last exchange. She really liked being with Fred. Every part of her was so bloody addictive. But that didn't mean love. It had never meant love before, so why would it now?

CHAPTER TWENTY-SIX

HER MUM BURST THROUGH the bedroom door without ceremony. "Time to wake up, sleepy head, or we'll be late."

"Mum, could you please knock?" Fred groaned, remembering it was Sunday.

"This is my house, Winifred. I'm looking for mugs to put in the dishwasher before we leave."

"I'm going to give it a miss today." She held her breath, waiting for the lecture to commence.

"Well, Father Michael is saying mass for your grandfather. He'll be surprised if any of you miss it."

Fred rolled over and shifted the pillow to find a cold spot for her throbbing head. "You only go to gossip with Aunty Peg."

"Well, when am I to see her otherwise? She's my own sister, and she never comes to visit. If I didn't drag myself to St Chad's, it'd be a lonely life, that's all I can say."

"A lonely life is it, Mum? With a house full of children and grandchildren."

"Christ, you think you lot are good company? You never tell me a damn thing."

Brian appeared at her mum's shoulder, mimicking her speech. Of course, he was already dressed for church. She'd been the last one to bed the night before, her temples still pounding from the whiskey chaser she'd added to the last orders. Ruby had been a bad influence in the best possible way.

"Fuck off, Brian." Fred rolled over and buried her face in the duvet.

"I won't have that language on a Sunday." Her mum turned to

catch him in the act. "You can stop that now, you daft bugger. The last thing we need up here is any of your nonsense. You wind her up."

Brian laughed. "Come on, lazy, otherwise you'll be sadly missed this morning. Don't worry though, I'll give young Sister Jackie your best regards." He winked, trying to provoke a reaction.

"There's a pot of tea downstairs, and I'll put you some toast in to eat on the way," said her mum.

Fred had two choices. She could put up with this guilt trip for the rest of the week, or she could get her ass out of the warm cocoon of her bed and stand under a shower for five minutes. "Fine. Could you two at least leave while I get ready? Tommy had better not be in the bathroom."

The rattle of Brian's laughter rang down the stairs, and her mum left the room, shaking her head.

Fred padded across the landing and locked the bathroom door behind her. She flicked the shower on, grateful for the sound of water filling the small room and blocking out the voices of her brothers from downstairs.

The urge to pack her bags and carve her own way out of here filled her head once more. Over the past year, she'd tried at least twice to move out, but it had never quite come to pass. Money, the housing market, looking after her dad... Things that had all conspired at one point or another to keep her firmly in her childhood bedroom for at least another few months.

Part of her didn't mind being back in the safety net of home. She knew her place here. She'd fitted back in like a worn armchair in the corner. A little bit of her resented her older brothers living their lives away from Manchester, but she'd stayed for good reason.

She showered and dressed, and before long, she genuflected for the final time and wiped the holy water off her brow. It had been a quick Mass, she'd give them that. A queue of worshippers exited through the gigantic oak doors and filed into the pub next door. She hesitated. Her father and brothers would be in there waiting for her, but the growl in her stomach warned her off any more beer for the weekend.

While she paused in the foyer, her mum hooked an arm through hers. "Coming home with me, lass?"

They hardly had any time alone together, so it'd be nice to help her mum prepare the Sunday roast. "Okay, but I'm not peeling potatoes. I always catch my knuckles."

"Jesus, you're a wimp. All that heavy lifting you do on the building site, and you can't peel a Maris Piper? I don't know who brought you up sometimes." Her mum put her head on Fred's shoulder.

"I don't like the feel of them." Fred shivered and grinned.

They turned into a side street and away from the crowd. The walk home was short, one they could both do with their eyes closed.

"It's a nice day for a stroll. Getting warmer, don't you think?" Her mum looked up towards the sky, flashes of blue poking through the dove grey clouds.

"Yeah, I guess so." Grateful for the fresh air, Fred gulped down a lungful, trying to rid her body of last night's toxins.

"What's with you, out all night? Have you nothing to say to me? I'm getting worried about you."

Fred sighed. Her mum had always been able to read her emotions, so there was little point in avoiding the incessant line of questioning. She bit her lip, not sure where to begin. "There's a person."

"Oh, right." Her mum shifted, clearly bracing for the conversation. "Go on then, tell me all about her."

"Don't be like that, Mum." Fred stepped away, breaking their linked arms.

"Like what? I'm waiting to hear about your new person."

"You're like this with the boys too. You never think we're serious."

"Well, are you? Because until you come home with rings on fingers, I'm the one still buttering your barms every morning."

Fred concentrated on the gaps in the paving stones. Some of

them needed attention.

Her mum looped her arm back through and pulled her closer. "Come on, you. Tell me about this new girl. Is she an improvement on the last one who broke your heart?"

Fred had almost forgotten she'd told her mum about Adrienne. "She was a mistake. And she didn't break my heart. We weren't even that serious."

"And this one? Does she have a name, for starters?"

"Ruby."

"Well, that's a lovely name. Is she local?"

Fred stumbled. She didn't want to get into southern-bashing. "No, she's here for a few months. She's originally from Abersoch, you know, in Wales. But she was working in London before she came up here to work at Boot Street."

"You work together, do you? Is she crew, as well? That's nice."

"God, no. She's part of the promotion team sent up by head office. She's lovely. You'd like her."

"Well, bring her 'round for tea this week. I'd like to meet her."

"It's a bit early for that, Mum."

"Nonsense. She mustn't know anyone up here. It'd be grand for her to have a proper meal."

Fred thought of Ruby's room she'd been renting. "I guess so. I'll see what she says this week."

"Were you out together last night then?"

"Yeah." A wave of nausea washed over Fred, reminding her of the volume of alcohol they'd consumed.

"You look worse for it. Who's the bad influence, you or Ruby?"

Fred considered the question, not wanting either of them to suffer the brunt of her mum's judgement. "Neither. We had fun, that's all." The truth was that they were both as bad as each other. Maybe bringing Ruby home wasn't a great idea. But she was a hit with people. She knew exactly how to make them feel at ease.

"Are you serious about her?"

"That's a question." Fred's cheeks ballooned as she puffed a huge breath into the spring air. "You know what? I'm having fun, she's great, and I care about her. And maybe, yeah, she could be special."

"Okay. As long as you're careful."

"It's not like I'm going to come home pregnant and strike shame upon the family, Ma." Fred laughed.

"You know that's not what I meant. You wear your heart on your sleeve. Always have. I know you want to settle down, my love, but make sure it's for the right person. That other woman gave you the runaround and left you in a right old mess."

Fred hadn't realised her mum had noticed how down she'd been when she'd broken things off with Adrienne. "It's completely different with Ruby. She doesn't want to hide away like we've got something to be ashamed of."

"Good. Because you've nothing to be ashamed of. I want you to be happy, that's all."

They turned and approached the back door.

"You can peel the carrots," her mum said as she dropped her coat on the peg.

Fred slid out of her boots and into her slippers. Home was for baggy jumpers and feeling comfortable in your own skin. Thank God she had parents who accepted her for who she was, warts and all. The idea of hiding a part of herself from the world filled her with latent shame. She was good enough for this family, and she was good enough to love. One day, she'd find enough love to force her to move out. For now, she had no pressing reason to.

The clock ticked loudly on the kitchen wall, reminding her that they were on a deadline until her dad and brothers burst in, demanding their dinner. Fred smiled, knowing this Sunday would feel like all the others. Like home.

CHAPTER TWENTY-SEVEN

"THANKS FOR MEETING WITH me." Ruby swallowed the lump of nerves in her throat. There was something about Hugo that intimidated her. It wasn't only her; everyone on the site steered clear of him when he visited.

"How long do you think this will take? I have to jump on a call at three." Hugo inspected his thick knuckles.

"Not long, I need a few details so I can write up a profile piece for *Construction Today*." Ruby gritted her teeth. She didn't want to be here either, but she had more grace and professionalism than to make it so obvious. This was going to be harder than she thought.

"Let's get on with it then." Hugo swivelled his chair in the other direction as if he was going to multi-task through their interview.

"If I could get your full attention, it'd make this quicker and easier for me." Ruby placed her phone on the desk. "Do you mind if I record? The transcript will help me with the interview."

He shrugged. "Fine, if you must."

The guy was something of an enigma. He drifted in and out of the site on a whim. Ruby hadn't been able to place his accent anytime they'd met previously. He appeared to have Adrienne's ear, but Fred despised him. Ruby's cheeks grew hot as her thoughts turned to Fred. She wondered if her heart would ever stop racing when she pictured her arms wrapping around her.

"Are we going to get this done?" Hugo's grunt brought her back from the brink of her daydreams.

"Yeah, sorry. Let's start with a bit of background. Tell me about how you got into construction."

"I studied engineering and finished top of my class. There were several offers on the table, but I was snapped up by an exclusive firm. Now I'm a partner in that firm."

Hugo's words landed flat on the desk like a dead fish. She was going to have to work hard to get anything out of this. "Tell me... which project makes you most proud?" An expectant silence hung between them. Ruby didn't dare take a breath in case she put him off.

"There is one. An old factory in London. It had been derelict for years. No one wanted to touch it, but I could see its potential. I worked with Delphine to create the vision of a glass structure and dropped it inside."

Ruby tilted her head in confusion. "You dropped glass inside a building?"

"No." He tutted, grabbing a pencil and paper from across the desk. "Look." He scribbled a few lines which looked like nonsense until they came together. "Imagine a gigantic Victorian red brick building. You see these huge gaps? They would have been the factory's windows. We wanted to create depth but retain the façade. So Delphine created a glass structure inside."

Ruby had to admit it sounded spectacular. "You kept the old and created something new? Like you've done here?"

"Exactly." Hugo set the pencil down with a satisfied finality. "That's our thing. These Victorian buildings have a sense of majesty about them that the modern world needs to respect. They'll still be standing far longer than the concrete blocks we knock up and call housing these days."

For the first time since she'd taken this job, Ruby stirred with a sense of pride in its artistry. She'd been fighting for so long against the cold and the mud, she'd not grasped the sheer beauty of what they were creating.

"Have I impressed you?" Hugo asked, an ugly smugness creeping into his voice.

That was what Fred hated, being talked down to all the time. "I hadn't really had the chance to think about the design intention here."

"Well, if you spend too much time with Fred Caffrey, all you'll get is bricks and mortar. She's more brawn than brains, let's put it that way."

Hugo had no way of knowing the insult detonated deep inside Ruby. She wanted to rise to Fred's defence and tell him that there was much more to Fred than he thought. Her breath caught in her lungs as she processed her thoughts, trying to get her words in the right order. "I don't think that's true. But let's get on with the interview." Despite heat soaring like a volcano, her professionalism had kicked in and saved her from spilling her emotions all over Hugo's desk.

He smirked. "If you insist."

He sank deeper into his chair. It was almost as if Ruby had passed some sort of initiation, and they could get beyond small talk.

"Tell me, Ruby, what excites you most about this project?"

Memories of the archives flickered in her mind. "You see these cobbles outside?" She gestured out of the cabin window. "Most people think they're trip hazards. It's all about flat lines and accessible paving. When I see them, I see the footsteps of the children on these streets. I hear them laughing as they run from their front door to their neighbour's. I see the pram stood outside in the fresh air, the washing billowing in the wind. Life has happened on these streets, and every stone left standing is worth preserving." Ruby sat back, wondering where the depth of her feelings had come from. She hadn't realised that Boot Street had made such an impression on her soul. If not the place, then the people at Boot Street...or at least one person, specifically.

"Of course, our job is to make this tired, redundant old space useable again in the modern world. And that's been the most exciting part of this project. Flipping the idea of modern living on its head, keeping the old, and injecting the new." He drummed his fingers on the desk.

The cabin door swung open, and Adrienne stood in its frame. "Oh, sorry to interrupt. That call's been brought forward, Hugo. Are you okay to jump on?"

He tutted even louder than before. "Not really, but I suppose I'll have to. Can't leave Sebastian hanging, can we?" He straightened in the chair, and Adrienne shut the door. "I've enjoyed our chat, Ruby. It's a shame to cut it short."

"Don't worry, I know you're busy. I think I've got what I needed to write something. Perhaps I can email you some background questions to fill in the blanks." Ruby stood, ready to make herself scarce. "I've booked a photographer for tomorrow. Hopefully you'll still be around, and she can grab a couple of headshots."

"Of course. Anything to lubricate the wheels of publicity." He smiled, but it didn't quite reach his eyes. "Ruby, I am serious about aligning yourself too much with our site manager. Be careful. There are others with power on this project who could be better allies for you."

She frowned, aggravation reigniting in her stomach.

"Fred is difficult. She can be controlling. And if you want to get creative with your plans, she might not be the right person to ask. That's all I'm saying. Anything you need, let me know."

His wink sent a nauseous shudder through her stomach. "Thanks. I appreciate your time," she said, desperate to leave. Once her boots hit the firm ground of the site, she took a few steps to put some distance between her and Hugo. There was something about being in that man's orbit that was intensely uncomfortable. Sure, he was successful, but he clearly had it in for Fred in a disturbing way. Why couldn't they all get on and work together?

Ruby realised she was walking towards Fred's cabin. It was like a magnet pulling her in, but her interaction with Hugo swirled in her mind. Still, she had a job to do. And she had been pretty inspired by what he'd said. There was no doubt to the depth of his passion, and Ruby could really use that in her storytelling.

The mechanics of the construction were interesting, but the

vision and reimagining the past was fascinating. If Hugo had a personality transplant to make him a half-decent human being, they'd be onto a real winner.

CHAPTER TWENTY-EIGHT

"MY MUM CAN BE a little intense, but she means well." Fred held Ruby's hand tight. "My brothers are plain annoying any time of the day. The only one worth talking to is Arthur, and he's so far down south he may as well be in a different time zone."

"Relax. I'm good with people. I can do a family dinner without embarrassing myself. Or you."

"Christ, I'm not worried about you. I'm terrified of them." Fred laughed. She didn't really mean it. She loved her brothers dearly, but they could be boisterous, especially in front of an audience.

"Your mum and dad have always been cool with you being gay?" Ruby sidestepped a discarded chip wrapper.

"I wouldn't say that. Mum made me promise to keep it all to myself for a couple of years, and when Dad finally discovered the truth, he was mute for a fortnight. But that was a long time ago, and they're okay with it now." Fred didn't often dwell on the dark days of her coming out. She'd been a lonely teenager, but once she'd found Stan and the crew, everything had changed. "To be honest, I think the worst thing was that I'm their only daughter so I'm not going to give them the big white wedding they'd always dreamed of."

"You're not?" Ruby stopped walking and nudged her in the ribs. "Well, I'm not sure I'm willing to take this relationship much further, Miss Caffrey. You've been courting me under false pretences." She giggled.

"As if. You're the one who has me wrapped around your little finger." Fred linked her fingers through Ruby's and drew her in for a kiss. They were far enough away from the house not to be noticed by anyone that mattered. Fred might be comfortable with herself, but she didn't want to be the talk of the neighbourhood.

Ruby whispered a little groan as Fred pulled away, and it made her want to tear off her clothes there and then.

"How quickly can we escape to your room?" Ruby asked.

"You're joking? Don't expect more than two minutes to yourself as soon as we get in. If mum's not chewing your ear off, Tommy will be showing off about something new." Fred caressed her cheek. "We'll slip away as soon as we can, I promise."

"You'd better." Ruby's reply dripped with intent.

Fred was already regretting the dinner plans. They could've spent the afternoon in bed together.

As they turned the corner, Tommy's legs were visible, stretching out from the front step. He jumped up as soon as he clocked them and bounded over like a newborn giraffe.

"Slow down, Tom." Fred raised her hand to stop him from knocking Ruby off her feet. "Sorry about my youngest brother. He's all legs and no coordination."

"Nice to meet you. Mum says we've got to be nice to you." He extended his hand to Ruby, and she graciously shook it.

"Good to meet you too, Tommy. Fred's been telling me all about her brothers."

"Well, I'm the best one. The youngest but the best. That's right, isn't it, Fred?"

"That's right." Fred mouthed a thank you as he turned his back, hoping that Tommy's enthusiasm wouldn't put Ruby off.

They followed him down the path and around to the side where the scent of boiling vegetables escaped through the kitchen window. Fred caught sight of her mum, her red face behind a curtain of steam, draining a saucepan into the sink.

"We're a back door sort of house," she said. "Anyone who knows us can come strolling in the back door. The front door's for the postman and the priest."

"Roger that. 'Round the back we go."

Out of habit, Fred shook off her boots at the threshold, and Ruby followed her. They were met by the official Caffrey welcoming committee, gathered in the modest kitchen. Tommy had clearly been sent out to scout their arrival.

"There she is, my girl," her mum said.

It was the first time in ages she'd used that turn of phrase and it reminded Fred of being little. She turned to Ruby. "Mum, Dad, this is Ruby Lewis."

"Hello there, Ruby Lewis. I'm Shirley. It's so lovely to meet you." Fred's mum took her in a welcoming hug while her dad hung back.

When Ruby was free from the embrace, he put his hand forward to shake hers. "Sean. Welcome, Ruby. Any friend of Fred's is a friend of ours."

Fred knew what he meant, but the term stuck in her teeth. They were more than friends, and she wanted everyone to know it and say it. She nodded at her dad and filed it away for later. There was no point in creating a fuss that would embarrass Ruby and the rest of them now.

"You take a seat in the sitting room while I finish up here," her mum said, wiping her brow with a tea towel.

Her dad needed no more encouragement and slinked off to take up his paper in the chair.

"No, what can I do to help? I insist." Ruby took off her jacket, looking like she meant business in the kitchen. "I'm not much of a sous chef but please, put me to work."

"I see. Well, you can give those pots a quick rinse if you like. That would be a huge help. Wash as we go. You're not work-shy like our Fred then?" Her mum laughed.

"I'm not work-shy, Mum. I just don't like the feel of wet vegetables." Fred cringed. She didn't want Ruby to think she couldn't cook or didn't pull her weight at home. Before she could give it much more thought, Brian made an appearance, his oversized frame dwarfing Ruby.

"Thought I'd better show my face and say hello." He gave her a short wave.

"Hi there, good to meet you."

Brian's lips twitched upwards when Ruby flashed her smile. She could win anyone over with that smile.

"Good, well now we're all settled in and Mum's got Ruby as her assistant, would anyone like a drink?" Fred asked.

"Beer, please." Brian sat at the kitchen table.

Fred passed out two beers. "Go and give that to Dad then."

"You're on your feet, you give it to him," he said.

"Brian." Her mum's warning shot made them both look up, but he backed down and took the beer. "That lad. You'd think this lot were still in school the way they go on sometimes." Her mum shook her head and drew Ruby into her circle of superiority.

"It's not me." Fred stopped, realising how ridiculous she sounded. Most of the time it didn't bother her that she lived at home. But she could at least be an adult about it.

"Do you fancy a beer for now, Ruby?" she asked.

"Listen, why don't you and Ruby relax for a bit before dinner is ready? Your dad's got the papers in the front room."

Fred stole a glance towards the back of her dad's head. He looked like he was already nodding off. She didn't want to spend more time in her brothers' company than was absolutely necessary. "Come on, Ruby, I'll show you the shed."

"Oh, yeah," Brian said. "She says that to all the girls."

"Brian, you're going to get into real trouble soon. Now behave yourself," her mum said.

Fred pulled the door closed. She caught Ruby's eye, and they both giggled. "Sorry about that. I did warn you about my silly brothers. Their hearts are in the right place, but they can be extremely annoying."

"Hello there." Mr J poked his head above the fence. "Sorry to frighten you. Fred's used to me popping up beside her."

Ruby held her chest. "You did make me jump."

"This is the famous Mr George Jensen. He put us in touch with his cousins who used to live on Boot Street."

"Great to meet you. We had such a lovely chat with your cousin. She's quite the character."

"That she is." He poked his fork into the mud and rested against it. "She called a few days ago to fill me in. Sounds like a wonderful project you're working on. I, for one, will be glad to see that area be lived in again. It's such a waste when people are needing homes and can't find anywhere."

"I know what you mean. It's a fantastic way to regenerate the city and to bring back people's memories."

"You ought to have a big party down there when it's done. There'll be folks who'll want to celebrate," he said.

Fred caught the flicker of what she now recognised as inspiration pass over Ruby's face.

"You're right, Mr Jensen. There's plenty to celebrate already," she said.

"Right, well, you get on. I expect Fred was going to show you whatever she's been cooking up in that shed of hers."

Fred laughed. "See you soon." She drew Ruby away from the fence.

"He's a gem, isn't he? I think your brothers are lovely too, by the way." Ruby grabbed Fred's hand as they walked down the garden. "They're so different from me and my sister. It's really strange."

"What do you mean?" Fred unlocked the shed and went in, brushing away the latest cobwebs.

"Melissa is very serious about everything. We don't really joke or bicker like you do. There's no banter. It's a very adult kind of relationship."

"Well, we're adults. It should be a grown-up relationship. Brian and Tommy are the worst. If the others were here, it'd be chaos." Fred stooped to light the fire.

"Wow, this is a lovely little space."

"Thanks. It's all mine, and I don't let the boys in unless they've been on their best behaviour."

"I feel privileged." Ruby stepped into Fred's space. "I've missed kissing you."

"Me too." Fred smiled. It had barely been half an hour, but the expectation of her lips touching Ruby's was almost too much. She was glad of the shutters against the window when she pulled Ruby hard against her chest. They kissed violently, hungry for each other.

When they broke apart, Ruby looked surprised. "I don't know why being on my best behaviour makes me so horny."

"Don't." Fred held her finger to Ruby's lips and her tongue darted out. "Cheeky."

"But this sofa looks so comfortable..." Ruby pulled at Fred's wrists, and they both fell onto the battered leather couch.

"We don't have enough time before dinner is ready. And for all we know, Brian is coming down the garden with some excuse to torment us as we speak." Fred pushed a stray hair away from Ruby's face and rubbed her lip with her thumb. "I'll make it up to you later though."

"You promise?" Ruby played with her belt and bit her lip.

Fred burned inside to touch her skin, to peel off each layer of clothing and kiss every part of her until she shook with desire.

"Dinner's ready," Tommy yelled from outside.

"I told you." Fred planted a final, steamy kiss on Ruby's lips, before drawing her from the sofa and towards the door. "Let's go and play nicely, and then I'll take you home and make it worth your while."

Fred locked up while Ruby went ahead. As she turned, the vision of Ruby entering her family home with such ease made her heart skip. Is this what she wanted? Someone who fitted into the jigsaw of her crazy family, who acknowledged and valued her for who she was. Someone who was proud to hold her hand sitting next to her at a dinner table.

If that was her search, maybe she'd discovered treasure. The thought was at once as thrilling as it was terrifying. If she'd found it, could she hang onto it?

CHAPTER TWENTY-NINE

"WHY CAN'T YOU POP on a train down to London so we can do this over cocktails?" Trix asked from the little square on Ruby's screen.

Ruby sighed and adjusted her duvet. Working from her bedroom should be comfortable, but it was cold and damp. "Because I'm up here now. I can't drop everything to go bar crawling with you. And I need to get these plans on paper for the board meeting. Adrienne has to sign off on all of this."

"And you need to butter Fred up beforehand, so she doesn't veto the whole shebang."

"Yes, that too. But I have that in hand."

"I've no doubt." Trix giggled.

Ruby brought up a virtual whiteboard in the video conference she'd set up. Trix was right, it would be so much easier to do this stuff in person but needs must. "Okay, let's start with a sketch of the site." She drew a box. "This is going to be a marquee full of tables. Imagine us having afternoon tea in here and a forties-style band playing on a stage."

"Sounds delightful. I hope I get a ticket for this one."

"Of course. I'll need all the help I can get, so you'll get a staff pass."

"Does Fred know you're building a marquee?"

"Yes, obviously." Ruby made Fred's support sound so much more concrete than it really was. "Anyway, by the time this event happens, they'll have the prototype suite finished."

"What the hell is a prototype suite? I thought I sent you to a building site up north, not some scientific research centre."

"It's a fancy name for a marketing office and a show house. It's where we'll have some flashy three-dimensional models of the streets. I'm so excited about it being finished, because then I'll have somewhere warm to work."

"You're such a softie. Too much time down south?"

"Ouch. Moving on. So, we'll have the media in the suite. I'll get some of the oldies to do some interviews."

"Is this the Historical Association?"

"Not quite. I'm trying to keep them away from any journos in case they give the impression there's something to dig up on the site. I want the old residents of the street to be front and centre. I've got one person in mind to be our VIP guest and media spokesperson."

"I'm with you. But the history geeks are going to be there, no?"

"Yeah, sure. It's a chance for them to have a nice cup of tea and a slice of cake. But we'll manage their exposure to any media."

"Gotcha."

Ruby drew more lines on the whiteboard. "I'm thinking we'll take guests on a walking tour of the site. They can go into some of the houses that have hardly been touched since they left."

"You should touch base with Caterina at the National Trust. She might be able to dress the houses, so it'll feel like the old days."

"Oh, Trix, what a brilliant idea." Ruby imagined the row of houses, each one bringing another decade to life, deeper into the timeline of the terraces. Her heart raced with excitement; she loved it when a plan started coming together. Even Fred wouldn't be able to rail against this one. "I need to find a decent band, or something like that, for the entertainment." She pulled up her browser and typed in the search bar. Her screen came to life with black and white photos of people beaming with pride and energy. She could almost hear the brass tones of the instruments.

"What have you found?" Trix asked.

"Hang on, I have to narrow down my search. Swing band, Manchester." Ruby clicked to share her screen. "Look at all these vintage bands for hire. I love it."

"There's one playing next week in the city. Why don't you check it out?"

Ruby zoomed in on the poster for a jukebox band. "Not sure, Trix. That's a fancy dress night."

"Take Fred with you. She can carry off a three-piece suit."

The vision of Fred in vintage threads sent butterflies through Ruby's tummy.

"Steady on. Save your fantasies for when we're finished our meeting." Trix laughed.

"Sorry. You're the one that brought it up." She mulled over the idea of the band. "It would be so cool to have live music. I'll speak to Fred and see if she's up for it."

"Oh, I forgot to tell you that there's a network thing at the end of the month. We're wining and dining the key clients. You're up to host one of the tables."

"You want me there?"

"You're running one of our biggest accounts, and it would be weird to entertain them without you. We're having it somewhere up north, so your lot don't need to fly down from Aberdeen."

"Really? Who's invited?"

Trix looked away from the screen to her left. "I haven't got the call sheet in front of me but from memory, Adrienne; some guy named Hugo; the architect. Oh, and Fred, of course. I squeezed her in. You can thank me later."

Ruby watched herself blush on the little screen. Of course she'd want to be there if Fred was going. A night in a fancy hotel could be a lot of fun. "I'm in."

"Thought you would be, sweetheart. I didn't even need to twist your arm."

***

It hadn't taken long for Ruby to source a Lindy Hop dress and a three-piece suit. Vintage was everywhere if you knew where to look. Convincing Fred to come with her to the club had been much more of a challenge.

"You can be very persuasive when you want to be." Fred kissed her forehead as they waited for the cab outside Ruby's flat.

"I've been told." She winked and then flinched as Fred went to touch her hair. "Careful, this blow-dry and set cost me a fortune."

Fred pressed her hands together. "You look so beautiful." Her eyes wrinkled as she smiled.

Ruby bathed in Fred's gaze, enjoying the moment of pure reverence. She took a breath, weighing up whether they should skip the band altogether and head back upstairs. "You look pretty good yourself." She stepped back to admire Fred's outfit and the way her waistcoat enveloped her chest, and how the trousers hugged her slim hips. Her hair was slicked back with a centre parting. Ruby took hold of Fred's lapels and drew her closer, and their lips met in a tender kiss.

Ruby broke away and squinted at the headlights coming into view. "Here we go."

They climbed into the back seat. She moved close, the gathers of her net petticoat flowing over Fred's lap. Underneath the folds, she rested her hand between Fred's legs and felt the squeeze of her thighs welcoming Ruby's touch.

She stared out of the windscreen, focusing on the orange tint of the city's street lamps. Her hand travelled further up Fred's thigh, stroking the tight weave of her vintage slacks. Fred's muscles tensed beneath her fingertips, flexing against her grip and arching, ever so gently, to meet her exploration.

Ruby smirked and pulled the zip of her trousers down, not wanting to meet Fred's gaze because she'd lose it and kiss her so hard, the driver would be outraged. She snuck a peek in her direction, and Fred closed her eyes, her chest rising and falling.

Ruby bit her own lip, stifling the swell of desire pulsing through her body. Maybe she could ask the driver to turn around and drop them back at the flat. The Lindy Hop band was probably fine and didn't need vetting before their event. But they arrived too soon, and the car came to a stop outside a tall red brick building in the old part of the city.

"I'll get this." Ruby withdrew her hand and threw her skirts wide across the back seat so that Fred could put herself together. She paid the driver and stepped out into the night.

"You're a bad girl," Fred whispered and scooped her closer.

"You can punish me later," Ruby said and grinned.

"I will, don't you worry." Fred took her hand and led them to a battered door. "This the place?"

"I think so."

The carefree sounds of a swing band bounced into the foyer, rich brass notes inviting them in. Through a set of double doors, the heat of the dancing hit them, and Ruby peeled off her long coat.

"Grab those seats, and I'll get us a drink." Fred nodded towards a cabaret table lit by a single candle flickering in its centre.

Ruby weaved her way across the room, ducking under a tray of drinks being carried aloft, and took hold of the heavy, upholstered seat. She paused, hypnotised by the rhythmic movements on the dance floor and the way each partner moved in sync but independently of each other, like they were autonomous but entirely connected.

The beats of the music brought the whole spectacle to life, breathing soul and fire into the movement. She'd never seen anything like it and stood mesmerised by the popping and breaking of the dance until Fred arrived with the drinks.

"It's something isn't it?" Fred took the seat opposite.

Ruby recognised the tranquillity in her body from the breath she took before she threw axes. "I love it. They look amazing."

Fred beamed across at her. "You want to try?"

"Definitely! But let's have a drink first. I don't think I'm ready for it yet."

"Me neither. Dancing in a room full of people dressed up in funny clothes is not my usual Friday night."

Ruby touched her hand. "Thanks so much for coming. If we could create an atmosphere like this, even half of this, at our event on-site, it would blow people's minds."

"What do you mean?" Fred asked.

"I mean, this would really tell a story of the history we're bringing back to life at the terraces."

"Yeah, I guess so. I think the bricks and mortar are more important. But you know more about telling stories than me, so I'll take your word for it." Fred raised her glass and gulped her beer.

Ruby ignored the echo of Hugo's words. Of course Fred would be concerned with the build, it was her job. That's why she needed to inspire the romance behind Boot Street.

Ruby squeezed Fred's thigh with gratitude more than sexual intention. She was thankful for Fred's support in making this happen and didn't want to let her down. She was more convinced than ever that bringing Boot Street to life with memories was the way to sell it. The future rooted in the past. She knew it. She needed to bring all the moving parts together in a few short weeks. But with Fred beside her on this, she was certain she could do it.

CHAPTER THIRTY

FRED STRETCHED HER LEGS on the bed. Drained from the day, all she wanted was to close her eyes to the world.

There was a knock at the door, and she grumbled quietly, not wanting to face another of her mum's heart-to-hearts.

"Can I come in?" Tommy asked.

She sat up on the edge of the bed. "Yeah, okay." She'd banished her youngest brother from her room years ago, but his appearance intrigued her. "What's up?"

"I need to ask you something." He shuffled back and forth in his white socks, leaving tread marks in her thick carpet.

"Did Mum send you?"

"No."

"Sit down then, you're making the place look untidy."

He collapsed into the bedside chair, his long limbs stretching into Fred's room. She shook her head, wondering if she'd forever be making space for her brothers.

"My college course finished, and Mum said I need to start paying for stuff."

She hid her smile. Of course, he wanted something from her. "And you want, what? Money?"

"No, of course not. Brian said that you were taking on more lads down the site, and I should ask you, because if you don't ask, you don't get. So, I thought... maybe I could come to work for you?"

Fred chuckled. He was a sweetheart really. A bit useless, but his heart was in the right place. She did need more hands. The labouring was dragging on, and they could make up time. "And you really want to work on the building site? It's either cold and miserable, or hot and miserable. For ten hours a day."

"I'm up for it, I promise."

"You'll need to work hard. We don't keep hold of any hangers-on." She cracked a smile. "A fella didn't turn up this week for labouring. You could take his place, but you'd need to talk to Champ, not me. And you'll need boots and a hard hat. I'll show you where to go."

He jumped out of the low seat. "Oh, sis, you won't regret it. How much will I get?"

"Talk to Champ about all that. I'm going away for a couple of days." She reclined back on the bed. "Shut the door then, kid, and start Monday."

He bounded out, and she heard the ruckus downstairs as he relayed the news to their mum and dad.

"Fred, you're a star," her mum called up the stairs.

She smiled. They didn't say it too often, but she knew they appreciated her help.

***

"I don't know why I need to be here. I'm the build, not the brass." Fred collapsed onto the king size bed, holding the phone to her ear.

"I know that, but you're the top of the build pile on this particular scheme, and it's important for the whole team to rub shoulders with the right people," Adrienne said.

"So, what? You called to make sure I was here?" Fred gritted her teeth and fixed her gaze on the smoke alarm on the hotel ceiling.

"I'm checking in with all our delegates. You're not special."

"Don't I know it." Fred hated that Adrienne might read into that remark. She was over their secret affair and didn't want to give her sideways boss any reason to think otherwise. "Luckily for you, Adrienne, I'm a professional. If the company wants me somewhere, I'm there." Fred stuck her tongue out as if she was vomiting the words onto the bed.

"Save the corporate bullshit, Fred. I can read your thoughts, even over the phone."

Fred huffed. Adrienne had gotten to know Fred's inner workings, and now they had to carry on as if nothing had ever happened.

"Please, make sure you're down in time for the canapés. And wear something nice."

Fred pulled a face. "I always wear something nice."

"Oh, I know."

Was she making moves again? Fred sat upright on the bed to fully concentrate on her next sentence. Her tone had to be distant and professional. There was no way she could encourage any flirting between them. The thought of Ruby checking into the hotel filled her mind, and her heart raced with excitement. Or was it panic? "I will wear something appropriate. Thanks for calling. I'll see you at dinner." Fred hung up. Adrienne was a pain in her ass. Couldn't she leave her alone to get on with her life?

She looked across at the suit bag she'd slung over the chair. She was looking forward to spending the evening with Ruby, but it was a crying shame they'd have to put up with a table full of other people. It'd be worth the wait when they made it back to one of their rooms.

Half an hour later, Fred double-checked her text message to make sure it was the right one and knocked on room four hundred. She scanned the wide corridor. Unlike every other hotel she'd ever stayed in, this one was far from long and thin. The whole hotel was an open-plan nightmare, with each room facing a tall atrium from the ground floor to the penthouse.

Fred looked up to see Delphine and Hugo closing their bedroom door a few floors above. If she and Ruby wanted to stay under the radar, they'd have to move around like spies. She berated herself for thinking that they should hide. It was everything she'd despised about her short time with Adrienne. That there was something to be ashamed of. That Fred wasn't good enough for

Adrienne to be proud of her.

Fred knocked again, wondering if Ruby had already gone down to the bar, when the door partially opened.

"Come in, quickly," Ruby whispered.

Fred recoiled before she stepped in. Was she worried about people seeing them too?

"Sorry, I was in the shower." Ruby stood naked, beads of water dripping down her chest.

"I can see." Fred chuckled, resisting the urge to flip Ruby onto the bed and forget the tiresome dinner ahead. "Come here, you." Fred stroked her cheek.

Ruby leaned in. "I'm running so late. It took ages for the lighting rig to go into the marquee."

Fred's shoulders sagged. She didn't want to think about the elaborate plans Ruby had forced her into agreeing to back at the site. "I thought it might. Let's leave the work talk and enjoy tonight."

"I thought you hated this kind of thing?" Ruby pulled on her lacy underwear.

"I usually do, but I have you to keep me company tonight." Fred dropped her gaze to Ruby's black panties, and she imagined tearing them off and throwing them to the floor.

"Don't undress me like that. You'll have to be very patient tonight." Ruby put her hands on her hips, clearly enjoying the reverse striptease she was treating Fred to.

Fred shoved her hands in her trouser pockets to avoid reaching for anything she shouldn't. "On second thoughts, this evening could be very uncomfortable."

Ruby tormented her for another half an hour of pruning, buffing, and layering items of clothing one on top of another. Fred pulled a beer from the minibar and stretched out on the bed to pass the time.

Before long, she'd dragged herself away from the comfort of the five star mattress to head to the function room. She'd expected opulence, but it turned out the hotel favoured post-modernist elegance. So she wriggled on the transparent, plastic chair and hoped her trousers wouldn't stick to her thighs with sweat.

"At least the candles are real," Ruby said, as if reading Fred's thoughts. She nodded at the flames flickering on tall sticks on each table. "Stop scowling; you look unapproachable."

Fred scanned the room and sighed. She didn't really want anyone to approach her. What she wanted was room service and Ruby.

Hugo caught her eye at the far side and raised his glass. Was that a sneer? She wouldn't put it past him. That man could patronise from a hundred feet.

"Adrienne, it's so lovely to see you again." Ruby rose from her seat to plant two kisses on Adrienne's cheeks.

Her cocktail dress hugged in all the right places and together, the pair looked ravishing. Fred cleared her throat and drew their attention.

"Please, join us." Ruby offered a seat, and Adrienne took it with a look of mild amusement.

"Thank you for hosting such a wonderful event, Ruby. I've been chatting to your managing director. He was singing your praises."

"DJ? He's a good guy. Thank you all for coming. It's lovely to spend some proper time together when we're not shaking the mud off our boots."

"So true. Don't you get sick of all the mud, Fred?"

Fred's cheeks warmed when Adrienne's gaze turned to her. She'd never really gotten used to them both being in the same room, and now she was sandwiched between them, unable to avoid their low-cut necklines. "After a while, you don't really notice it."

"But look at our Fred tonight, all scrubbed and polished."

Fred tried to inch back on her chair as Adrienne stroked her collar. The plastic gave nothing, and she remained pinned to the spot.

Ruby bit her cheek and reached for the empty bottle of wine.

"Can I refill anyone's glass?" She looked to the others around the table. "I'll pop to the bar and get some more white."

"Ruby is your new squeeze then? Fascinating." Adrienne sniggered.

"No—"

"Don't deny it, Fred. It's fucking obvious. You're like a puppy around her."

Fred straightened her shoulders, unwilling to roll over and accept humiliation. "Jealous?"

"Please. Don't flatter yourself. We were over before we even began." Adrienne sank against the solid back of the chair and sighed. "Go for it. She's lovely."

Fred considered her ex-lover for a moment. "Are you being nice?"

"Fuck off." Adrienne laughed as Ruby returned with an ice bucket and a full bottle of sauvignon blanc. "I was saying to Fred that you two should enjoy yourselves tonight. Never mind those work rules about personal relationships. It'll be our little secret." She winked at Fred then rose and left the table.

"Was she talking about us?" Ruby asked, her forehead scrunched up in confusion.

"She's trying to wind me up. Ignore her." Fred gulped her red wine. "She likes to get inside my head and make me overthink everything."

"Why would she do that? She seems cool to me."

Fred bit her lip, knowing she had to be honest. "Listen, we had a thing. It was over and done with quickly. But since then, she's sort of been weird with me." Fred's stomach turned over. She hoped that Ruby wouldn't react badly. "I didn't mention it before because it was so trivial. But Adrienne has... You know... You saw her." Her voice stalled, and the background music filled Fred's ears. The soundtrack had been muted all evening, but now it threatened to overwhelm her.

"It's okay, I get it. It makes sense now. I wondered if you two had some sort of backstory."

Fred hesitated. "There's nothing between us."

"I know. She might be a bit jealous, that's all." Ruby smiled and leaned in. "I find it hard to imagine you two together though. She's so..."

"Yeah. She really is. We weren't really together though. Please don't try to imagine us." Fred took Ruby's hand under the table. She held her delicate fingers, enjoying the warmth of their palms together. "I want to hold your hand properly," she said, wanting to know that they were back on track, despite Adrienne's attempt to derail them.

Ruby dipped her head. "We can't. Not tonight. It's a work thing for me as well, you know? DJ won't be thrilled if I start flaunting you in front of clients. It's not a great look, and I need to tell him properly, really."

"Okay. But I want you to know that if I could, I would show the whole room that we're—"

"We're what?"

"We're making out." She laughed it off, but the truth was she wasn't sure what they were doing. She wanted a relationship with someone who'd hold her hand in public and kiss her on a crowded street. She wanted that with Ruby. Did that make them serious? Was she falling for Ruby?

CHAPTER THIRTY-ONE

"MIND YOUR BACKS," CHAMP hollered through the foyer, scattering the team of room dressers. He carried a piece of staging with one of the labourers across the marquee and set it in place at the head of the makeshift dance floor. "That all right for you, Ruby?"

"Perfect. Thanks, guys." She admired the vision that had come to life. Since the marquee's erection, she'd flooded the space with nostalgic details, evoking a time before, where memories were made. She'd assembled Manchester's best set-dressers, a team of theatre designers who had worked their magic to create the atmosphere of a bygone tea dance with modern twists. She nodded her approval at the positioning of a flower garland at the top table.

"Ruby, come and see the time tunnel."

The lead designer, Tala, led her into the room where the team had constructed a mysterious exit to the marquee. Ruby ventured into the darkness, behind a velvet curtain the colour of moss. The first thing to hit was the smell. "This is unbelievable. It smells like the past. How have you done that?"

Tala laughed. "It's a trick from our immersive experiences. We pump scent through the air vents. It works really well, doesn't it?"

"It sure does. People are going to lose their minds over this." Ruby followed the flickering flames of the fake oil lamps over her head. Fred's voice entered her head. "I think we might need some floor lights to avoid any trip hazards."

"I guess so."

Ruby squirmed. "You know, some low-level strip lights. It's just that our site manager is pretty hot on risk."

"Cool. We can sort that." Tala led Ruby around the corner. "And here, the time tunnel emerges into the last century." Tala spread her hands in a ta-da gesture.

Ruby marvelled at the warm glow bathing the space. "Wow, that really is stunning. You guys have done such an amazing job." She twirled around, taking in every detail. The flocked walls begged for her touch. "These details... Where are we?"

"You mean, when are we?" Tala asked. "We're going to lead each of the guests in the marquee through the tunnel. There'll be some sort of soundtrack that glitches so you know you're going back in time. This is what a living room in the nineteen twenties would have looked like."

Ruby lifted a cushion and brought it to her chest. This was even better than she'd imagined. "I love it." She pulled out her phone and dialled Fred. She knew she'd be in her office doing the monthly project update. "Fred, you have to come over to the marquee and see what we've done in here. It's going to blow your mind."

"I don't really have the time right now. Can it wait?"

Ruby recoiled slightly. "I'd love you to see it, but if you're busy then of course, it'll wait." She glanced at Tala, hoping she hadn't heard the brush off.

Fred sighed down the line. "It's okay. Give me ten minutes to wrap this up."

She must've run across the yard because she made it in five, and Tala was still halfway through demonstrating the open-hearth stove.

"This is quite something," Fred said. "You're going to need some lights in that corridor. It's pitch black, and someone will take a tumble."

"Don't worry, we've already spotted that." Tala smiled politely.

Fred always saw the negative in everything, and it was getting Ruby's hackles up.

"This is all getting so elaborate for what was a little event to welcome an insignificant history group," Fred said.

"I'll leave you guys to it," Tala said and left back through the dark void.

"You'll need a hard hat back out there. Don't forget this is a building site," Fred called after her. "Ruby? Is this really what you wanted?" she asked, her hands on her hips.

"What are you talking about?" Ruby wasn't going to let Fred dampen her spirits or veto her vision this time. "This looks brilliant. I couldn't have expected them to translate my little sketches into this. They've built a time machine back to the past."

"It's a stage curtain and some old charity shop clutter which is probably a fire risk."

"Christ, can't you leave the constant vigilance at the door?"

'No, I can't.' Fred stiffened. "You know why? It's my name on those boards at the entrance. It says I'm in charge of this place and anything that goes wrong. Bringing fixtures and fittings without any fire treatment into a live environment is adding to my growing list of worries this week."

Ruby bit her bottom lip to constrain her frustration. She couldn't unleash her anger; people were still working beyond the heavy drapes that separated them from the rest of the world, and she would never embarrass Fred on her own site. But swallowing Fred's ridicule took everything she had. She stared down at the mustard carpet that Tala had lovingly sourced. "I don't think you really get what we're trying to do here. What I'm trying to do."

Fred stared back. A clock on the fake wall ticked like a bomb between them.

"I'm trying to get what it is. But it's difficult. You see, I'm demolishing bits of houses and rebuilding them, brick-by-brick. I'm doing it all under the scrutiny of some sort of tyrant, control-freak director, a frustrated board, and restless crew. We want to get on with stuff."

Fred released her tousled hair from her hard hat. The strands stood on end, and Ruby blinked away to ignore how gorgeous she looked right now.

"This job is at constant risk of overrunning, it's on a tight-rope budget, and all you come to me with is barmy ideas and outlandish execution," Fred said, getting a little louder. "Taking Champ off his day job was the final straw today. He should be supervising the demolition of the factory wall, not building your stage."

"What's got into you? Why are you being like this?" Ruby threw her hands up in frustration, suddenly not caring who heard through the curtain.

"I told you. I'm trying to get a job done, and you seem to be amusing yourself and embroiling half the crew."

Ruby straightened, her blood beginning to boil. "Yeah, I can accept that I have gotten a little distracted, but I think this is a great way to build morale. To build your team." She took a deep breath. "I'm sorry if you think I've been such a pain in the ass. But I think I'm achieving something here beyond spades in the ground."

Fred ran her hand through her hair. "Oh, really? Is that all I do? Shovel mud and dirt? At least I'm doing more than wasting money on theatre companies and brass bands. They've arrived at the gate, by the way."

"They're here for their rehearsal. They wanted to check the acoustics." Ruby looked up, tears springing to her eyes.

"Don't do that." Fred put her hands on Ruby's shoulders. "Don't get upset."

"I'm not upset. I'm furious. You could've supported me in this, but you've ripped the rug from underneath me at the very last moment." She shook her head, shock rolling over her. "I know you don't really believe this about me, but I'm quite good at my job, and my clients usually love everything I do for them." She sniffed, defiant, but aching from the hurt of Fred's criticism.

"Well, maybe your clients are more interested in getting their faces in the newspapers than actually doing their job." Fred dropped her hands to her side. "I need to close down for the day. You get on with whatever is going on here."

Somewhere deep down, Ruby accepted that Fred cared more

about the cement holding this place together than the people in it. "Wow, you're going to leave after all that?"

"Some of us have got a site to run. When do people arrive?" Fred asked.

Ruby's shoulders froze. "Tomorrow. We've got a rehearsal for the dancers later and then the caterers will set up their stations."

Fred's jaw stiffened like she was biting her tongue.

"Champ said he would lead the tours. If that's okay with you?" Ruby said deliberately, putting as much emotional distance between her and Fred as possible.

"Of the old houses? Tours, plural?" Fred swallowed. "Fine. But Champ is in charge. No wandering off."

"I know." Her shoulders dropped another couple of inches. "Don't you trust me to even get that right?"

"It's not like you've got a perfect track record for following orders, is it?" Fred's radio buzzed, and Champ spoke over the airwave. "I'd better get back." She rubbed her hands together.

"Fred?" she called. "It might be best if we don't see each other tonight. I'm going to be busy here for a while."

She stared back. "If that's what you want."

"It is."

As Fred disappeared into the tunnel, Ruby flopped onto the couch. She held her head in her hands, going over what they'd said to each other. Fred's frustration had burst from nowhere, and Ruby had been blindsided.

This wasn't about selling houses. Ruby had invested herself in the fabric of this place and yearned to see her stories come to life so that future generations would understand where it had all come from. Hugo had seen it, so why couldn't Fred? Maybe he'd been right after all: Fred simply couldn't see past laying bricks. The walls of the makeshift room closed in around her, and Ruby struggled to force air in and out of her lungs.

Fred had shown such contempt for her efforts, it was like an axe in the chest. She was trying to do her best for this project and had constantly come up against pushback after pushback.

She'd show Fred that she could do this, with or without her support. She was great at her job and pulling off an event like this was her bread and butter.

She summoned her strength to steady her breath. Fred wouldn't break her with this. She had a job to do. She'd won awards because of her laser focus on detail and a flair for telling a cracking story. If Fred couldn't stand by her side, then she'd go it alone.

CHAPTER THIRTY-TWO

FRED SLAMMED THE CABIN door behind her and saw Hugo sat in her chair. "Can I help you?"

"Trouble in paradise?"

Fred clenched her fists. "Not at all. I've no idea what you're talking about."

"That's not what I heard." He leaned back. "You and lover girl were arguing in the gigantic tent she's had put up at the back of the show houses. I admire her vision, if nothing else."

That stung, but Fred wouldn't let Hugo have the satisfaction of knowing that she was pissed off with Ruby. "Ruby's done a grand job of pulling it all together. You should be pleased, you're the keynote speaker."

"Oh, yes, my assistant told me I'd been given a speech to write. Like I haven't got enough to do around here."

"What are you doing here?" Fred asked, not hiding her frustration at Hugo's hostile takeover of her office.

"I came down early to see what all the fuss was about. I'm glad I did so I could see your face."

"I don't know what you're talking about. Everything is fine. If you don't mind, I've got plenty to be getting on with here."

"I'm sure you have, what with oversized publicity stunts springing up around you. I imagine it's not really your thing. Have you lost control of your site, Fred? Do I need to talk to the board about it?"

The burn of anger rose to Fred's cheeks, and she cleared her throat. "I have not lost control. Ruby and the team sought my permission for everything they've done." That was a white lie she could live with. "And I'm looking forward to welcoming folks from the community into the site tomorrow."

Hugo smirked. "I can see through your precious attempt to support your little girlfriend, *Winifred*. The trouble is, I know only too well how all this mess must be doing your head in." He flicked a pen across the desk. "She's a bit of a liability, isn't she? I mean, friendly enough, gorgeous legs. But naive."

Fred clenched her jaw in a vice-like grip. She was furious with Ruby for overstepping every boundary she'd set. But she was livid with Hugo for coming in here and pulling at the scab. "Why don't you stick to oiling the cogs of commercialism, Hugo?"

"I would, my dear, but everywhere I look, your girlfriend has parked a temporary installation over the top of my plans. It's like we're running a theme park all of a sudden. Is Adrienne aware of all this?"

It was the one thing Fred could affirm. "Of course she is. And she's the one that brought Ruby down here, so if you've got an issue with it all, you need to speak to her."

"Oh, I will, don't you worry. I have plenty to tell Adrienne the next time we speak."

Fred caught the threat in his tone. She wasn't scared of what Hugo could throw at her. Despite their mutual spiky attitude, Adrienne had demonstrated her faith in her time and time again. Even when they'd split, she'd remained a professional ally. Surely the business with Ruby wouldn't change that.

"You look worried?" Hugo scrunched his beady eyes together like a cartoon villain.

"You mistake boredom for worry." Fred leaned against the wall. "Are you finished?"

"You think you own this place, don't you? But one day, all your power is going to come crashing down around you and no one, not even Adrienne, will stand at your side picking through the rubble."

Fred couldn't fathom the depths of Hugo's feelings for her.

What had she done to make the man so irate? "You care an awful lot about my future. I sometimes wonder why... You're not jealous, are you?"

"Of you? Some labourer who landed on the fast track? You've made it because at the right angle, you're almost fetching, and the lads fancy you."

Fred scoffed. "You sure you don't fancy me? If I had a pound for every excuse you made to visit my cabin—"

"Do me a favour. I can't bear the thought of my build being executed by you. It deserves better."

A dull ache began to spread under Fred's ribs. She'd been standing tense for too long, and Hugo was beginning to breach her armour. "I'm good at my job. You're jealous that I have the respect of my crew without needing to sleep with any of them."

"Except Ruby."

"She's not my crew. She's Adrienne's contractor. That's completely different." Fred's breath quickened. "If you want to make a big deal of me and Ruby, go ahead. I don't care if the board knows. Adrienne can fire her." Fred almost crossed her fingers, praying that wouldn't happen.

"They might fire you." His words ricocheted onto the cabin walls before he slammed the door.

Fred trembled. "Jesus," she whispered to herself, slumping into the vacant chair and running her hands through her hair.

She couldn't take any more friction today, she was spent. There was too much going on for her to focus on the day job, which was keeping the build on target.

***

"What would you do though, Stan?" Fred set her pint down on the oak bar.

"You know Hugo. You have to ignore him. If you get sucked into that kind of drama, nothing but bother will follow. I'd kick him off the site unless he has a board meeting to come along to."

Fred nodded. "I can stay out of his way but if I ban him from the gate, that's going to bounce all the way to the top."

Stan grunted his agreement. "And what's all this business about a big do tomorrow? Do you want me there?"

Fred had forgotten she'd even mentioned it. "Well, only if you want to. There'll be cakes and sandwiches. Champ's going to take people on a bit of a tour."

"Right then, I'll be there."

Fred smiled for the first time all day. It would be great to have someone on her side at Ruby's event. She wanted Stan to enjoy some of the perks now that he'd retired. "There's a big tent and a sort of interactive thing, but don't worry too much about that. Enjoy your food and drink."

Stan furrowed his brow. "Interactive, you say?"

Obviously, he had no clue what Fred was going on about. The last time he'd managed a build, it was about bricks and overtime, not publicity stunts. "Yeah, you'll see." She blew out a long thin breath, her shoulders weighing heavy. "I've been wound up about it all day, but actually it's going to be great."

"Everything okay?" Stan asked.

"I think I might have been a bit of an asshole at work."

"That's the boss's prerogative. I could be a hard bastard sometimes, but it always came right in the end."

Fred worried that it wasn't the site lads she'd been harsh with, it was the person she had grown to care for. "Anyway, I'd better get going. I've got loads to do tomorrow, and Mum will have dinner on."

"Okay, lass. I'll see you tomorrow. I'll wear my best suit."

"Your only suit, you mean?" She leaned into their shared laughter, cherishing their cocoon of friendship in the bustling bar. "Thanks for the pint."

Despite offloading to Stan, she still carried the burden of the afternoon all the way home. She banished the business with Hugo to the back of her mind, eager not to spend any more energy on him. But her frustration with Ruby had festered as the day progressed. Rather than fading, the stain of their fight had set into the fabric of their relationship. Fred tried to shrug it off, but thoughts whirled through her mind faster and faster, gathering speed and energy with each rotation.

She hadn't wanted to lose it with Ruby. She simply had to control what was in her domain. The fear of something going wrong had settled in the pit of her stomach with such permanence. She ran through what she'd said. Worse still, how she'd said it. Why had she been so spiteful? Ruby had been so excited to show her the marquee and whatever the hell she'd installed behind it.

Raised voices tumbled from her kitchen window. Brian and Tommy were in full flow. She looked up at the inky sky, tuning into her own thoughts before her head exploded with her brothers' chaos.

Life wasn't going to pause for her to work out what was happening. She recalled the tears that had pooled in Ruby's eyes and vowed to mend the rift in person first thing, so it didn't spoil the day. She detested letting her obsessive need for control get in the way of their relationship.

She pulled out her phone and typed.

Let's talk tomorrow. Hope tonight has been okay. x

She sent the message to Ruby, pausing to see if she'd seen it.

"Fred, is that you?"

"Yeah, I'm coming." Fred plastered her best poker face on so her mum wouldn't twig that something was wrong. She wanted a quiet tea and early bed. The sooner she could get to tomorrow morning, the better, then she could make it up to Ruby. Fear coiled in her stomach as she circled the possibility that it was too late. She'd been so horrible that Ruby might not even entertain an apology. Boot Street had been the best thing to happen to her in the last few years, mostly because Ruby Lewis and her helter-skelter of ideas had turned up when Fred had least expected it.

CHAPTER THIRTY-THREE

Ruby TWISTED THE HAIR straighteners and a warm curl tumbled against her cheek. "I don't want to see her."

"I hear what you're saying, but you can't get away with it today. Not with all this going on," Trix said.

"You don't understand how she spoke to me. When I came out of that marquee, it was so obvious the whole bloody crew had heard every word." Ruby nursed the sore spot in her chest every time she thought about it. Humiliation didn't sit easily for her, and she wasn't used to the ripples of self-loathing that came with it. Fred was meant to be the person she could turn to, not someone who would tear down her ideas.

"You need to rise above this. You have a job to do, and I have every faith in you to get it done. Adrienne and the board wouldn't have appointed us if they thought we'd tumble at the first pushback." Trix drummed her square fingernails on the countertop. "Ignore Fred, stick your lipstick on, and show those old folks a good time. The press will lap it up, and we'll be counting the column inches all the way to the next billing period."

Ruby tutted. It never took long for Trix to bring it back to the bottom line. "This is about more than the assignment. I was really getting somewhere with Fred. Like, maybe we could have been a thing, but it's all been such a waste of time." She'd spent the whole night going over it in her head, and the layers of rehearsed conversations grew heavy around her heart. She hadn't seen it coming. She hadn't realised she was falling so hard for Fred and that rejection would sting so sharply.

The door knocked, and Champ poked his head in. "The first

guests are starting to arrive. Thought you might want to make your way down to the entrance. I've got everything roped off, like you said."

"Thanks, Champ." Ruby turned to face him, wishing that Fred had made one last attempt to see her, that she'd raced over to apologise for her explosion. "Have the journalists arrived yet?"

"No cameras yet, but some guy with a notepad has signed in. The rest are the old folks."

"I'll come down now." She wrinkled her nose at the sight of her safety boots against her satin trousers. One day soon she'd be able to look glamorous all the way to her toes again.

Outside, she brushed a mark from her jacket sleeve. For the first time in weeks, she smelled the demolition in the air, particles floating in the breeze.

At the gate, cars queued and people spilled onto the pavement. She watched as they climbed out of the vehicles, aided by sticks and frames, and sometimes, with a helping hand.

A woman examined the gaps between the cobblestones as if she was reading a story. She dabbed a handkerchief at her eyes and took the arm of her male companion.

Ruby walked towards the couple. "Miss Walsh? It's so lovely to see you. I'm Ruby. We spoke on the phone last week." Ruby scanned Florence Walsh's face for sign of understanding.

"Thank you, my dear. It's nice to see you in person." She extended her cold hand, and Ruby took care in shaking it.

"Don't worry, I've still got all my marbles. It's my knees that might give out on us."

"It's marvellous that you could come. Everything's set up inside. You're our guest of honour today." Ruby hooked her arm through Florence's and took stock of her cousin next to her. "Welcome, Mr. Walsh. Thank you for coming along too."

"Couldn't pass up the chance to have a nose around. Be nice to see the old haunts."

"Come inside, we've got refreshments and Northern TV are

here. Miss Walsh, they'd like to interview you first, if that's okay?" Ruby led them through the bright foyer of the marketing suite, grateful to Champ for polishing the floor at dawn but now fretting it might be too shiny for the most infirm guests.

Florence stopped at a tabletop model. "What's this?" She ran her finger across it, her rounded, arthritic knuckle snagging on the smooth rooftops.

"It's a three-dimensional model of the project. We'll be demolishing the back of each of the houses but preserving the historic façade. Then we'll build a new modern house behind it with glass which lets light into the living space." Ruby puffed her chest with pride. She'd been practicing her elevator pitch for days. "When we're done, we'll have a row of houses which look exactly how they would have in the 1900s, but they'll be family homes for the future."

"How wonderful." Florence scanned the room, her brow furrowed as if she was looking for someone.

"Are you ready for us, Ruby?" A local reporter flicked her thick hair over her shoulder. She beckoned to a haggard-looking cameraman. "I'd really like to film out in the street. The rain is holding off, and I want to see the cobbles behind you, yes?"

Ruby sprang into action and led Florence outside where she'd arranged for cameras to get the best possible angle for TV. She helped her into an old-fashioned armchair on the cobbled street, avoiding the impatient glare of the reporter.

"Ignore the camera, just talk to me. My name is Rebecca Strong from Northern Television. You've probably seen me on the evening news." Rebecca fiddled with a microphone, and Florence looked blank. "Anyway, let's kick off with what it means to you, coming back to your childhood home."

Ruby held her breath. This interview would make or break this coverage. She'd either pull off a major press event or have to admit that she'd wasted more than a few thousand pounds. Her stomach churned waiting for Florence to answer.

"It's been such a long time, I'm not sure where to start."

Ruby flashed a thumbs-up behind the camera, hoping she'd catch it.

"How about how you're feeling right now? Sitting in the street where you played as a child?" Rebecca asked.

"Well, it's a bit strange. I never thought I'd be back here. When I left, it was for good. But it's bringing back many memories today." Florence's shoulders sagged.

"What do you think about the plans for the area? It's been derelict for nearly a quarter of a century, so you must be pleased to see life being breathed back into these houses."

"Yes." She squinted into the sun then scraped at her hand, her eyes flicking from side to side.

Ruby scratched her own head, begging for her to say something powerful while the camera rolled.

"I spent my childhood here, and it was a wonderful place to grow up. But these Victorian terraces grew shabby, and this area wasn't very fashionable for a long time. I'm so pleased that new families can make the back-to-backs their homes. Whatever modern take they've dreamed up, I'm sure they'll be so happy here. I know that we were." Finally, Florence beamed at the camera.

"Great. Thanks, that's all we need." Rebecca scrolled through her phone and turned her back.

"That's all?" Florence chuckled.

"Ruby?" Trix called. "It's almost time for the first tour."

The street had filled up with people, and the cordon that Champ had erected was holding up well. Anyone without a hard hat was steering clear of any dangers. Ruby exhaled. A few more hours and she could relax.

Taking her position on a raised step, she put the megaphone to her lips and flinched at the piercing noise it made. "Can I have everyone's attention, please? We'll start our first tour in two minutes. We'll be setting out to see an example of the old, terraced house and our phenomenal architect, Delphine Garre, will be on hand to explain her vision for the new development." Ruby nodded to Champ to start lining people up. "Everyone, please put on a vest and hat. You'll need to follow me and stick to the paths provided. This is a live construction-site, so we've got to observe the rules." She handed out the safety equipment. "Miss Walsh, please follow us on the tour." Ruby waved a pink flag in the air, beckoning the group of pensioners she'd invited for tea.

She forced the emptiness in the hollow of her stomach deeper, out of her consciousness. There was no time to stew over Fred's frustration and hurtful behaviour. But like a cloud, it hovered over her every move across the cobbles. She glanced to her right, watching the elderly woman she'd made her spokesperson. She admired her courage to speak when the world had so obviously dealt her a rough deal. There was a melancholy in her eyes that Ruby understood. She was sad today too; sad that Fred wasn't at her side, cheering for her success. She wondered whether they'd said too much yesterday to be able to repair the rift between them. Were they so fragile that one argument would rip them apart? Or was she kidding herself that there was much to break up? Were they a hook-up of convenience while Ruby was in town?

It broke her heart a little more to think like that. Fred was no hook-up. But maybe the feeling wasn't mutual. Fred had never said she loved her. And it wasn't like she minced her words. Ruby shook the distraction from her head and tried to focus. This event was a big deal and if she lost her mind now, Fred might be proved right.

CHAPTER THIRTY-FOUR

THE BEATS OF THE brass instruments carried through the foyer as Fred sped through the doors. She stopped short at the edge of the marquee, which was filled to the brim with people, and she could barely make out her crew from the visitors. She weaved her way through the tables, careful not to bump into the delicate towers of cakes and sandwiches suspended in the air by the waiting staff. She shook her head, dismayed at the sight of silver service wandering through her building site.

The swing band burst back to life, and the dance floor filled with netted petticoats and tweed slacks. At another time, Fred would have joined in, holding Ruby's slim waist close to her hips. She pushed the thought from her mind, tired of wrestling with her feelings and the pressure of keeping everything on track.

She spotted Ruby at a table, entertaining two older women. She looked radiant, her hair tousled from her hard hat, a stray lock falling towards her shoulder.

Fred went towards her, bumping into a tray of mimosas held aloft by a young waiter. "For fuck's sake," she said, wiping the spilled liquid from her sleeve.

"Sorry, mate."

She frowned, hating the familiar term that was so prevalent on a building site. "I'm not your mate. Can you clean it up and make sure no one slips on it?"

"I'll get someone over."

Fred stiffened. "No, you'll sort it yourself. Take responsibility for that hazard and see that it's done quickly." The edges of her temper were so frayed, she could blow up at anyone in her way this morning. She met Ruby's gaze and strode across the room. "Can we talk about this?" She took Ruby's arm and steered her towards the back of the room, searching for somewhere quiet. "Why've you been avoiding me?"

Ruby looked at the floor. "Listen, I want to get this thing done and over with. Once I've packed up, I'm going to take a few days off. We'll see how we both feel after that."

"What?" Fred shuffled, trying to work out what was happening. "I've been trying to track you down to talk properly about this."

Ruby looked away. "I need to focus. Delphine is about to come on."

A spotlight shone on the stage, and Delphine cleared her throat. "Good afternoon, folks. It's delightful to see so many of you here for the launch of our new scheme. Before we start our last tour of the site, I'd like to take you through my vision for Boot Street."

Fred raised her eyebrow at the ten-foot screen which illuminated the room.

At this angle, the terraces loomed over them, every detail of the past flickering on the canvas. The camera led them through the faded front doors and behind the brick façade, where each house was flipped upside down in a computer-generated animation. The film finished with light streaming through the glazed structure and into each of the families' lives. Fred had to admit that Ruby had done a fantastic job with the film.

As the room came back to life, Fred guided Ruby back into the time corridor where they could talk without disturbing the rest of Delphine's speech. "I don't need to hear any more of Delphine's sales pitch," she said, holding Ruby by the hand.

"I really do have to—"

"Please. Hear me out."

"The last time we were in here, you had nothing but criticism for everything I do. So, unless you're going to start with a massive apology, I have to be somewhere." Ruby twisted away.

Fred cleared her throat. Was she sorry? She had meant all

the things she'd said. "I'm sorry for hurting you. That's not what I wanted. I'm just so stressed out with everything here." She gestured back to the room. "This is huge. You've done an amazing job, but it really is taking our eye off so many things that are happening. I had to suspend the demolition of the lower terrace this week."

"Why?" Ruby looked back.

"Because it's not okay to have bits of buildings falling onto old people." She touched her arm, aching for Ruby's forgiveness.

"I'm sorry. I didn't mean to get in the way like this. I'm good at my job, Fred, but sometimes you treat me like I'm a fool. It's like if you're not in control of something, you can't fathom anyone else being."

Fred flinched. The thought of anything not being in her control pushed her buttons. "I get it. It doesn't help that Trix is here, egging you on."

Ruby wrinkled her nose in that adorable way that made Fred's insides melt.

"It's not her fault. *I* wanted to impress everyone. Especially you. I guess that's backfired."

The curtain behind Ruby flickered, and Champ appeared. "Boss, you okay to run this next tour? I need to fix the cordon at the gate."

Fred hesitated. Their conversation wasn't over yet.

"They're ready for you now." Champ clearly wasn't going to leave without her.

Trix had gathered a small group of old folk. They huddled to put on their safety vests and hats.

"Ruby, I'll take this one out while you stay here with the dancers," Hugo said.

Fred stirred. "You can't do it alone, Hugo." She tried to temper the disdain in her voice.

"I won't be alone, will I? You'll be with me." His smirk spread over his fat face. "And Ruby's already dealt with the press tour, so it's just a few pensioners. We can handle it, can't we, Fred?"

Fred shrugged at Ruby. She didn't want to cause a scene in front of the visitors.

"Okay, I'll wait for you back at the marquee," Ruby said.

Fred led the way, skipping over the detail in the tunnel which she still thought was ridiculous, and they reached the first house, which had been preserved like a little time capsule.

"This house was in the Taylor family. The fathers worked in the textile factory," Hugo said.

He took centre stage as the group filed in, looking like a plump ringmaster.

"This would have been kitchen, sitting room, family space, and possibly even a bedroom for a couple of people. Pretty miserable having to squeeze your whole life in this tiny space."

Fred zoned out from Hugo's monologue and counted the hard hats, making sure everyone was inside. People murmured their interest in the fixtures. A couple of older ladies drew their coats tighter around them. She wondered how short they could make the tour, desperate to get back to Ruby and smooth over the growing rift between them.

"We could maybe skip the yard, Hugo, and carry on."

Hugo edged to the rear of the small room. "Shame to miss it, let's head outside and see how the terraces stand back-to-back."

The yard was a small square of quarry tiles edged by tall brick walls on three sides with a mirror image of the same yard and house opposite.

One of the women came forward. "I'd really love to see number thirty-three. That's where my family lived."

She reminded Fred of her own grandmother, her face worn with kindness.

"That's not too far, I'm sure we can stroll back that way," Hugo said and didn't make eye contact with Fred.

The whole party looked his way, soaking up his authority.

"That's not possible, I'm afraid," Fred said from the back of the yard. No one turned around so she repeated herself, only louder this time.

"Oh, I'm sorry. I don't want to make a fuss. I haven't been home for such a long time, and it's brought back so many memories of my own parents." The woman's eyes watered, and she reached inside her handbag for a tissue.

"Fred, don't be such a spoilsport," Hugo said and wrapped his arm around the woman. "We can easily go past number thirty-three on the way back to the marketing suite." He nodded towards Fred. "Our site manager takes her responsibilities very seriously."

Everyone chuckled, and Fred shrunk into her boots, wishing she'd left Champ to this tour. Anger rose in her throat, but she couldn't bear to lose it in front of all these people. They hadn't come to witness a showdown. She checked her phone screen. The site crew hadn't sent any messages to say today's plans had changed, so it should be safe to go a bit further into the terraces without getting in anyone's way. She gritted her teeth, thinking through a safe path back to the event. The quicker she got these civilians off her site, the better. "Fine," she said.

"How wonderful. Let's make our way there now, everyone. Mrs?" Hugo held out his hand for the woman in question.

"Mrs Gladstone. Used to be Farnham all those years ago."

"Follow me."

Fred held up the rear as they made their way through one of the tiny alleyways at the side of a row of houses. For a moment, they were plunged into darkness with only a beam of light at the end to show them the way. Fred listened to her own breath, hoping for time to quicken and this day to be over. They turned back onto the cobbled street where Hugo held a clipboard high, as if he was running tours around Rome. Everyone followed like little ants.

The screech made them all duck. Terror smacked Fred in the stomach. "Out of the way."

The crane fell, and time slowed down. She reached, every muscle stretching, to push a man to the kerb. The debris that followed sent a cloud of dust down the street. Her face smacked into the cold edge of a cobble before a lump of a person landed on top of her. They all panicked, tripping over their own feet and falling to the ground. From this angle, she could see at least one of them was badly hurt.

A brick fell at her ear, and she covered her head, realising her hard hat had rolled away from her as she'd fallen. "Stay still if you can and cover your heads. There are falling bricks from the demolition." Fred rolled over and went to get up, but pain jolted through her leg. She looked down and saw a twist in her leg that shouldn't be there. "Fuck." Now she'd seen it, the full force of the wound seared her flesh and her vision blurred. "Hugo?"

"I'm here."

The world went black.

CHAPTER THIRTY-FIVE

NAUSEA SWIRLED IN RUBY'S stomach as the crack of steel against stone reverberated through the tent, the canvas sides proving no barrier to the sound. "What the fuck was that?" She turned to Champ, clenching his sleeve so tight that her knuckles blanched. The band faltered, and a confused hush fell over the dance floor.

"I don't know." He already held his radio to his mouth. He coughed. "Control to Fred. Are you receiving?" Champ walked towards the door at speed. "I'd better go and see what that was."

Ruby followed the broken voices on his radio. "Collapse... demo team."

Fred. She couldn't breathe.

"Ruby, I need you to keep people in here where it's safe." Champ held her arm tightly. "Ruby, can you listen?"

"I can't... I need to see if Fred's okay."

He broke away toward Trix, and she nodded. Ruby remembered to breathe through the panic that rose and threatened to crush her ribs. She ran out towards the cobbles and down the terraces to see what had happened.

She'd gone a hundred yards or so before she saw the crane on its side, its criss-cross pattern twisted into submission. Rubble had fallen and was concentrated at its epicentre. The folks who had been on the second tour steadied themselves like walking wounded, huddled together in shock.

Two figures lay on the ground with a crowd around them. Ruby sprinted towards the first, Fred's body broken in a way she'd never seen before. "Oh my god. What happened?"

"Call an ambulance," Hugo said as he stepped forward.

Ruby froze.

"Do it. Call an ambulance."

Champ stepped in. "It's already been called in. Guys, check these folks for injuries and if there's nothing wrong, take them to safety, please." He gripped his radio and the crew assembled.

Swallowing nothing but dry air, Ruby dropped to her knees at Fred's side and nudged her. "Can you hear me?"

"She was hit by some bricks that fell across the wall. I don't know how it happened, but it's a fucking shitshow."

Hugo continued to speak but his voice faded as Ruby leaned into Fred's neck, tears streaming down her cheeks. She stroked her face. "Please, wake up."

Sirens blared from the gate, and Champ shouted instructions down the radio. Within a minute, a paramedic jostled for space and someone guided Ruby away to the kerb.

"Sit down. I think you're in shock," Champ said. "I need to deal with this. Tommy, can you take Ruby back to the office please and get her some tea?"

Tommy...

"No, I'll go with her." Ruby stood tall, shaking the fog from her brain. "I want to go with her. Tommy too. We should both go."

Champ stared between them as if he was weighing up the fight.

"Okay, you two. Let's get out of the way for the paramedics to do their job, and we'll see what happens." He pulled up his radio. "Can someone get me some water and two cups of sugary tea out here for Ruby and Tommy, please."

Another lad pulled some barriers around the accident and made them move further away. "I need to make this place safe."

"Tommy, are you okay?" Ruby realised she wasn't the only one desperate for Fred's eyes to open.

His skinny frame was dwarfed by the safety vest, making him look like a little boy who'd come to work with his dad.

"Tom?" She touched his arm.

"I'm fine." He dabbed at a cut on his face, and blood seeped out faster under the pressure.

"Shit, you're hurt too. Champ, can we get a first aid kit out here?"

"I'm fine. Don't fuss over me." He shrank beneath her attention but didn't take his eyes off the green uniforms fitting a neck brace and lifting Fred onto the stretcher.

Ruby sobbed. "Will she be okay, Champ?"

"She'll be grand," he said, with dead eyes that betrayed the lack of belief in his words.

"It's a shame she led us so far into the site really." Hugo blew steam across a mug of tea.

"What do you mean?" Ruby asked.

"She was taking us a bit further than planned when the crane collapsed on the factory side."

Ruby's breath stuck in her chest. She hadn't had time to contemplate what had happened.

Hugo shrugged. "It's a wonder why she took the risk. I'd better get back to the marquee and make sure everyone else gets home safely. You might have some paperwork to fill in, Ruby, since this was all your idea."

Ruby's jaw ached, her stomach lurched, and she vomited into the gulley. The weight of responsibility almost crushed her, and she knelt against the hard pavement. She pressed her knee further into a tiny stone, wanting the burn to sear against her bone instead of inside her head and chest.

They'd only just found each other; the threat of losing Fred now was unthinkable. How could she have let this happen?

CHAPTER THIRTY-SIX

"Go." Trix forced her towards the door and thrust Ruby's coat into her hands. "I'll sort everything here."

"I'm going to need to talk to you about what happened," Champ said, approaching from the yard. "I've got to take statements."

"She's in no fit state for that though, is she?" Trix turned to Ruby. "I don't know why you didn't leap into that ambulance with Tommy."

She shook her head, grateful that Trix filled the gaps because she couldn't seem to anchor any words. "I couldn't... Hugo said I had questions to answer."

Trix glared in Champ's direction, and he took a step back. "The questions will wait, I suppose."

As Fred's deputy, he was in charge, but the poor thing was no more ready than any of them to deal with a major incident. Fred had a steady grip for these things, and they were all worse off in her absence.

"What about all the guests? How will they get home safely?" Ruby asked, scanning the room of panicked, frail people she'd gathered here for a silly party.

"I'm going to make sure they're all fit and well, and then we'll get them into taxis." Trix drew her in for a hug. "Get yourself to the hospital and see how Fred is. Don't worry about this."

"I'm going to need to talk to them too." Champ held up a clipboard. "Have we got everyone's phone number?"

"All right, Champ. Give us a break with the health and safety audit you're running over there. Let Ruby get out of here, and I'll help you sort everything else."

"What about the other chap?" Ruby asked. "He looked awful

when they took him off." The sight of the man, limp on the stretcher, flashed into her mind. How could she have let this happen?

"He's in the right place." Trix swallowed, her cheeks pale with fear.

The whole company would be liable if the worst happened. They might never recover. "DJ…"

"Don't." Trix held her hand up to stop the conversation. "I can't think about that right now. Get in the taxi. I have all this under control."

Ruby made her way to the waiting cab. Streets flashed by, and she opened the window to help with the nausea that threatened to overcome her again. She picked at a seam on the back seat of the cab, replaying the scene she'd walked into. She'd felt it, right in her bones. She'd never lived through a proper earthquake, but she imagined that the tremor might feel the same. A sudden sense that the earth beneath you couldn't be trusted. That something, somewhere was shifting so completely, that everything afterwards would be changed.

The car came to a stop outside the city's main hospital. Ruby drew a breath, filling her lungs with air. Through the automatic doors, she stared at the countless rows and rows of directional signs. Baffled, she approached a porter with a kind face. "Where's accident and emergency?"

"You're not the first to stand like a lemon in reception. This place is three times the size it used to be. They keep adding corridors and still expect people to find their way. It's a maze."

She followed his trolley until he sent her to the right, where every one of her senses came under attack. Her nostrils filled with the stench of vomit, her eyes stung from chemicals she couldn't place, and her pores opened with sweat to cool her skin. The temperature soared despite the double doors opening and shutting every three seconds to admit another desperate patient.

Ruby coughed, the dry air tickling her throat. At the desk, she waited her turn behind a line of people at different stages of anguish.

At the front, she opened her mouth to speak, emitting a tiny fraction of her voice. She put more into it to rise above the crowded waiting room. "I'm looking for Fred—Winifred Caffrey. She's come in from an accident at Boot Street?"

A woman behind a mask typed into a computer. "Was she brought in by ambulance?"

"Yes, that's right." Ruby pressed her temple where the mother of all headaches was in labour.

"Date of birth?"

Ruby paused. "I don't know."

"Right." The woman rolled her eyes. "And you are?"

Ruby knew it was relatives only. "I'm her sister," she said too slowly to be convincing.

"Okay. I can't give you any information, I'm afraid." The woman moved onto the next person in the queue.

"Ruby." Brian waved from the other side of the room. "We're in bay eleven."

Ruby sighed. At least she could get beyond the guards. "Brian. I'm so glad I found you. Can I see her?" She followed him through more indistinguishable corridors until they reached their destination, and Brian nodded towards a curtain. Behind it, Fred laid in the bed, hooked up to monitors, a head guard stabilising her neck and obscuring her face. Ruby swayed and had to steady herself against the wall before she leaned further into the bay. "Will she be okay?"

"We don't know yet, love," Fred's mum said, sniffing into her tissue.

"We can't stay here. There are too many of us," Brian said. "Tommy's down in the canteen."

"I'll go," Ruby said. "I wanted to see her, that's all."

"No, you stay with Mum. I'll go and get us a cuppa." Brian disappeared before she had time to argue.

"Let's sit out of the way. The nurses have been coming and

going." Fred's mum led them to a short row of plastic chairs.

Ruby perched, unable to relax, and dragged her shoe along the vinyl floor. "I need to do something."

Fred's mum smiled through her tears. "I've seen my kids come and go through this hospital. Tommy was in here every week when he was little. Always spraining something or breaking another bone. Our Fred's a fighter. She'll bounce back in no time, I'm sure of it."

Ruby hoped so. Her shoulders ached from holding herself together when all she craved were Fred's arms around her. She stood and paced the corridor.

"Mrs Caffrey?" A woman in scrubs appeared. "I'm Ms Chambers, the consultant on duty today. We're worried about Winifred's head injury, so I'd like to book a CT scan for her. Once that's done, we'll know more." The doctor pressed down on the tablet she carried and handed it to her colleague. "Immediately, please."

Fred's mum followed her as she walked away, leaving Ruby scraping her nail against the moulded seam of the chair. She didn't belong there with Fred's family. She was taking up space for her dad or one of her brothers.

Before she left, she snuck another look behind the blue curtain at Fred's still body. Her shirt had been cut to fit a cannula, and it revealed bloody scrapes on her skin and the promises of bruises to come. Her gaze followed the blood down her wrist to her pale fingers, still against the waffle blanket of the bed.

Ruby closed her eyes, shutting out the dizzying guilt that swarmed around her face. "I'm sorry," she whispered. She gathered herself and made for the exit, determined to take up no more space where she wasn't needed. She couldn't make this right, but she could get out of the way. It was her fault. The whole wretched thing had been her silly idea. She'd forced every decision through like it was a game.

But it wasn't a game. People had been hurt. She remembered

the other man. Was he okay? She pushed through the crowd gathered in the reception. Overwhelmed, she steadied herself against the wall and reached for her phone. "Trix. It's me."

"I thought you were at the hospital?"

"I am. I found Fred, but her family is here, and there's too many of us. Have we heard anything about the other chap who was injured?"

The pause on the other end silenced everything. Footsteps, chatter, and the roll of trolley wheels all came to a hush as she waited for Trix to speak. "Are you there?"

"I'm so sorry. Champ heard a few minutes ago. He died in the ambulance."

Ruby choked on the dead air in her throat. "What?"

"He didn't make it. His name was Ambrose Walsh. He'd missed the end of the first tour, so he went out again and wanted to see down the street. So, he was further along than everyone else when the crane collapsed, and he took the brunt of the debris."

Ruby's legs faltered and a fresh wave of nausea hit her.

He'd died... The man who had brought Florence Walsh for the TV had lost his life that morning. And for what? A few column inches in the local rag and Ruby's self-esteem.

She closed her eyes and saw his face. It wasn't his actual face because she'd barely seen him to be able to recall it. But someone's face filled her vision. It was grim. A slackened jaw and lifeless, piercing eyes stared back at her.

Ambrose Walsh was dead. It could have been her father. It could have been Fred.

The world turned again. How could Fred forgive her for this? The thought that Fred had to wake up in order to forgive her was too much to bear, and she stumbled at the door frame.

She saw herself back at the centre of the marquee. Earlier today she'd admired her work, defiant against Fred's judgement and determined to pull the whole thing off. The speed at which her world had shifted was dizzying. Her stubborn ambition had taken someone's life. She swallowed the lump in her throat and followed its descent to her heart, where it faltered. The shame engulfed her, snuffing the oxygen from around her. *How could this have happened?*

CHAPTER THIRTY-SEVEN

THE BLURRED CEILING CAME into view, and Ruby focused on more mould spots creeping from the edge. Her tongue stuck to the roof of her mouth, and her skull ached from sobbing herself to sleep last night.

The door cracked open, and Trix carried in a steaming mug. "Good, you're awake."

Ruby groaned and lifted the duvet over her head. She didn't want to face the day.

Trix perched on the end of the bed before flicking last night's socks onto the fraying carpet. "How're you feeling?"

"Honestly?"

"Always." Trix laid her hand on Ruby's knee and gave a quick squeeze.

Tears welled and spilled down her cheeks. "I want to go home." She closed her eyes, collapsed onto the pillow, and shut out the world. Maybe if she stayed still for long enough, it would all disappear.

"I hate to bring this up, but DJ is sending a crisis team to handle things."

Ruby squeezed her eyes tight. How could Trix talk about work when she was still spiralling. "What's happening with Fred? How is she?"

"She's stable. I spoke to Tommy an hour ago."

The brick in Ruby's stomach shifted, and its sharp corners spiked another fear inside her. "Is she going to wake up soon?"

Trix held her gaze. She was braver than Ruby, able to ride out this sort of stuff in life. But she didn't answer.

"Tell me."

"I don't know anything. I don't know any more than you do." Trix jumped off the bed and opened the curtains. Bright light pierced the room, and they both shielded their eyes. "Drink your tea and get showered. We're going into the office before we go to the hospital."

As the door closed, Ruby sat with the fear that Trix blamed her for what had happened. They all blamed her. She picked at the flaky skin on her dry lips, wondering if everyone else had got home safely last night. Everyone except Ambrose Walsh and Fred.

She skipped the shower and dressed in slow motion, hovering on the outside of her own body, watching everything happen to her. At Boot Street, a cordon ran around the perimeter of the accident and a police car was parked at the front gate.

Champ sat at Fred's desk, typing. Bags of fatigue gathered under his eyes. "Are you okay?"

"I'm all right. What about you?"

"I've been going over the accident logs all night, writing up a report for the board, completing the health and safety forms. The police got here a while ago. They have to attend to check nothing untoward happened, like someone tampering with the crane. There'll be an inquest, no doubt. Maybe more." He scratched the stubble on his chin.

"Do you know what did happen?" Ruby asked.

"In layman's terms, the crane fell apart and brought the factory wall down with it. That part of the site was unstable because the demolition was underway," he said. "I don't know why the crane would have given way. We've got the demolition contractors on-site to talk to the police."

"I shouldn't have brought all those people here." Ruby gripped the back of the chair to keep herself upright. This conversation wasn't helping her nerves.

"But folks weren't anywhere near the demolition-site. It was an accident."

The cabin door swung open, and Hugo strode inside. "Morning, you two. Champ, you look a right state. Have you not been home?"

"No, I haven't. What time is it?"

Hugo glanced at his gold wristwatch. "Ten o'clock." He looked Ruby up and down as if to remark on her appearance too but kept it to himself.

"Can I help you?" Champ asked.

"There's an emergency board meeting at eleven in the marketing suite. You've been called in Fred's absence to explain what happened."

"I know. The bosses have already been in touch."

Hugo's lip curled as if he was put out that Champ had a direct line to their management. "Did they tell you that Fred will likely get suspended?"

"What?" Ruby said. "She can't be suspended; she's in a coma. And she did nothing wrong."

"It's simple protocol. Nothing for you to worry about, but having a fatality on your site leads to a big investigation. Fred can't be allowed on-site in case she tampers with evidence."

Fury bubbled inside Ruby's diaphragm, and she wanted to scream at the injustice of it all. But Hugo was right. Someone had died on Fred's watch. It was all her fault, and Fred could lose everything. She stumbled to the door and kicked it back on its hinges. She lurched to the edge of the cabin and vomited the tea she'd had. The stomach acid burned her throat, and she heaved, hurting her ribs.

"Hey." Champ kept his distance. "Ignore that. There will be an investigation, but it'll find the truth. There's nothing untoward here, and nothing for Fred to worry about."

Hugo emerged from the cabin. "Except that she let you run riot across this building site with a load of pensioners. And that she turned a blind eye to every single breach of site rules because she was having a steamy relationship with the new office girl. Isn't that right, Ruby?"

She had no fight left to stand up to the accusations. She knew the truth but put like that, maybe Hugo was right. Maybe Ruby had glossed over some of the details, and maybe Fred had let her.

Ruby gathered the strength in her limbs and walked to the mess room. Inside, she slumped onto the wooden bench to take off her boots. If Hugo was going to say all of those hateful things at the board meeting, she had to make this right.

She unlaced her boots, remembering the day Fred had brought them to her. She tucked them into the cage on the wall. She folded her vest and placed it on top. She should never have come here. This wasn't the place for her. The only thing she could do to protect Fred's reputation was to take responsibility for the entire fiasco and leave.

The suite had been cleared as much as possible, but evidence remained of the previous day's chaos. Glitter trodden into the carpet, the broken stems of flowers hung from vases, and a sagging arch of balloons.

Ruby turned her back on the sad echoes of the party that went so wrong. The board filed in, and Adrienne stood out from the crowd as usual, though her face was drawn and tired, and there were black rings around her eyes.

Ruby took a seat at the back, and the introductions washed over her. Her knee bounced with nerves, and she couldn't shake the vision of Fred and Ambrose lying in the street.

"I'd like to invite Robert Champers, deputy site manager, to give us an update on the situation—"

"Wait, I'd like to speak." Ruby approached the table. "This whole thing is my fault."

"Ruby, please sit down," Adrienne said.

"No, I need to explain. I invited the historical society here because they were interested in the site. Then I thought it would be great to bring back previous residents of Boot Street to their family homes. I really was trying to do my best to get people interested in what we're doing here and to tell its story. I forced Fred to do the tours and then she went out on her own, and this horrible accident happened. It's not her fault. Nothing is her fault. It's all my fault." She came to a grinding halt with ten pairs of eyes wide around the table. Her breath stuck in her throat and every muscle twitched in unison, propelling her towards the door and out of the room.

Ruby bounced straight off Trix's chest at the gate.

"What the actual fuck is going on?" she asked, holding Ruby at arm's length.

"We need to go. I can't be here."

She'd said her piece, but she imagined Hugo tearing Fred to shreds back in the boardroom. The only thing left to do was to say goodbye and make herself scarce. If she wasn't around, they couldn't accuse Fred of anything like an improper relationship.

***

Sirens screamed around the bend, off to the next emergency. Someone else in need of help. Ruby bowed her head, shame creeping over her like a weighted blanket.

Blank faces filed in and out of the hospital, shoulders hunched with the burden of worry. Ruby summoned whatever dwindling courage she had to go in. She couldn't bear another day without holding Fred's hand.

Pausing at the ward entrance, she cleaned her hands and scanned the board for Fred's name.

"Who're you looking for?" a nurse asked gently.

"Winifred Caffrey."

"She's still in high dependency. Sit in the visitors' room, and I'll see if one of her family can come and see you."

Ruby fiddled with her door keys and wrapped the metal keyring around her knuckles. She peeled off a layer of clothing in the stifling room and folded her jacket on the arm of the chair.

Tommy's frame filled the doorway. "Are you kidding me?"

She hadn't expected such a hostile reception.

"It's your fault she's in here. Do you think she wants to wake up and see your smug face bearing down at her?"

"Tommy, I—"

"The whole crew is blaming you for what happened. If it hadn't been for your stupid tours and wacky ideas, no one would've been in the way of that crane."

She knew he was right. "Can I just see her for a moment? I didn't come here to make a fuss."

Shirley appeared at his side. "Ruby, love, come on through. It's only one person at a time while she's in the HDU, but you can pop in."

Tommy whipped around to his mother. "I don't think so, Mum."

"What do you mean? Ruby will be okay for a quick visit."

"I don't want her in there. Fred wouldn't either."

Shirley stared at them both, clearly begging for some sort of explanation.

"It's the investigation at work," Tommy said, sidestepping into the room and fidgeting with something in his pocket. "They're mouthing off about Fred's judgement, saying she made mistakes because of her goings-on with Ruby. If they see her here, it'll be the final nail in Fred's coffin."

The turn of phrase dropped like lead into Ruby's stomach.

"Don't say things like that, Tommy." Shirley turned away, running her hand through her wild hair. "Listen, I don't know what's going on at Boot Street. All I can focus on right now is whether my daughter is going to wake up, and whether her brain is still going to be as sharp as it was on Friday morning. The rest, I don't care."

"They were barely even together, Mum. They'd had a massive row on Friday night."

Ruby's legs shook. Part of her could understand Tommy's attack. None of it would've happened without her actions, but would Fred really not want to see her? Would Fred hate her? Her questions whirling around, she didn't have the space or energy to figure it all out. She fought the tears welling in her eyes, but the guttural sob which escaped surprised her.

Shirley sat beside her. "Tommy, go and get some tea. Come back in twenty minutes." Her direction had a finality to it. She picked up Ruby's hand and held it. "From where I'm sitting, you're in a right mess. I'll take you through to Fred. She's still asleep, but you can have a few minutes together."

Touched by the softness of Shirley's words, she followed her into the unit. The lights were dimmed, and each bed was surrounded by many more pipes and machines than she'd expected. Fred's body lay slack in the bed. Ruby hovered at the end, paralysed by fear. Their whole world had turned upside down in a matter of days. She'd failed Fred in the worst possible way. While Fred took great care of everything in her charge, Ruby had ripped up the rule book and stamped through the warning signs.

Her tongue clamped to the roof of her mouth, unable to form any words. Her breath quickened as she panicked.

Fred would never run away from her responsibilities. But staying put couldn't help. It would only make things worse. Fred had to understand that. She gritted her teeth, determined to see it through, despite every fibre of her body screaming in torment.

CHAPTER THIRTY-EIGHT

WITH HER EYES CLOSED, every other sense was dialled up. Somewhere next to Fred's head, a machine bleeped. It was a constant rhythm that she zoned in and out of. The chatter of the nurses' station sounded further away, and every now and then, one would approach with the swoosh of the curtain and lift her wrist.

Sharp fibres of the sheets itched her bare skin, and she ached to scratch but her limbs wouldn't move at her command.

"When will the physio arrive?" her mum asked.

"They'll start this week. We need to assess Fred for some gentle movement to keep her muscles active. It'll help with her recovery."

The bleeping faded and returned, along with a hand in hers. She twitched, recognising its size and weight. *Ruby*.

"Fred." A pause. The bleeping filled the void. "I wanted to see you and explain."

A sniff. A tremor.

It's okay. You don't need to worry.

"It's all so awful." She kissed her hand, her soft lips running over each knuckle.

I'm going to be fine. I need to sleep a bit longer, and I'll be right as rain.

"I made a mistake coming here. I pushed you too far, and it's my fault people got hurt. It's my fault..."

The beeps quickened.

"Hugo is making all sorts of noise about the accident. And about us. So, it's best if I get out of your way. You can deny everything."

I'll never deny you.

"I'm going home. I'm sorry I've caused such a mess."

Teardrops fell onto Fred's hand, and she almost burst from her body to reach Ruby. Deafened by her internal scream, her lungs filled with a raw, agonising cry of frustration. Why couldn't she do anything? The question terrified her. If not now, when Ruby was right there, then when? When would her brain decide to reboot?

The footsteps faded down the corridor, the volume falling slowly before the door swung back on its hinges. Agony seared through Fred's chest, and the beeps returned with vengeance.

***

Her eyes opened this time like it was nothing. As if all the other times, they would've sprung open if she'd tried a bit harder.

"She's awake! Sweetheart, it's okay. You're in the hospital."

No shit, Mum. Fred blinked against the blinding fluorescent tubes hanging overhead but forced her eyes open again in case it was a fluke, and she couldn't really wake up. She licked the sandpaper cavern of her mouth and lifted her hand. "I..."

Her mum put the ice to her lips. "Brian, get the nurse. I'm not sure what she can have."

A nurse arrived with their signature swoosh of the curtain.

"Hello, Fred. It's nice to see you've woken up. I'm Karen, your nurse. You've had a bad head injury, and you've got a little break in your leg, but there's not too much we're worried about now. We were waiting for you to wake up so we can run a few more tests."

Words still failing her, she blinked. The shutters came down on the florescent bulb, then sprang up again.

"You had us worried, our kid," Brian said.

"I'll page the consultant, and we'll see if she can pop and see Fred on her rounds. That'll speed things up."

"Tired," Fred whispered.

"I know, you must be." Her mum sank into the chair. Her hair lank with the vigil she'd kept at the bedside, pillows of worry under her eyes.

"Ruby?" Fred coughed and caught the look Brian gave her mum.

"We'll talk about all that later, shall we? Let's see if we can get you a bit more comfortable."

Her mum plumped the pillows and straightened the sheets. Fred couldn't argue. Her eyes had opened, but the rest of her body was still catching up.

"You're awake?" Tommy loomed over the bed, grinning like a cat.

"Sort of," she whispered. He crushed her hand too tight, but she couldn't wriggle away.

"Fred, you're not going to believe what's been going on down at the—"

"Tommy, that's enough," her mum said with an unfamiliar steel in her tone. "She needs to focus on getting her strength back."

"I was only going to tell her that Hugo is..."

She glanced between them, trying to interpret the unsaid exchange. "What?"

"You should get some rest," her mum said.

The conversation was over, and Tommy retreated into the bay and sulked in the chair. Something was off. What did Tommy want to tell her? A heaviness crept over her shoulders, and she sunk further into the mattress, letting the sleep come.

Sometime later, she flicked open her eyelids hoping that this time, she had control over waking up.

The doctor stood at the end of her bed holding a tablet. "Great to have you with us. We're going to run another CT scan to be sure that the shadow we saw wasn't a bleed. But I'm pretty confident that now you're awake, you'll start to feel much better."

"What happened?" Her memory swirled in her head, and she couldn't put anything in a logical order.

"Your head injury was serious enough to knock you out for a couple of days, and we had to check your brain for signs of bleeding. I want a second scan to rule that out."

"My head injury?" Fred fiddled with the drip in her wrist, trying to work out what was going on.

"There was an accident at your place of work. A crane fell and part of the building collapsed. You were underneath it all."

Fred flinched as red brick flashed in her mind. It had hit her square in the face. She touched her cheek, covered with gauze, and it smarted as soon as her fingers made contact and the memories burst like fresh wounds across her body. "I was hurt."

Her mum appeared at her side. "You were, but you're going to get better, and that's all that matters now."

"There was someone else." She saw a man in front of her—she'd tried to push him away. She'd seen the crash and tried to force him off the street. "There was a man."

The doctor excused herself, leaving her mum and Tommy inspecting the floor tiles. Tommy shuffled and rubbed his nose with his sleeve.

"Mum?" Fred rose up onto her elbows, her ribs creaking in agony. She'd beg her mum for information if she had to. But part of her, cloaked off, already knew what happened. She needed help to lift the curtain of confusion.

"There was a man with you when everything came down. You tried to get between him and the falling rubble, but it wasn't possible." She held her hand. "He died, sweetheart. You couldn't have done anything more than you did."

The sob that came stuck in Fred's throat, and pain spread through her abdomen. "What was his name?"

"Ambrose," Tommy said. "It's all over the papers."

She laid back on the cotton wool pillow, too flimsy to hold the weight of her sorrow. "Why did it happen, Tommy? What did the investigation say?" Fred's mind kicked into overdrive, ignoring the frailty of her body.

"It's too early. That's what Champ said this morning. But it wasn't your fault."

"I know it wasn't my fault." How could it have been? She wasn't on the crane. "Why? Who said it was my fault?"

Her mum stepped between them. "Tommy, can you go and ring your dad, please, and tell him to come over?"

He gathered his jacket, kissed Fred on the cheek and sloped off.

"I don't want you to hear this in dribs and drabs from your little brother." Her mum perched on the bed and stroked a tuft of hair from her face.

Fred leaned into the touch, wanting nothing more than to rest in her mum's hug for a while and forget the world. "Go on, then. Let me have it."

"That Hugo is causing trouble. He's claiming that risks were taken last weekend that could have been avoided."

Dread filled Fred's hollow legs. "He might be right there. Hosting a hundred pensioners wasn't exactly top of my list."

"Yeah, but he's spreading rumours that you let it happen and turned a blind eye."

"Where are you getting all this from?"

"Champ has been keeping me posted. Tommy's been at work too, but he's not reliable." Her mum patted her arm. "Champ has your back on this. That Adrienne too, she's been quite the advocate. They're standing up for you."

Threats and accusations burst inside Fred's head. All she could hear were Hugo's toxic monologues. "Has he blamed me for all this? Tell me the truth. I can take it."

"Yes, he has. They've suspended you pending the investigation, but Tommy said that's protocol."

"Fuck that." Fred knew better. That screamed Hugo and his meddling. "Where's Ruby?"

Her mum rubbed her eyes and held her palms at her cheeks. She looked exhausted. "I didn't know if you'd heard her."

"Heard her? Is she here?"

"No, sweetheart. She put her statement into the board and said it wasn't your fault, and that it was hers." Her mum's gaze dropped to the floor. "Then she left."

"Left?"

"Gone home. That's what she said."

An echo of this replayed in her mind. She knew that Ruby had gone. She'd felt her absence, laying in the cold bed alone with nothing but itchy blankets over her skin. She'd craved Ruby's touch. But it hadn't come.

She pressed her eyelids, releasing the tears. Her career shattered, her reputation in pieces, and the person she thought she had a future with had run away. Was it too hard for Ruby to face up to her responsibilities for this?

Fred wasn't sure whether she was even to blame. It was an accident, wasn't it? Could she even be sure of that? One thing was true, Ruby had sure as hell run away from it all pretty quickly. How could they be something and then nothing. Just like that?

CHAPTER THIRTY-NINE

THE DOORBELL CLANGED THREE times, reverberating through Ruby's temples.

"I'll go." Melissa set down her book and padded through the hallway.

"Is she here?" Trix had arrived. "Is she bloody here or not?"

"A pleasure as always."

"Sorry, Mel." They double kissed with maximum volume.

Ruby drew her knees into her chest, waiting for the onslaught. Trix on her own was bad enough. Trix and her big sister was big trouble.

"You ran away?" Trix pulled a wheelie suitcase behind her. "It wasn't bad enough to drag me all the way to Manchester, but then you make me get the train to Bangor and ride a bus all the way down here. There weren't any taxi drivers who'd travel this far south. Do you know what I've been through?"

Under different circumstances, the whole farce would've made Ruby giggle, but there was no fun to be had today.

"Aren't you going to say something?" Melissa asked, her hands on her hips. She'd obviously been waiting for backup to arrive.

"Did she tell you where I was?" Ruby glared at her traitorous sister.

"She didn't have to; you're an open book. Plus, you could hardly skip back down to London and stay in your sub-let flat. When you said "home,' I assumed you meant here in the middle of nowhere."

Trix collapsed onto the sofa, pushed off her boots, and flung her legs over Ruby's. "Now I'm here, we can work it all out. Pop the kettle on, Mel, I'm gasping. Have you got any of that nice tea you have up here?"

Mel left the room, shaking her head.

"Have you told her what happened?" Trix asked.

"In a roundabout way."

"You mean, your messed-up version?" Trix leaned further into the oversized cushions and was almost swallowed by the goose down. "You know it's not all your fault, don't you?"

Ruby didn't need a pep talk right now. She needed to wallow in her pool of guilt, raising a toe every now and then to see how much filth clung to her.

"The crisis team have handled the fatality."

"Don't do that." Ruby's bottom lip trembled. "Don't minimise that man's death to a PR issue."

"I'm doing nothing of the sort." She sat upright. "I've been in Manchester for three days trying to wade through this mess. I'd still be there if I wasn't worried sick about you."

Ruby looked to the ceiling, trying to tip the tears back into her head. She sniffed, screwing her face up in shame. "I can't believe it."

"Can't believe what? That there was a freak accident on a building site?" Trix gripped her shoulders. When she wriggled away, she held her chin. "This isn't on you."

Melissa came in with a wobbly tray. "Oh, have you set her off again? She's done nothing but sob since she got here. I can't get much sense out of her."

"Don't talk about me like I'm not here." Ruby threw herself down on the couch, hoping they'd both disappear if she closed her eyes. A vision of Fred in the hospital bed came to mind, refuelling the self-loathing inside her head. "Did you see Fred?" she asked.

"No. It's family visitors only. But I spoke to Tommy last night. She's doing loads better." Trix held her hand. "Don't you want to go and see her?"

Ruby wanted nothing more than to sneak into that hospital bay and curl up at her side. She'd do anything to feel her close right now. "She won't want to see me. I need to keep my distance so this whole thing about me and her goes away."

"You mean the accusation that Hugo is making? It's being investigated, and they won't find anything in it. They're much more interested in how that crane collapsed for no good reason. The demolition crew are shitting themselves. They're sub-contractors, so if they're to blame, well, who knows..."

Ruby's stomach crawled with doubt, and she couldn't sit still. She threw off her blanket and went to the window.

"Let's go outside. It's warm—for Wales, at least," Trix said, taking her by the hand.

Her shoulders straightened with Trix to lighten the load a little, and she followed her out of the French doors.

"Put some shoes on, Ruby. It's not that warm," Melissa called after them.

She slipped on the sliders at the door. "I'll take you down to see the view," she said.

Trix was right, the air warmed her neck and the sun beating onto her chest felt good. As they reached the top of the garden, her lungs expanded. "I can breathe." She held onto the fence post. "I don't think I've taken a full breath since it happened."

"You're stressed out. It's normal when something horrible happens. And for someone like you, this feels like a failure. I understand."

It wasn't a stress that she'd ever lived through before. This was suffocating, stomach-cramping, breath-bending panic.

"What are you going to do about Fred? I thought you two had something going." Trix squinted into the sunshine.

"I don't know. We fought before the accident and then... I've made a mess of everything."

"Have you?"

Ruby tasted the salty air. "God, it's good here."

"If you like peace and quiet. And rain."

"It's not raining now."

"You left home because you wanted more. I get it. You can

retreat back here whenever you want to. It's your safe space. But soon you're going to need to come to terms with what happened, accept you're not at fault, and speak to Fred. She really likes you. Possibly more than that. And you've run away when she's in the worst shape."

Spoken out loud, the truth kicked Ruby in the guts. She'd left Fred alone when she needed her most. "How could I stick around when I'm to blame for everything? Fred needs me out of the way if she's going to defend herself against Hugo's lies."

"Does she? Or would it be a whole load better if you were by her side right now, helping her to recover?"

Ruby stared at the thin line between the land and sky. "I hate you and your truths."

"I know. But who's going to give it to you straight, if not your straight bestie?"

"I can't go running back though."

"I'll go with you. But first, we really need to talk about that accident. I want you to believe you couldn't have predicted it or done fuck all about it. You were inside the marquee with me."

"Only because Hugo took my place."

"Right then, you two. Let's go for a walk." Melissa dumped two pairs of wellies and a couple of waterproof jackets at their feet.

"Fine." Trix took one of the coats. "But you owe me a gin and tonic for this assault on fashion."

"Come on. No one will spot you out here." Ruby huffed and led the way to a break in the hedge.

"Watch this stile, Trix. It's higher than it looks," Melissa said.

"She gets her leg over most things." Ruby surprised herself that she was still capable of cracking a joke. Then guilt washed over her. How could she laugh when Ambrose Walsh was lying in a morgue waiting to be cut open?

Trix shook Ruby's arm. "Don't do that."

"What?"

"That, with your face. Don't make me laugh and then look

miserable. The world came crashing down. We have to dust ourselves off and rebuild it."

It was easy for Trix. She'd always been able to bounce back from adversity, but Ruby struggled. Her time in Manchester had changed things for the better. She'd seen the potential of something grow from nothing. Her mind wandered to the last client she'd entertained: the family of futon makers. It had been a quaint story once she'd worked her magic. But it sparked nothing like the passion she'd shared for those damn houses.

The love she felt for Boot Street wasn't just the day job. It was Fred. Everything about it had been down to Fred's energy, her determination, and her will to succeed.

"I don't know if I want things to go back the way they were."

"So, what then? You're going to tip your whole world upside down because of this? It was an *accident*."

"Stop it, you two, and enjoy the view." Melissa opened her body wide, pointing toward the vista as if she'd conjured it herself.

Ruby swallowed the lump in her throat. She'd seen this horizon many times but today, it continued forever...at least until it reached land on the other side of the bay.

"Oh, for fuck's sake," said Trix. "I really try and hate this place for being at the arse end of nowhere, and then you go and show off."

Ruby smiled properly this time. The little beam reached into her heart and tugged at the strings of her safety net. Her best friend and her sister were here, as they always were, wrapping her in their warmth and keeping her safe.

But there was something missing. Their limbs were warm, but they lacked Fred's strength. They weren't a patch on the way she wrapped herself around Ruby's body and held the world at bay. Could she ever get that back? The rolling sea stretched ahead of her. Above it, the sky leaned in like a blank canvas. Years ago, she'd stood frustrated and alone at this cliff edge, wanting to escape to the bright lights and endless opportunities of the big city.

Now, the possibilities shrank to a pin point. The one thing she wanted, the one person she craved was absent. She'd gambled with her career and lost the most precious thing she'd ever held: Fred's heart.

CHAPTER FORTY

FRED SAT ON THE bed with a sigh, shattered from a trip to the bathroom. For the first time in her life, she didn't trust her own limbs to carry her weight.

A shadow appeared at the curtain, and she fixed her robe, making sure to be decent for the doctor on her rounds.

"Hello," Adrienne said softly, as if she didn't want to disturb anyone.

Fred couldn't mask her surprise. "What are you doing here?"

"I came to see how you're feeling." She sat without an invitation. "The chairman would've come, but the board thought that sending a female would be more appropriate."

"Of course they did." Fred laughed, arching her back as her core spasmed. "Did they think you'd have a better bedside manner?" That slipped out before she'd thought about it.

"If you mean that they thought I'd be kind and sensitive, I guess so." Adrienne shuffled on the seat, seemingly arranging herself to stay for a while.

Fred edged back into the bed, almost dropped her crutch, and failed to look strong and graceful.

"Do you want me to help you?"

"No." She needed help, but she didn't want it from Adrienne. She hadn't managed to get back into bed yet without her mum or a nurse. Her body wasn't performing in the way she expected.

"Let me help." Adrienne hooked her arm under Fred's and pulled her backwards. She lifted Fred's good leg onto the bed and stood back, her face softened.

Fred liked it.

"How are you doing?" she asked again, obviously not ready to give up without an answer.

"Have the board sent you here to make sure I'm still alive?" Fred regretted the phrase. She was still alive, and Ambrose Walsh wasn't. Now was no time to be flippant about it. "Sorry, I didn't mean that."

"Well, if you must know, I volunteered to come and check in on you. I'm worried about you, and I wanted to satisfy myself that you're doing okay. Your crew is pretty tight-lipped. I think they're paranoid that you're going to get fired or something."

"Am I not? I thought I was suspended pending an investigation. Surely someone has to take the rap for it all?"

Adrienne went to hold her hand but then drew it back. She sighed, the shadows beneath her mascara deepening in the glare of the hospital light. "You're not suspended. You have a leave of absence because you've been in an accident. There's an investigation, but you wouldn't expect anything else, would you? We need to know what happened to that crane."

"You don't know yet?" Fred asked, sitting upright.

"No, not yet. The inspectors are still on-site. We had to wait for the police to release it back to us."

Fred sank down a little further, weighed down by the uncertainty of the whole thing. "Tommy said I'd been suspended."

"Not on my watch." Adrienne looked her straight in the face with some unspoken promise to make up for all the hurt and rejection she'd caused.

"Why are you being so nice?"

"I care about you." She put her hand on the bed. "I know I messed it all up, but I wouldn't want anything bad to happen to you." She cleared her throat. "I'm trying, but Hugo is going after you, Fred. I don't know if I can protect you from the full weight of that."

"What do you mean?"

"He's saying you broke protocol to protect Ruby."

"Did I fu—"

"He's put in a formal complaint, and it's being investigated by the directors." She pulled an envelope from her bag. "It's in this letter. I asked to be on the panel, but Sebastian said no. I think he might have an idea that we had something last year."

Fred stared up at the ceiling, wishing she was anywhere but here. "What can I do?"

The sound of the tea trolley rolling past filled the silence.

"Nothing, for now. It's not like there's any counter-evidence to present. You need to wait to be called to an interview. They'll want to speak to Ruby too. Where is she?"

"How should I know?"

"Well, you're in a relationship, aren't you?"

"Not as far as I'm aware."

Adrienne took a breath. "What do you mean? Just tell me what's going on and I can help."

Fred thought twice about the next lie to come from her lips. For once, Adrienne was being kind, and she didn't want to deceive her. The problem was, she hadn't really come to terms with the last few days. She and Ruby had been something, but it obviously wasn't enough for her to stick around and see her through this. "We were together, I guess." She shrugged, hoping that her answer would suffice.

"And what about now? Has she left you after all this?" Adrienne frowned.

"You tell me." Fred twisted the sheet around her finger, trying to ignore that she was lying in her pyjamas talking to her ex-lover. "My mum said she came to say goodbye, but I don't remember it. The last I recall is leaving her in the marquee and going off for the tour with Hugo."

"What else do you remember?"

"Looking up and seeing the crane melt out of the sky. Then nothing." Fred closed her eyes and saw much more than nothing. "Sometimes when I'm drifting in and out, I hear someone scream.

It sounds like Ruby, but it can't have been 'cause she wasn't even there."

"It must've been frightening."

"Not really. I got myself in the way, and I must've reached the man... Ambrose. I remember his body against my hands. I wish I could've pushed him further." Fred swallowed the lump in her throat that threatened to burst. If she started to sob, she might not stop.

"It wasn't your fault."

"Everyone keeps saying that. But I don't know if it's true." The more she heard it, the less value it had. What could she have done? Did the crane need an inspection? Was there unplanned demolition that she should have known about? "I have so many questions," she said, inspecting the thread count of the sheets.

Adrienne fiddled with her necklace. "The inquest will answer some of those, I hope. Then there'll be a health and safety investigation."

"An inquest? Like the coroner?"

"Yeah. Ambrose Walsh died on our site. The family are now saying he had a heart attack in the ambulance, but we need the coroner's verdict to draw a line under the cause of death."

Fred's chest itched like insects were crawling over her. "I want to get myself out of this fucking bed and back to work."

"Steady on. There's no way you're in a fit state to go anywhere near Boot Street. Or any other building site."

"Who says?"

"The board, remember? You've been signed off until you're recovered and a qualified doctor says you're fit for work. I know how stubborn you are, but this is non-negotiable," Adrienne said. "If you're on-site, you'll probably invalidate all our insurance. You don't want us to get into even more trouble, do you?"

Fred smiled. "Looking out for me or the company purse?"

"A bit of both."

"As usual." They laughed together.

Adrienne gathered her things. "I have to go."

"Already? I was enjoying your company."

"Makes a nice change. I'll come back and see you soon." She kissed Fred's forehead. "For now, don't fret about work. Put the investigation business out of your mind and get better. We miss you."

"When's the funeral?" Fred called after her.

Adrienne stalled and turned back. "There's a post-mortem first. The family are hoping it'll be in a couple of weeks. We're covering all costs."

Fred bit her cheek, hoping to taste blood in her mouth to avoid the anguish in her heart. She'd never seen a dead body before, but Ambrose's lifeless pupils pierced her dreams every night. "I'll be there," she said, as Adrienne span around and out of sight. "I'll be there."

It was the least she could do to mark his life when she hadn't been able to save it.

CHAPTER FORTY-ONE

"THIS IS TOTALLY UNNECESSARY. I can walk." Fred stood, sending the wheelchair spinning backwards.

"No, I will not let you go like that. We've been through all this. You might fall." Her dad threw his hands up in despair. "The consultant only discharged you on the grounds that you followed the guidance and kept yourself safe."

Fred bit back her next sentence. She was going to argue that it was her job to keep people safe. She'd spent her working life keeping people safe. But the reality smacked her in the face. She was going to a funeral for a man who'd died on her building site. She sat back down. "Fine, you can wheel me there. But there's no way I'm going into the church in this thing."

Brian huffed from behind. "Get in the fucking chair, Fred, and we can all get a move on."

"Don't be so disrespectful. We're about to go to Mass," her mum said.

"It's not Mass, Mother, it's an Anglican funeral."

Fred rolled her eyes. Only her family could get stuck in the semantics of Roman versus Anglo Catholic funeral traditions. She stuffed an envelope into her jacket. It contained the letter from the bosses outlining the scope of their investigation. They'd been careful not to single her out, but it was clear that her management was under the microscope. "Are we walking or not?"

"Well, we are. You're not," Tommy said.

He'd been laid off the site too after Fred's accident. She wasn't sure whether that was down to Hugo or whether he'd lost his way without her there. Either way, he was under her mum's feet again.

Ten minutes later, they approached the church, a modest building at a busy junction.

"Shall I get out and walk, Dad?"

"And what will people think then? That I've performed some kind of miracle?"

"Well, we are at church," Brian said.

"Fuck off." Tommy punched his arm.

"Will you two stop it? We're almost there, and the last thing your sister needs is her brothers making fools of themselves. Give it up."

"Stop." Fred raised her hand and turned in the chair to force her dad to come to a halt. "No more. I'll go in on my own."

"You will not."

"No arguments. I'll meet you in the pub in an hour." She rose out of the chair, took her crutches from the back of the seat, and steadied herself. "I have to do this myself," Fred said, stroking her mum's hand as she nodded her approval.

As she reached the corner of the building, she sucked in the city's air to give her the courage to go in. She had to do this herself. *Be brave.* She had to say goodbye properly to this stranger who fell at her feet.

Inside, the carpeted room was warmer than she'd imagined. Sunlight dappled the wooden chairs. It looked friendly in here. She strained to make out the faces in the congregation, heads bent, in sadness or prayer. She picked out the Boot Street crew. Champ had dug out his best suit and looked like he was going to a wedding. Adrienne sat a few seats down. How did she manage to look like she was at Paris fashion week on a Thursday morning in Manchester? And there was Hugo, scowling at the world for whatever reason. Fred sat at the back before any of them saw her. She hadn't come to take up space or attention. She simply wanted to pay respects to a man who'd lost his life too early.

***

Ruby hunched against the carriage window, trying to avoid eye contact with anyone. A queue of people filed in, forming a line through the carriages, jostling their bags for space.

Steam clung to the window, the damp evidence of people breathing. People still alive. Ruby drew her initials in the condensation and ran through the possibilities ahead. Fred might be there if she was well enough. Why didn't she know if she was well enough? The guilt crushed her.

"Stop it." Trix slid a lidded coffee cup across the table. "I know what you're doing, and you need to chill."

"What am I doing?"

"You're going through all the chaotic possibilities that might befall you over the next five hours. This is what's going to happen. We're going to arrive on time for this funeral. We're going to blend into the crowd because we're dressed in our finery." She waved her hand across her suit. "We're going to pay our respects, and then we'll leave and have a huge glass of wine at DJ's expense."

Ruby fought the urge to argue with her. How could she act so normally when this was such a fucked-up day?

The train hugged the coastline and rounded the country's edge, almost tipping them into the waves below. It was beautiful on any day, but a day like this, with the steel blue sky stretching forever, there was the promise of something. The wave of optimism crushed her, breaking its pact and leaving nothing but grief in its wake. She'd gotten used to its ebb and flow over the last few days. Hurt would come and go again. Then come back, even sharper than it was before.

At some point, she rested her eyes, and the red clouds of the sun strobed behind her eyelids. She awoke in Manchester, her mouth furry with sleep and dehydration, and took Trix's hand, happy to be led across two platforms under the criss-cross rooftop of the city's station.

Ten minutes later, they arrived at the address Trix had scribbled on the back of an envelope. St Martin's. Ruby's heart ached as she lifted herself out of the cab.

They sat at the back to avoid attention. At the end of the short service, Hugo made his way toward Ruby before they could escape. He wore his usual smugness. Even behind a pair of overpriced sunglasses, he glared, and his lips were turned up in disgust.

"Good of you to turn up. I thought you'd gone off back to London."

There wasn't a question, so Ruby stayed silent.

"Still, it's for the best, I think. You don't want to cause Fred any more trouble than she's already in."

A fire in Ruby's stomach rekindled. Could she fight back? She was sure of neither her strength nor her chances. "Now isn't the time." Cutting him off seemed the only possible option at this stage. Ruby scouted the church for a sign of Trix. *You had to leave me now.*

"You know she'll lose her job."

"She doesn't care what you think," Fred said as she limped towards them.

"The woman of the hour. How lovely to see you two reunited. Can't keep you apart, hey?" Hugo peered over his sunglasses and flashed his veneers. "I'll leave you to it. You must have all sorts to catch up on. Don't forget to get your stories straight for the inquest." He turned and headed down the aisle, his noisy footfall making heads turn in his direction.

"I wasn't sure I'd ever see you again," Fred said, breaking the awkward impasse.

"I'm so sorry." Ruby looked around to see who was listening. "I thought it was for the best to get out of your way. Hugo made all sorts of claims against us both."

"You don't need to explain. I know why you left."

Ruby yearned to say so much more. She'd rehearsed her explanation so many times in her head. But now, face-to-face, all she could do was stare into Fred's stern face and silently beg for forgiveness. "How are you?"

"I'm well, thank you."

Fred talked like they were sat across the board room table, with every syllable rounded off to provide no way into her thoughts and vulnerability. The crowd dispersed, and they were alone, save for the organist and the verger tidying chairs. Ruby flinched as the door swung back open and Adrienne returned.

"Fred, I'm driving to the wake. Will you be wanting a lift?"

Ruby looked between them. Before she'd only ever seen hostility, but today there was something more, a reverb of that old connection they must've had. Adrienne's expression softened, and her head tilted as if she had the patience to wait.

"Hi, Ruby. Sorry, I didn't know you were here. Do you want a lift too? If you want to go together, I can wait."

Ruby hadn't expected that offer. She glanced at Fred, her shoulders freezing at Adrienne's turn of phrase. They weren't *together*. That was the one thing she needed people *not* to think, especially the bosses. Fred's whole world could come tumbling down if they were.

Before she thought any more about it, she opened her mouth. "We're not together." It wasn't a lie. But it felt like sawdust in her mouth. "I'm heading back home. But thank you."

Adrienne frowned, deep creases settling between her eyebrows. "I'll wait for you outside. Sounds like you have some talking to do."

"We don't." Her face full of fury, Fred edged towards the door, holding the chairs to support her exit.

"That's it then?" Adrienne asked as if she was questioning so much more than whether Fred was ready to leave.

"That's it," Fred said.

Ruby held her burning cheeks. With no other choice, she had denied the woman she thought she could love. But if the company wanted to, they'd make their lives a misery. And Adrienne was one of the directors. She had as much opportunity as anyone to throw

Fred to the wolves to save Boot Street's reputation.

Ruby screamed inside, the frustration of the whole episode eating away at her. She knew how much Fred valued her job—it was all she'd ever wanted. She'd never forgive herself if she caused it all to crumble around her.

CHAPTER FORTY-TWO

"ARE YOU ON THE mend?" Stan sat in Fred's sitting room, rattling the cup on his saucer.

Fred's mum had got the best china out for him, despite his protests.

"I am. I've told Sebastian I'll be back next week." Fred turned the volume down on the daytime chat show.

"That soon? You sure you shouldn't be taking a bit longer, kid?" He slurped his tea and shot Fred's mum an apologetic glance.

"I've told her she shouldn't be going in, but she's gone back to the shed to avoid my nagging."

Stan winked at her. "I see. Well, if she's back in the shed, she must be getting better."

"You're no help." Her mum moaned as she lifted herself out of the chair and went to the kitchen. "I'll cut you a slice of cake."

"Grand. Thank you, Shirley."

As the door clicked shut, he leaned forward in his seat and set down his cup. "Now you can tell me what's going on at that bloody site and what they're trying to pull."

Fred smiled. Even though he'd retired years ago, Stan was still one of her most fervent supporters. "They're trying to scapegoat me for the safety checks."

"Not being done?"

"They were done. They're in the logbooks."

"Nothing to answer for then."

"It's the demolition schedules. There shouldn't have been a crane that close that day. I don't know why it was."

Stan's brow furrowed. "Sub-contractors?"

"Maybe. I'm not privy to the whole investigation yet. Champ says they're looking at the ground that the crane had been positioned on before the fall. One of the theories is that the soil was too soft and one of the legs gave way."

"If that's true, that would explain why a crane could fall out of the sky. Those four legs need to be on solid foundations. But the demo crew should know all this unless they had some rookies on shift that day." Stan stroked his chin. "Have you got legal advice?"

"Yes. But I'm not convinced they're asking the right questions."

"I'll look over the papers when you get them."

"There's something else." Fred picked at her nails. "Hugo's launched a smear campaign against me. He's claiming my judgment was impaired because of my 'relationship' with Ruby."

Stan pursed his lips. "Had you declared it?"

"Not in so many words. But folks knew."

"Is he onto something?"

"Is he fuck." Fred stood and balanced on her crutches. "He's spiteful and vicious, and if it wasn't this crisis, he'd have found another way to get rid of me."

Stan arched his eyebrow. "Well, hold the line and ready yourself for a fight." He sipped his tea. "You and Ruby will need to be united on this though. You'll need to work together."

Fred's heart sank into the midnight zone of her ribcage. Working together felt like a very distant memory. "Easier said than done. She hasn't really spoken to me since the accident, and she made it very clear at Ambrose Walsh's funeral that there was nothing between us." The hurt of that denial reopened every time she recalled it.

"I'll come with you and meet with your lawyer. We'll crack this between us," Stan said.

Fred stopped mid-pace at the window. "You'd do that for me?"

He smiled. "Two heads are better than one, aren't they? That's what we always said."

Warmth flooded over her as if Stan had got up and delivered a bear hug. "Like a defence team?"

"Yeah, if you like." He chuckled. "We've got work to do though, if you're going to show that Hugo where to go."

Fred nodded. Stan was right; there was no time to lose in gathering her defence. She might have lost Ruby in all this, but there was no way she'd lose her job and her reputation too. They were the only things she had to keep her going.

***

Fred polished the windowpane and stared out into the pitch-black garden. Her shed had gathered dust while she'd been recovering, and she was glad to be back. Two shadows moved across the lawn, and she shook her head, awaiting their interruption.

"Knock, knock. It's only us," said Brian, not waiting for a welcome.

Tommy brought up the rear, cradling a six-pack of pale ale. "We've come to cheer you up."

Fred puffed her cheeks, as if anything she could say would change their minds. Her brothers had kept vigil at her bedside while she was in the hospital. Since she'd come home, they'd only let her out of their sight a handful of times.

"I don't think I'm supposed to be back on the beers, boys." She inspected one of the cans for its strength.

"Nonsense. It's been two months since you took that knock to the head. You can have a little shandy." Brian produced a bottle of lemonade from the carrier bag at his side. "And you've got your stick for balance."

"Fair enough." She laughed. "You don't need to worry about me."

Brian collapsed on the sofa, sending a dust cloud up to the exposed timber joists. Tommy dragged a chair across, and she put her feet up on an old potting table.

"We are though," Tommy said, his forehead creased with lines of concern that didn't belong on such a young face.

Fred remembered that he was there that day too, and he probably still felt the tremor when he closed his eyes at night.

"What're you thinking about, Tom?" she asked, giving him the space to offload.

He cracked the top of his can with a hiss and brought it to his lips. "It's all gone to shit, hasn't it?"

She could confirm that the worst had happened or shrug it off like another day at the office. "Yes, it has."

"Well, what can we do to help?" Brian asked, raising his own tin in solidarity.

"It's good to know you're thinking about me, that's all." Fred tipped her enamel mug free of dirt and mixed herself a shandy, more lemonade than beer. "I'm going back to the site next week. They can either kick me off or let me work. But I'm not sitting around here any longer. Mum's starting to do my head in with all the fuss."

They murmured their sympathy.

"What if they kick you off though?" Tommy asked.

"They won't. Why would they?" Brian squared his shoulders.

"I'm going in whether they like it or not." The fight reignited inside her chest. Saying it aloud to her brothers fanned the flame. "I'm not going to sit down like a victim waiting for someone to trash my career. I've worked damned hard to make it on-site, and I deserve that job. If they want to take me down, I'll take them down with me."

Two tins crashed above her as the brothers saluted her fighting call.

"Bring it on!" Brian laid his big hand on her shoulder. "We're with you all the way."

It meant the world to her to know her family, and her friend Stan, would fight alongside her. But the void between her lungs reminded her that someone was missing from the infantry. If only Ruby would stand up for her. If only she'd stood alongside her that day at Ambrose's funeral. But Ruby had denied her and denied their unity. Sometimes, in quiet moments, her mind played tricks, convincing her that Ruby acted in her best interests. She fantasised that she'd walk back through the door to make everything right. A kernel of hope lay in Fred's heart. She doubted it would seed but rather that it'd wither in the misery, dry and forgotten.

CHAPTER FORTY-THREE

RUBY SWERVED TO AVOID another oncoming commuter clearly in no mood to slow down. London was at its worst when the weather warmed up. Stifling Tube stations, sweaty buses, and no room to walk was a recipe for frustration and impatience.

She was no stranger to the uniquely disgusting stench of someone else's armpit in your face while an underground train lurched its way across the city. The network of tunnels still fascinated her, but after six months in the relative fresh air of the north, it suffocated her.

It wasn't just the Tube. Ruby couldn't breathe. Every rise and fall of her diaphragm stuck in her throat, and her muscles were tense, her brain fuzzy. She couldn't get past the feeling of panic that had consumed her since that day the crane fell.

Her flat was still under contract, so she climbed the stairs to Trix's apartment and used her key to let herself in.

"Is that you?" Trix called from the kitchen.

"Yep. Only me." Ruby hardly had the energy to respond. She dumped her bag at the door, slipped off her shoes, and went straight to the spare room to throw herself onto the unmade bed. She lay still, going over the day she'd had. Nothing much had occurred. She'd walked. She'd consumed junk food and milky drinks. At some point, she'd gone down a rabbit hole on social media and lost a couple of hours.

Trix leaned against the doorframe, wiping her hands on a luxury tea towel. "Have you been in the office today? Or are you still wandering the streets?"

Ruby hadn't been able to face going into the London office

since she returned to the capital. She imagined the little pods of productive people, and all the ideas and joy bouncing around the room. It made her stomach roll. There was no way she'd keep up.

"You know DJ is going to start asking some tricky questions soon. You can't avoid it forever."

"Fuck DJ." She screwed her eyes shut, sorry that had come out so forcefully.

"Charming."

"Well, he's the one who sent me up to Manchester in the first place. It's all his fault. I told you I wanted to work on that art gallery."

Trix sighed and shook her head. Even *her* patience seemed to be ebbing away with Ruby's inertia.

"We both want you to get back on track. It's not about rushing you. But the quicker you get a handle on some sort of routine, the better." She sat on the end of the bed. "If you're not ready to come back to work, then maybe you should go back to Melissa and spend some time in the fresh air? The weather is warm, and it'll be beautiful up there."

"Are you working for the tourist board? You hate Wales."

"But you don't." Trix threw the tea towel at her head and laughed. "You seemed better there, that's all I'm saying. Did you phone the doctor?"

Ruby shut down. She didn't want to talk about how fragile she was. "No, and I'm not going to. I'm fine. If you want me out of your hair, then I'll go back up to Abersoch in a couple of days."

"That's not what I said." Trix put her hand on Ruby's shin. "I want you here. But only if London is a good place for you to be, and only if you can get back on track." She paused, her eyes shifting around the room as if she was searching for anything that would change the situation. "Do you want to go out tonight? Fancy throwing some axes?"

She did. Ruby wanted to throw axes at Hugo's head for causing so much trouble for Fred. "Yeah. That'd be good."

A couple of hours later, Ruby brushed the creases from her

shirt and pushed at the heavy door to the old place.

"It still stinks of beer," Trix said, tottering across to the bar.

Ruby laughed, her own shoes sticking to the timber floorboards.

"You're back!" James came around the bar to greet her with a wide grin. "It's been ages. How's it going?"

"I'm doing fine," she said, desperate to close down the line of questions. "How're things here? Speedy around?"

"She's out with a new girl. Talking of which, where's your lovely lady?"

Ruby stumbled. She regretted ever bringing Fred here and wished it had remained her sanctuary. "She's back up north."

"What a shame. I liked her." He winked. "You looked good together. A real match."

Ruby shot Trix a look warning her not to wade in on this conversation.

"They are a good match, aren't they? I think so too. Sadly, Ruby is having second thoughts."

James tipped the bottle of whiskey towards them both. They nodded and he poured two measures. "Well, you know what they say..."

Ruby didn't need any more advice on her chaotic love life.

"What do they say?" Trix downed her drink and leaned into the bar.

Ruby held her head, waiting for the pearls of wisdom to bounce between her best friend and her favourite barman.

"Love is like a fine whiskey. Don't waste it."

Ruby groaned. "You've made that up, and it's rubbish." She shoved his shoulder.

Trix nodded. "That was a bit shit, James. I thought you were going to lay some profound truth bombs on us."

He laughed. "I'm not a poet, you know? I get paid to pull pints and measure liquor."

"Drink up, Trix. Let's go and throw something. Is that okay, James?" Ruby swung around on the chair, ready to take on the axe-throwing world. She missed the weight of wood and steel in her grip.

"Sure. Leave me on my own." He grinned. "Take Speedy's lane. She won't be in this evening, and the rest are booked."

"We'll be back before you know it. I need to blow off some steam." She pushed the door through to the alley. A couple of stag dos gathered at one end. "Follow me," she said, leading Trix to the other side. Ruby stood a little taller. Speedy's lane was reserved for VIPs and regulars.

She took her place like she'd never been away, scuffed her shoe against the mark and polished her axe with her breath. The weight of it centred her, and she blocked out the chaos around. The whip of the three blades made her heart race. So much jeopardy surrounding their journey to the target. A little off track, and they could rebound and cause some damage.

Turning back to their table, she caught a familiar shape at her side.

"Hello, you," Speedy said, coming in for an embrace.

"Good to see you. Remember Trix?" Ruby signalled between them.

"I do. Hey there." Speedy extended her hand then turned back to Ruby. "I've missed you down here. That sub-let doesn't show his face much. And it's not as pretty as yours."

Ruby smirked. "Ever the flirt, hey, Speeds?"

"Only in the right company."

Glad of the distraction, Ruby relaxed into herself. She enjoyed the attention, if she was honest. Apart from the whirlwind with Fred, it had been a while since she'd allowed herself to bask in someone's gaze.

"You mind if I join you?" Speedy asked.

"I thought you were out on a date?" Ruby handed her a blade.

"No one special. I cut it short. James texted to say you were back for the night."

Ruby frowned. Speedy had come home to see her? Doubt

nagged, but she ignored it. It was hanging out, nothing more. She focused on Speedy's throw. From her hands, the axes flew like arrows, with purpose and drive.

Then it was her turn. To her surprise, she landed a trio of smooth, definite hits.

"Have you been practicing?" Speedy asked.

"There's not been much opportunity. Busy at work, and the axe places up there are for hens and stags."

Speedy nodded towards the groups. "Gotta bring the cash in somehow."

Trix fidgeted behind them. "Mind if I leave you guys to it and grab a drink at the bar? Come find me when you're ready."

"Sure," Speedy said before Ruby had the chance to object.

She took another three throws. Silent, deadly releases at the middle of the target, each bang on.

"Looks like I'm on my game tonight." Speedy held Ruby's gaze a moment too long. "What do you reckon?"

Ruby weighed up the question. Speedy wanted more from her than throwing axes. She thought about throwing herself under her sheets and giving up till dawn. But that would destroy the tiny piece of self-worth she clung onto every night when she closed her eyes.

Speedy inched closer, and she knew what was coming. A night of abandon. The chance to revel in the fog and pretend the world didn't exist. Her lips parted, and Ruby recalled her last kiss. In that moment, she saw Fred. She tasted the sweetness, unique to her.

She coughed and stepped back, holding her hand up to halt Speedy's advance. "I need a minute."

Blood pumped through her heart, and with every breath she took to steady her pulse, another curl of panic crushed her. The world began to spin.

"Here, let's sit down." Speedy held her hand, the touch no longer charged with lust but gentleness.

Ruby had almost forgotten the friends she had here, and the routines she'd made. Maybe she could come back and make a go of it in London. But who was she kidding? Leaving Fred in that hospital bed had been the worst thing she'd ever done. The emptiness it left behind haunted her still. It didn't matter how much she tried to fill her days with food, drink, work, or play, nothing would fill the hole that Fred had left in her heart.

And nothing quieted the hollow scream inside.

CHAPTER FORTY-FOUR

"WHAT'S THE PLAN?" TRIX dumped her purse on the side and stretched out on her sofa.

"Can you get me a meeting with Sebastian?" Ruby paced, tapping her fingers with frenetic energy.

"The chair of the board? Why?"

"Because I have to convince him that Hugo is a no-good liar."

"So this isn't about you taking the blame for the accident?"

"Not entirely." Ruby paused mid-step. "But I am going to explain that I drove those plans, not Fred."

Trix rolled over and pulled her phone out of the bag. "I think DJ went to college with him. That's how we got the contract in the first place. If anyone can get you a meeting with the top dog at Boot Street, it's our main man."

Ruby bounced on her toes. She was finally taking control of something. Maybe she couldn't bring Ambrose Walsh back, but she sure could save Fred from a near-certain career crash. And maybe their relationship could survive this too.

"Wow." Trix sat up.

"What is it?"

"DJ says he's catching up with Sebastian at Olivia's Bistro tomorrow at noon. You can come for the aperitif if you really want to."

"Wow, that's quick."

"It is. But you don't want to sit on this for any longer, do you?"

"I guess not."

Ruby turned over and over all night, the sound of Trix's little snores drifting through the wall. She tossed the twisted duvet off her legs and padded down the hall to get a glass of water. She had to be at her best to convince Sebastian that Hugo was the rotten core at the heart of Boot Street, but with bags sagging at her eyes, she screamed desperation.

At some point, she must've drifted off to sleep on the sofa, because she awoke mid-morning with a crick in her neck and dribble down her chin. Feeling no more revived, she stood in the shower and let the warmth of the water dissolve her doubts.

"It's only me," Trix shouted from the front door. "I'm popping back between clients. You nearly ready? I'll drop you off in my cab."

Ruby turned the shower off. "Almost done."

In twenty minutes, they'd crossed the river and pulled up to a swanky hotel.

"You going to be okay on your own? Are you sure you don't want me in there?" Trix put her hand on Ruby's shoulder.

"It's my mess. I should be the one to fix it. Or at least start to." The more she ran over her arguments, the less convinced she was of success. But she had to give it a go.

DJ stood at the bar in a tailored suit. "Well, if it isn't Ruby Lewis, my star player. Long time no see."

She mirrored his beaming smile. For all his faults, he was a good guy. "Thanks for setting this up for me."

"Hey, you know we've all got your back. What happened at Boot Street was a tragic accident. But, jeez, we can't be held responsible for the legs on a crane."

She shivered. He'd oversimplified what had happened, but she couldn't blame him. He didn't know the people on that site like she did, and he hadn't met any of the old residents.

"Seb is a good friend of mine. He'll hear you out, but I'm not sure why you want to bend his ear over all this. The investigation hasn't implicated you."

"I know that. But it is pointing the finger at Fred Caffrey, and I can't see her get shafted over this."

DJ smirked. He knew there had been something between

them. "You're a sucker, Ruby. While the rest of us would turn our backs, you're fighting the good fight."

"Is Sebastian here yet?" She wanted to get this over with.

"He's sitting at the window at the best table in the house, obviously. I told him to expect you." He winked.

Her legs shook as she made her way over, she hoped they didn't betray her. "Mr Sanders?"

He stood, the perfect gentleman, and shook her hand. "Please call me Sebastian. You must be Ruby?"

She nodded and took a seat opposite when he offered it. "Thanks for seeing me. I'll be brief. I don't want to take up your lunch time."

"Please, I can do without Dominic bending my ear about stock prices. I'm assuming this is about what happened at Boot Street. A terrible situation. Go ahead." He leaned forward, his kind eyes narrowed with a hint of concern. "Would you like a drink?"

"No, thank you." She inhaled, her breath sticking in her chest despite her efforts. Nerves gathered. "Hugo Garre is trying to blame Fred Caffrey for the accident. He's making up lies about Fred's practices and motivations."

Sebastian sipped his water, giving nothing away.

"The truth of it is, sir, that Hugo has been bullying Fred for months, and it came to a head with the accident."

"I've heard Hugo's claims." He touched the cutlery next to his empty plate. "Chief among them is that Fred's judgement has been impaired by her feelings for you. What do you say to that?"

The noise of the restaurant faded while her ears drummed with a hundred beats. Still scorched by her previous denial, Ruby knew that to reject this claim would leave a scar that would never heal.

"Fred and I have had a relationship. I won't hide that."

"You tried to hide it though, as Hugo claims in his evidence. That looked suspicious, you have to agree."

Ruby picked at her thumbnail, shrinking under the table. What had she been thinking, running away? "I thought I was protecting

Fred from the fallout of our relationship. But I was wrong. Hugo has twisted the truth."

"Tell me your version of events." He raised his empty wine glass towards the sommelier. "Are you sure you won't join me?"

She ignored the invitation. She wasn't here to sip fine wine but to set the record straight. "The simple truth is that I've fallen in love with Fred. But that has nothing to do with the event at Boot Street and the crane accident. Fred's risk radar was as sharp as ever, and she insisted I change my plans when they pushed the safety boundaries. She was a professional in every way." Ruby took a breath, her mouth sticky and dry with nerves.

"Is that it?" he asked.

"She loves that job, and she's given everything to your firm. She's been there since she was a teenager. Please don't take it away from her."

"Ruby, I need to tell you that our investigation into safety practices at Boot Street is separate from the coroner's inquest. I appreciate what you've told me here, but you really need to put in a witness statement to the investigating team."

"But I'm telling you. You're the man at the top, aren't you? You'll see the report."

He placed his hands on the tablecloth. They looked soft, too soft to have done a day's work on a building site.

"Could you send DJ back over on your way out? I've heard you. Leave it with me." Sebastian rose from the table, signalling that their conversation was over.

Ruby stood and left the restaurant, her legs turning to jelly with the adrenaline racing through her body. She ran down the road, dodging tourists on Park Lane. The urge to move came from nowhere and within a few minutes, a fire raged in her lungs. Sebastian hadn't given any indication either way, but she'd done it. And anything was better than the passive grief she'd kept company since she'd walked away from Fred's hospital bed. She could hear the beeping of the machines now, matching the rhythm of her thudding stride through London's most exclusive borough.

There was only one place to head. She turned the key in Trix's lock and stuffed everything she could fit into a bag. She paused at the fridge to crack a bottle of water and took huge gulps, swallowing back her cough.

Euston wasn't far, and she picked up her feet despite the lactic acid burning her shins. The train would take her north, back to Fred, where she'd beg for her forgiveness if she had to. It didn't take long to pack, but the journey to Manchester took forever. Ruby eventually set her bag down at the Boot Street boards and tied the stray lace on her shoe. The terraces sparkled in the afternoon light, the promise of something new shimmering off the red brick façade.

The scent of summer hung in the air and for the first time in a while, she looked forward and stepped towards the open gate with her head high instead of hanging.

"I can't let you back in without your pass," Rattle said, popping out of his tiny window. "All the rules have been tightened that extra bit since, you know..."

She knew. The memory blasted through the fresh air and optimism she'd been breathing. "Don't worry. Maybe Champ will come and get me."

He smiled with a look of pity. "Sure thing. I'll radio through."

She tapped her boot on the dusty ground, inspecting a piece of loose gravel. Rattle handed her a hat and a vest.

In a few moments, Champ strode through the courtyard. "Ruby," he said, waving. "Where's your badge?"

"I handed it in when I left." She shuffled, not wanting to go over the whole thing.

"Come on in. Are you starting back up?"

"No, not quite. I've come to see Fred."

He sucked his breath, making a screech which set her teeth on edge.

"Does she know you're coming? She's on desk duty for the next few weeks and I'm in charge."

"I'll find her." Ruby went to walk away, but he rounded in front to stop her.

"Two things. First, you need to stay with me, otherwise you're not insured. Second, I'm not sure she'll welcome the visit. She's not been herself since she returned to the site."

Ruby could imagine the inner fury that Fred stoked. She was back at work but not back on top, and that would do her head in. "I'll try my luck." She hesitated. "Will you take me there?"

Halfway across the yard, he stopped short. "Looks like she beat you to it."

Fred's icy glare stretched across the site, and the summer temperature plummeted. She was still on crutches and dragged her cast behind.

"Thanks, Champ. She'll be okay with me." Fred discharged her deputy with a wave. "What are you doing here?"

Ruby stuttered, unable to form a sentence.

"I thought we'd cleared your locker and sent it on to Trix?"

"You did." Ruby coughed. "I wanted to talk to you."

Fred's eyes blazed. "I don't think we have much to say to each other. I'm trying to get back to building houses." She looked away.

"Please, don't go. I need to say something."

"You're making a scene," Fred whispered and gestured to the assembled site hands nearby.

"Then listen to me. It won't take long." Ruby swallowed her fear. "I love you."

Fred froze on the spot and checked the yard. Everyone and everything stopped.

Ruby had to finish what she came for. "I'm sorry about leaving. I never wanted to, but it was the only way I could think of to get you out of trouble. I've been utterly broken without you in my life." She stepped into Fred's space and took her hand. "Please."

"You ran away because you can't stick anything out, Ruby. Trouble came, and you wanted to be as far away as possible." Fred pulled away, leaving Ruby empty-handed.

"That's not it. I came to the hospital to come up with a plan. Hugo had already mounted the attack against you. Against us both. Then Tommy said it was best if I disappeared."

Fred frowned. "What has my little brother got to do with this?"

"He said—"

"And you do whatever Tommy says now, do you?" She laughed, her throat rasping.

"No, but I thought it was for the best."

"How would you know what's for the best? When do you ever do what's in anyone's best interests but your own?"

Tears sprang to Ruby's eyes and threatened to overwhelm her. She didn't want to lose it in the yard. "You're right, I guess. I don't know what's for the best." The tears fell, streams on her cheekbones. "I know we were good for each other. I know I fell in love with you. I wanted you by my side."

Fred scanned the audience, almost every member of the crew held their breath for her next word.

"Me too," Fred said, with an audible sigh. "But it wasn't to be. You're like fire, Ruby. You rage without control, and I can't handle the chaos." She shoved her hands in her vest and brought out the radio. "Champ, can you come back and escort Ruby off-site?"

CHAPTER FORTY-FIVE

FRED COULDN'T MOVE. HER bones ached in places she'd never really thought about. But it was nothing compared to the wound in her chest. Ruby *had* betrayed her. She'd left at the worst possible moment. Fred had run through every possibility, but her hope had been in vain. There was no escaping the sad truth that Ruby had walked away from her hospital bed.

Fred's family had swarmed around her, willing her recovery on with love and attention. But she longed for Ruby. She wanted to link her fingers through her own, pull her into her chest, and hold her while she rested her eyes.

But she'd given up the opportunity. Her arms remained vacant. And now she'd pushed away that final chance.

She looked out of the cabin window and pulled her vest up around her neck.

Adrienne approached from across the yard and came in, disturbing the trance she'd fallen into.

"I thought I'd give you some time to calm down. That was quite the show." She bumped Fred's shoulder. "Are you letting her walk away? That's it?"

"What?" Fred asked. She shook the last half an hour from her head and tried to focus on the next thing. "Why are you even here?"

"I told you on Monday; I'm down here all week for the PR agency pitches, since you insisted that I fire the last agency. Remember?"

"Yeah." Fred blinked, struggling to make sense of the detail.

Adrienne skipped at her side. "You know you could make my life a whole lot easier by letting Ruby back."

"Don't be funny. The last thing both you and I need is Ruby

here." Fred collapsed onto her chair, tears springing to her eyes.

"Get her back, Fred. You want to. I want you to."

"What the fuck has it got to do with you?" She didn't want to take it out on Adrienne, but she was there, right in front of her, getting caught in the fire.

"You want me to list the ways?" She perched on the desk, her legs swinging off the end. "She's a great PR. The best we've ever had. And you know it."

Fred rolled her eyes. Is that all she had? Because there was no way she was going to entertain that kind of relationship carnage for good copy. "Anything else? Because I'm really busy."

"Busy doing what? Looking at site plans?" Adrienne chuckled. "Get over yourself, Fred Caffrey. You've fallen in love with her. You reek of romantic desperation. Go. And. Get. Her."

Fred's jaw dropped at the outburst. "You're the last person I expected to say that."

Adrienne rolled off the desk and kneeled at Fred's eye level. "You're made for each other. Jesus, she just announced that she loved you in front of your whole crew. That's the kind of public display of affection you always wanted." She looked down. "It's the validation you deserve."

"I told her where to go. I can hardly row back on that, can I?"

"Do you love her?"

Fred tuned into the monologue playing non-stop in her mind. She plummeted into the gap inside her chest then further still to the gnawing in her stomach she'd had since Ruby's disappearing act. "Do I love her?" She bounced her good leg. If she said no, it would be denying the obvious. "Yes."

"You need to tell her." Adrienne held her hands and drew her to a standing position. "You might need to apologise too. You can be awful when you're angry." She pulled her in for a hug. "Come on."

"Where? She's gone off. How am I supposed to go after her? I'm not at my athletic best at the moment."

Adrienne tilted her head, a smile developing. "You know where she might be heading?"

Fred studied the muddy footprints on the floor. The smaller ones reminded her of Ruby's boots. Where would she go to? Back to London?

"I don't know, but I can call Trix and find out."

Adrienne chuckled. "Allow me. She's much more likely to pick up my call if she thinks there's a contract at the other end of it." She pushed Fred into a seated position and opened her phonebook. "Hey, Trix."

Fred stared up at the woman she'd rejected a matter of months ago. Could it really all work out? Her mind fixed on one thing: getting to Ruby.

"Listen, I'm not getting in the way of this... No, she's not in trouble..." She rolled her eyes.

Fred held out her hand. "Give me the phone."

Adrienne tutted and passed it over.

"Trix? It's Fred. Where's Ruby?"

"How the fuck should I know?" Trix groaned. "I'm not her keeper. She left here to come up to you. For all I know, she's still in Manchester."

"She left a little while ago. Do you think she'll come back to London?"

Trix paused. "No." Her voice softened, with a hint of regret. "Hold on. I can find her. Our phones are linked in some weird techie way."

The agony of waiting stretched on.

"She's at the train station." Trix finally revealed. "Wait, the picture's moving. She's on a train track. I think she's going to her sister's."

"Uh huh, well, where exactly is her sister's?" Fred rifled through a drawer for a pen and scrawled across the back of an envelope.

Adrienne took the phone back. "Thanks, Trix. How about lunch next time I'm in town? Sure thing. Email me." She put the phone down.

"Fancy a road trip?" Fred asked, a renewed flame burning

inside.

"In the Porsche?" Adrienne blanched.

"What else? I'm not taking one of those trucks to Wales."

***

"I think we'd have been better in a truck." Fred tried to cling onto whatever surface she could as the car took another bend on the single track.

"Nonsense. We'd still be stuck in that motorway traffic without this little speed machine and my handling of rural back roads." Adrienne winked.

"Why didn't you ever take me out in this when we were dating?"

"You never asked." Adrienne pouted cheekily. "And you were always covered in mud; I didn't want to shell out on the valet." Adrienne swerved to avoid a pothole. "Jesus, these roads are unbelievable."

"Aren't they as bad in Scotland?"

"I guess, but I don't tend to venture much further than Aberdeen." She wriggled against the leather seat. "I'm going to need a pitstop soon. I don't think I'll make it all the way."

Fred nodded. "I need to stretch my leg too." They'd been on the road for nearly two hours. She looked up the options on her phone. "There's a tearoom coming up soon on the left. It might still be open."

"Lovely."

Adrienne continued a couple more miles and followed the brown signs down a dirt track. The light faded under the tree canopy until an imposing Georgian building came into view. She cut the engine, and they both sat for a moment. The trees swayed around them, the shadows of leaves dancing as they were taken by the breeze.

"I'm desperate. Shall we go in?"

"I'll wait for you by the car," Fred said, fatigue setting in. She got out and leaned against the stone wall. What was she doing racing across the country to find Ruby? The fear of what she was going to say started to eat away at her confidence.

Recalling the last few hours, she cringed over her actions. She had been so awful to Ruby when she'd opened up her heart. And then she'd made a snap decision to drive miles in her wake. It wasn't only her body healing from the last few weeks, it was her mind too, and she didn't trust her own judgement.

Adrienne returned. "You doing okay?"

"This is all a bit much."

"Isn't it? Who knew we'd be taking a road trip to win back your new girlfriend." She grinned. "It's exciting. And it's a whole lot more positive than the past few weeks have been. Lean in, baby."

Fred swallowed, blinking tears from her eyes. "I don't know what I'm going to say when I get there. How far are we?"

"I don't know. Twenty minutes, longer if we get stuck behind another tractor." Adrienne took Fred's hand. "You could start with the truth. You both deserve some time to talk."

"How are you being so rational about all this?" Fred thought back to the time she'd rejected Adrienne.

"We had some fun together, and I didn't take you seriously. I didn't take *us* seriously enough." She dipped her head, unable to meet Fred's eye contact. "But when I see you with Ruby, I can see what I was missing out on. You can't throw this away because you're scared of the repercussions of the accident. Because that's exactly what it was."

Fred rested her head in her hands. "I've really missed her. But I don't get why she did a disappearing act."

"Well, ask her. She tried to explain herself back at the site. Maybe it's time you listened."

"Like I did that time you came to my house?" Fred looked up, pursing her lips. "I'm sorry I didn't give you a fair hearing."

Adrienne waved her away. "Enough of that. This is about the future. Let's get back on the road."

Fred nodded. "Let's go. I know what I need to do."

There was no going back now. She had to find Ruby and tell her how she felt. If it all went to shit, then so be it. But she had to try.

CHAPTER FORTY-SIX

"THANKS FOR COMING TO get me," Ruby said, leaning against the window until it proved too bumpy a ride.

"Well, I was hardly going to leave you at Bangor, was I?" Melissa huffed. "You could've given me a bit more warning, though. I haven't changed the beds."

The state of the guest rooms was the last thing on Ruby's mind. She couldn't shake the image of Fred banishing her from Boot Street. She'd looked so different, her skin grey and limbs skinny.

"What the hell is going on? You've been up and down here like a yo-yo for weeks."

Ruby had no energy to explain the latest episode in the saga her life had turned into. "It's over with Fred."

"That's a shame, lovey. I mean, I didn't even get to meet her."

"Don't make me feel even worse about it."

A speeding car pulled ahead of them. "Second-homers." Melissa tutted. "There are even more now than there used to be."

Ruby shut her eyes. Retreating into her own head was worse than listening to Melissa's commentary, but the evening sun was too harsh to keep her eyes on the road. Everything hurt. The ache in her neck had spread to her shoulders. The effort of breathing through her sobs had left her ribs sore. Her eyelids scratched against her pupils, dry as the desert after the floods of tears that she'd succumbed to on the train up here.

"What's this joker doing?" Melissa frowned at the car in front, its brake lights flickering on and off. "It's like they've never seen a country road." She slowed down, giving them time to move ahead without bearing down on them. "How long are you staying for this time?"

Ruby shrugged. "I don't know what I'm doing. The sub-let is almost up, but I don't have a plan."

"Are you taking a few weeks off though? You're a wreck."

"Thanks, Mel. I could do without any more home truths today. I need some sleep, that's all. And to put all of this behind me."

The road twisted and turned another few times before they took the left turn towards Abersoch. Hope rekindled in Ruby's belly. She had once hated living here, but her return anchored her once again. The coastline snapped in and out of view, and Ruby breathed easier when she opened the window to welcome the salt on the breeze.

"Feeling better?" Melissa smiled.

Like most people who make a home next to the sea, she knew its healing powers.

"I guess so."

They turned onto a single-track road which wound its way higher into the hills surrounding the beach, tightening like a screw towards the summit. The silhouette of their family home perched, overlooking the shore.

Melissa's eyes narrowed, and she blinked at the oncoming headlights. "That car is still ahead. I wonder where they're heading?"

"Who are you? Neighbourhood watch?"

"Well, you have to keep an eye on things out here. People look after each other." She shielded her eyes. "Hang on, they're heading up our driveway."

Ruby flipped her head to see the car disappear behind the hedge. "No..." *It can't be.* But hope flickered deep inside.

Melissa's eyes widened. "Has she followed you here?"

"She can't drive with her leg in plaster." Ruby shook her head, unwilling to believe it could be Fred. But her familiar frame stepped out of the passenger door, and Ruby's legs dissolved once more. Stuck to her seat, her breath came faster. Her hopes of a second chance had been shattered back at Boot Street, and she didn't trust what was happening. Slowly, she reached for the handle and stepped into the drive, coming face-to-face with Fred.

"Beat you." Adrienne emerged from the driver's side determined, it seemed, to break the tension. "I'm Adrienne. You must be Ruby's sister." She strode over to Melissa and held out her hand.

"Enchanted to meet you. Shall we leave these two to it?" Mel chuckled and shook her head, leading Adrienne into the hallway. "Would you like a cup of tea?"

"Ever the hostess, my sister." Ruby took a hesitant step forward, closing the gap between them. She fought the urge to run to Fred. "I wasn't expecting to see you again." She burned to say so much more, but fear held her tongue.

"Watching you walk away..." Fred stalled, her eyes closing. "I couldn't let you go."

Ruby's breath stopped, and her stomach tensed with anticipation. "What do you mean?" She needed Fred to spell it out. She couldn't risk laying her heart bare just to be rejected again. "You did let me walk away. You sent me away."

"I'm so sorry. You deserve more." This time Fred inched forward, her body opening with a hint of a promise, with a trace of reconciliation.

"It's such a mess. I don't know what to do." Ruby trembled all over, her hands shaking at what had happened and what might come.

"It is a mess. But it's not your fault, and you can't blame yourself." Fred took hold of her fingers and held them still. "It was an accident. We can't let it destroy what we had."

Ruby frowned, unable to digest the words. "But at the site, you said—"

"I was wrong. I'm still angry and tired. My body hurts in places I've never known. But I'm certain of this: you turned my world upside down the minute you walked into my site. You're chaotic, Ruby Lewis. You're a ball of energy. You don't play by any rules."

She smiled, her eyes filling with unspent pain. "There was a horrible accident that wasn't your fault, and the investigation report is clear: the soil that the crane was on was too soft that day. It should have been checked by the contractor, and they're liable for that."

Ruby stared ahead, trying to take in the words. "So you're not in trouble?" Ruby asked.

"I've got the proof to show I asked the demolition crew to position elsewhere, on firmer ground."

"But Hugo said—"

"Hugo has been moved on. The board saw through his vendetta against me. He's probably sipping cocktails and spending his payoff as we speak." Fred bit her lip. "Ruby, listen. You weren't to blame, no matter what you think. I should've listened when you tried to explain back at the site. I was shocked to see you, and it all hit me again. I was so angry that you left me back at the hospital. But I think I understand why. I *want* to understand."

"I've tried to make it better." Ruby's agony caught in her throat.

"I know that." Fred paused. "I can't let you walk away."

"Why?" Ruby asked.

"Because I need to be near you. I don't work without you."

Ruby broke, tears falling down her cheeks as she sank against Fred's chest.

"I love you, Ruby." Fred tipped her chin upwards. "I think I've loved you since you ran into me in your heels."

"You have?" Ruby's heart faltered. It was everything she'd wanted. Together, they could heal through the pain. Together, they'd be stronger than ever. She looked up into the watery blue of Fred's eyes and saw their future. She kissed her softly, tentatively leaning into the lips she'd hungered for. She drew closer, inch by inch easing the hurt inside, softening the scars. "I love you."

CHAPTER FORTY-SEVEN

FRED HELD RUBY'S HAND tight as they walked through the back door. The theme tune to her dad's favourite TV show carried through the hallway. She parked her bags at the foot of the stairs, and her mum came out to investigate the noise.

"It's you two." She wrapped Fred in a hug then took Ruby by the shoulders. "I'm so glad you're back here, love. Fred missed you terribly."

"Mum..." She rolled her eyes. "Where's Tommy? I want a word."

"He's out the back messing around with car parts. Brian's at the pub." Her mum hovered at the kitchen door. "Shall I get the kettle on?"

"Yes, please, Shirley. I'd love one," Ruby said.

"Stay here. I won't be long." Fred gave Ruby a quick peck on the cheek and shuffled outside as fast as her dodgy leg would take her.

Tommy looked up, his face smudged with oil. "Hey." He wiped his hands with a rag, transferring more dirt onto his fingers. "Where've you been?"

"That's what I want to talk to you about."

His eye twitched. "Oh, yeah?"

"I went after Ruby." She studied the change in his expression as the realisation that he'd caused a rift in their relationship dawned.

"Listen, Fred. It's your business, but she's trouble–"

"You're damn right it's my business. You had no right to tell her that the accident was her fault. You scared her off, and you knew it."

He scuffed his shoes against the concrete. "It wasn't like that. I told her what everyone else was saying. Not just me. It did my head in."

Fred bit her lip. She could lose her shit with Tommy, but he wasn't the root cause of all this trouble. "Don't be Hugo's mouthpiece. Out of everyone, you should've been standing up for us, not taking Ruby down."

He shoved his hands in his pockets. "I did stand up for you. I got into a row with that Hugo and lost my fucking job because of it. You don't understand, Fred. You were in hospital, that poor bloke was dead, and the whole place was caving in on itself. Hugo and his hangers on said that if it hadn't been for Ruby, you'd still be okay. I wanted to get her out of the way. I wanted to do you a favour."

She digested his words. He was right, in a way. He'd been caught in the tornado which had ripped through the site. Blame and speculation had left a mess in its wake. She blew her cheeks out and hoped to expel her frustration. The last few weeks had been too much and she wasn't used to spiralling out of control like this. "I understand why you did it, but I need you to apologise to Ruby and tell her the truth. She ran away thinking that I blamed her for what happened. That's on Hugo and people like you."

He raised his eyebrow. Her little brother wasn't used to being held to account for his misdeeds.

"I mean it. A man lost his life that day because of careless actions. I won't let it destroy what could be our future. You need to stand up on this one and no shrugging it off like it's not important. Me and Ruby are a thing. A serious thing."

His head bowed. "I'm sorry. I'll tell her too."

"Get on with it then. She's inside."

He slinked off, shoving his hands in his pockets. It'd be a lesson for him, and she was glad of it, in some ways. Fred took the path of least resistance to her shed and sank into the couch. She hoped that Ruby would accept Tommy's version of an apology and that they could, finally, put some of this behind them.

She looked up at Mr J in his garden. She and Ruby weren't the only ones who'd been battered by this accident. The memory of Ambrose Walsh filled her heart. Would she ever be able to live with the guilt of not reaching him, not pushing him hard enough?

"Hey." Ruby appeared at the door.

"Did Tommy speak to you?" Fred pulled her in.

"He did. I get it." Ruby raised her head and kissed her softly on the lips. "We're going to be okay, aren't we?"

Fred gazed into the well of possibilities deep in Ruby's eyes. Their whole lives seemed to stretch ahead. "We really are." She wrapped Ruby's arms around her waist. "All that matters is that you hold me tight, and I hold you back."

"Do you promise?" Ruby asked.

Fred recalled all the doubts she'd had. She'd second-guessed herself and Ruby so many times since they'd met. But they all melted away in the heat of their embrace. She knew, deep in her soul, that Ruby was fire. Not so long ago, she was scary and out of control. Now, Fred saw it was Ruby's flame that would nourish her, warm her, provide life and energy when she needed it most. For her own part, she'd take care not to wash away the chances they had, nor drown out the possibilities for their future.

She stood toe-to-toe with the woman she loved. "I do promise. I promise to always love you."

Ruby beamed back. "Me too, Fred Caffrey. I will always love you."

EPILOGUE

Two years later

FRED STILLED HER TROWEL, distracted by the scent of potatoes roasting in the oven. Up on the hill, she caught a glimpse of a tiny figure at the edge of Melissa's garden. She was probably home tending to her own weeds. She smiled, relishing the deep contentment she'd gotten used to.

The door to the caravan swung open, and Ruby wiped her hands on her thigh-length apron. Fred grinned at the sight of her smudged lipstick and loose ponytail. Despite all her efforts, the stove and its accessories would not be tamed.

"Are you almost done with that? Dinner is nearly ready." Ruby brushed flour from her hips, stirring Fred's desire.

She flicked at the remaining cement. "Let me lay this last row, and I'll wash up."

"Don't be too long. I have puddings rising in the oven, and who knows what might happen if I leave them."

Fred chuckled. "Come here, my domestic goddess."

Ruby closed the distance between them, her eyes on fire. She leaned in, kissing Fred hard. "Listen, you can't be distracting me or I'll end up burning down the caravan, and then where will we be?"

Fred shrugged and rubbed the sweat from her top lip. "I'm almost done with the first floor."

"We can't live in a house without a roof, never mind any bedrooms." Ruby wriggled out of Fred's reach.

"Oh, no, we can't live without any bedrooms. That would not do at all." They laughed in unison, lifting their joy to their own patch of sky. "Let me wash these tools, and I'll come in and help." Fred kissed her on the nose, and she skipped across the garden to the van.

Fred stood for a moment, admiring today's progress. It had been a while since she'd dug foundations and laid her own line of bricks, but like riding a bike, once she got going, there was nothing to think about.

The sound of tyres spinning against the dust disturbed the silence. A few moments later, Adrienne drove her new Porsche across the gravel that Fred had laid as a makeshift driveway.

"I told you to bring a truck." She laughed, shaking her head.

"That would be no fun, would it?" Adrienne shrugged. "And I wouldn't get to see your face when I turned up in this beauty."

"Is that what you've spent your bonus on?" Fred tutted.

"That and some other lavish extras." Adrienne chuckled. "Don't tell me, you've popped yours into the building society before Ruby spends it on interiors?"

Fred laughed. "Not likely. Every penny is being poured into this place."

Adrienne squinted and surveyed the progress. "You're doing well. It's amazing what can be achieved in a couple of months. But I hope you're ready to come back. We need to talk about the new build."

Fred dusted off her hands. "We've only just finished Boot Street. Can't I take a breath?"

"You've been enjoying the Welsh fresh air for long enough. It's back to the grindstone for you and that lovely wife of yours." Adrienne nudged her in the ribs. "Come on, you know you love it."

Fred smiled, the warm glow of topping out at Boot Street still fresh in her memory. It had been a hard but rewarding job.

"You've got Tommy and his crew to complete this." Adrienne nodded at the half-finished house standing proud on the plot of rural land. "Why are you getting your hands dirty with it?"

"Because Tommy needs supervising. He's still new to it. And

there's nothing like seeing it rise from nothing like this, with your own sweat and tears. Don't you think?"

"I prefer houses when they're finished and sold, but I know what you mean." Adrienne screwed her nose up at the filth surrounding them. "How long are you going to be living in that caravan? At least back in Manchester, you'll have somewhere comfortable during the week."

"It's not so bad." Fred nodded towards the open door. "You're going to love what we've done with the place."

"I doubt that very much."

They entered the van to the smell of a roast dinner that filled her up with anticipation and nostalgia. "Adrienne's arrived."

"I thought I heard voices." Ruby kissed Adrienne on the cheeks. "How are you?"

"Perfect. I'm missing you two like mad. Head office is so quiet, and I've got nowhere to bolt to for fun."

"We'll be back at it before you know it." Ruby winked.

"Thank goodness. You're going to love this new project. It's right up your street."

"Tell me more," Ruby said, shaking cornflour into a pan of thin brown water.

"Coal heritage. Big mining community. They're very vocal about how the land should be used."

"Coal mines? Sounds like the surveyors will be busy," Fred said.

"That's all done and dusted." Adrienne waved away her concerns. "They're ready for a top construction crew and..." she beamed in Ruby's direction, "our new director of marketing."

Ruby blushed. "Stop it, you. I'm still pinching myself."

"I don't know why. You're the best in the business."

"Isn't she?" Fred kissed her cheek and shuffled the envelopes on their kitchen table. She sat down to her sketches. "Have a seat, Adrienne."

"You're going to have to move those, darling, if we're eating at the table," Ruby said, stirring another pot on the stove.

"I know. I just wanted to show you both what I added last night."
She unfolded one of the pages and stroked her finger across its
pencil lines. She'd scribbled in the margins with arrows pointing
here and there.

"Did you finish them?" Ruby wiped her hands on the skirt of her
apron.

"Sort of. It's not perfect, but it'll do for now." Fred frowned,
doubting herself for the hundredth time since she'd started this
project. She looked at Adrienne. "Do you think it's enough to sign
off the design budget?"

Adrienne considered the sketches and bit her lip, as if reading
her thoughts. "Absolutely. I can work with this. You've done a great
job. But someone else could lead on this if it's too much for you."

Fred leaned back on the bench. "I promised that I'd help mark
Ambrose's memory. I don't want to move on from Boot Street until
we've completed this."

Ruby rested her hand on Fred's shoulder.

"I'm okay." Fred stroked her fingers. "I just want to make this
right."

"I'll take the designs back with me, and you can follow on
Monday and talk next steps," Adrienne said.

Ruby grinned. "You'll be in Manchester on Monday? Can you
pick me up some shampoo? The nice one that I like."

Fred laughed and shook her head. "You can take the girl out of
the city..."

"You wouldn't have it any other way." Ruby planted a kiss on her
lips, squeezed next to her on the bench and put her hand on Fred's
thigh. "Show us your plans."

"Okay. So, these are rough sketches, but the architects will
work their magic. I was thinking that this will be the Ambrose
Walsh Sports Pavilion." Fred pointed to a rectangle on the plan,
adjacent to the Boot Street terraces. "I want them to design the
front elevation, take out a couple of walls internally, see what they
think about a new eco roof. There'll be a kitchen and two dance

studios. And a big space." She smiled. "People can use it for all kinds of things."

Ruby rubbed a tear from her cheek. "Florence will love it."

Fred brought to mind the elderly lady who'd appeared on the news for them two years ago. "She knows what I had in my head, but I'll pop in and see her while I'm in the city to take her through these sketches and see how she is."

"She'll like that." Adrienne squeezed her hand.

The rattle of a saucepan lid jolted them all from dwelling too much in the grief of the last two years. "Sorry, let me just see to the dinner." Ruby rose and left the table.

"I'm going to grab my things from the car. I have the new project plans for you to keep hold of. And I brought you an early house-warming gift." The caravan door swung back on its hinges as Adrienne left them alone.

Fred closed her eyes. Each day, she tried to think less of what had been lost and more about what had been created. "Hey, chef, come back here for a minute." Fred patted the seat next to her.

Ruby sat down. "What is it?"

"Are you ready to go back to Manchester?"

Ruby laid her head against Fred's chest. "It's not like we're giving up what we have here. We'll work our butts off in the week, and we'll do what we can to finish the house at the weekends."

"It's going to be tough."

"I know that. We both knew that when we took on this build." She looked up into Fred's eyes. "But it's not forever. Sometime soon we'll look out over our own piece of the horizon. This place will be our home whenever we need it to be."

"Our retreat from the city?"

"Yeah. One day it'll be our forever home."

"Thank you, Ruby Lewis."

"For what?"

"Wandering onto my building site with your pointy shoes that day. Making me happy. Building a life with me. Bringing me to this perfect parcel of land and letting me build our dream home." She took Ruby's hand and stroked the contours of smooth skin which she knew by heart. "I love you."

Ruby planted a long, lingering, joyful kiss on her lips. "I love you too."

Fred sat in their cocoon of unrivalled happiness. Everything, almost lost, was now forever hers to keep, to cherish, and to hold safely in her heart.

THE END

AUTHOR'S NOTE

Hi there, I just wanted to say a big thank you for reading *Back to Back*.

I hope you enjoyed it. If you did, I'd be thrilled if you could leave a quick review on Amazon or Goodreads. Reviews mean the world to new writers.

If you're hungry for more Boot Street drama, you might want to read my short story *Back in Time*. It follows Florence Walsh at Ruby's event as she visits old haunts with her childhood sweetheart, Agnes. More than memories are rekindled in this sweet tale.

You might also want to check out my debut novel, *Here You Are*. You'll meet romantic artist Elda and sexy barrister Charlie. Can these two strong women heal past wounds to find love?

Thanks for your support. And happy reading!

www.jofletcher.com
Follow me on Instagram, TikTok, and
Facebook at JoFletcherWrites

Other Great Butterworth Books

Here You Are by Jo Fletcher
.Can they unlock their hearts to find the true happiness they both deserve?
Available on Amazon (ASIN B0CBN935ZB)

Heart of the Storm by Ally McGuire
Sometimes a storm is just what you need to clear the skies ahead.
Available on Amazon (ASIN B0CYTSQXWW)

Sanctuary by Helena Harte
Passions ignite and possibilities unfold. Welcome to the Windy City Romance series.
Available from Amazon (ASIN B0D4B42RRW)

Dead Ringer by Robyn Nyx
Three bodies. One killer. No motive?
Available on Amazon (ASIN B0CPQ8HFK7)

Medea by JJ Taylor
Who will Medea become in her battle for freedom?
Available from Amazon (ASIN B0CK2FB7GW)

Virgin Flight by E.V. Bancroft
In the battle between duty and desire, can love win?
Available from Amazon (ASIN B0CKJWQZ45)

Fragments of the Heart by Ally McGuire
Love can be the greatest expedition of all.
Available on Amazon (ASIN B0CHBPHR6M)

Stunted Heart by Helena Harte
A stunt rider who lives in the fast lane. An ER doctor who can't take chances. A passion that could turn their worlds upside down.
Available on Amazon (ASIN B0C78GSWBV)

Dark Haven by Brey Willows
Even vampires get tired of playing with their food...
Available on Amazon (ASIN B0C5P1HJXC)

Green for Love by E.V. Bancroft
All's fair in love and eco-war.
Available from Amazon (ASIN B0C28F7PX5)

Call of Love by Lee Haven
Separated by fear. Reunited by fate. Will they get a second chance at life and love?
Available from Amazon (ASIN B0BYC83HZD)

Where the Heart Leads by Ally McGuire
A writer. A celebrity. And a secret that could break their hearts.
Available on Amazon (ASIN B0BWFX5W9L)

Stolen Ambition by Robyn Nyx
Daughters of two worlds collide in a dangerous game of ambition and love.
Available on Amazon (ASIN B0BS1PRSCN)

Cabin Fever by Addison M Conley
She goes for the money, but will she stay for something deeper?
Available on Amazon (ASIN B0BQWY45GH)

Breakout for Love by Valden Bush
They're both running from their pasts. Together, they might make a new future.
Available from Amazon (ASIN B0CWHZ4SXL)

The Helion Band by AJ Mason
Rose's only crime was to show kindness to her royal mistress...
Available from Amazon (ASIN B09YM6TYFQ)

That Boy of Yours Wants Looking At by Simon Smalley
A riotously colourful and heart-rending journey of what it takes to live authentically.
Available from Amazon (ASIN B09V3CSQQW)

Scripted Love by Helena Harte

What good is a romance writer who doesn't believe in happy ever after?
Available on Amazon (ASIN B0993QFLNN)

Call to Me by Helena Harte

Sometimes the call you least expect is the one you need the most.
Available on Amazon (ASIN B08D9SR15H)

What's Your Story?

Global Wordsmiths, CIC, provides an all-encompassing service for all writers, ranging from basic proofreading and cover design to development editing, typesetting, and eBook services. A major part of our work is charity and community focused, delivering writing projects to under-served and under-represented groups across Nottinghamshire, giving voice to the voiceless and visibility to the unseen.

To learn more about what we offer, visit: www.globalwords.co.uk

A selection of books by Global Words Press:
Desire, Love, Identity: with the National Justice Museum
Aventuras en México: Farmilo Primary School
Times Past: with The Workhouse, National Trust
Young at Heart with AGE UK
In Different Shoes: Stories of Trans Lives

Self-published authors working with Global Wordsmiths:
Steve Bailey
Ravenna Castle
Jackie D
CJ DeBarra
Dee Griffiths
Iona Kane
Maggie McIntyre
Emma Nichols
Dani Lovelady Ryan
Erin Zak

Printed in Great Britain
by Amazon

46382788R00176